ARTHUR C. CLARKE'S
VENUS PRIME™

D0950361

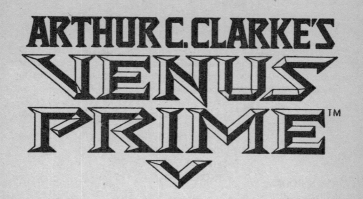

ARTHUR C. CLARKE'S
VENUS PRIME™

VOLUME 3
HIDE AND SEEK

PAUL PREUSS

A BYRON PREISS BOOK

AVON BOOKS ◆ NEW YORK

ARTHUR C. CLARKE'S VENUS PRIME, VOLUME 3: HIDE AND SEEK is an original publication of Avon Books. This work has never before appeared in book form. This work is a novel. Any similarity to actual persons or events is purely coincidental.

Special thanks to John Douglas, Michael Kazan, Russell Galen, Alan Lynch, and Mary Higgins.

AVON BOOKS
A division of
The Hearst Corporation
105 Madison Avenue
New York, New York 10016

Text and artwork copyright © 1989 by Byron Preiss Visual Publications, Inc.
Arthur C. Clarke's Venus Prime is a trademark of Byron Preiss Visual Publications, Inc.
Published by arrangement with Byron Preiss Visual Publications, Inc.
Cover design, book design, and logo by Alex Jay/Studio J
Front cover painting by Jim Burns
Library of Congress Catalog Card Number: 88-91380
ISBN: 0-380-75346-4

First Avon Books Printing: June 1989

AVON TRADEMARK REG. U.S. PAT. OFF. AND IN OTHER COUNTRIES, MARCA REGISTRADA, HECHO EN U.S.A.

Printed in the U.S.A.

K-R 10 9 8 7 6 5 4 3 2 1

PROLOGUE

Dare Chin was not a nervous man, but he was edgy tonight. Mainly it was that damned plaque, the infamous Martian plaque. It had been discovered ten years ago, somewhere near the edge of the north polar icecap, no one knew where exactly, because the guy who found it wanted to keep it a secret. And he had, long enough to blow himself up in a drilling accident.

The plaque was a mirror-finish scrap of alloy the size of a broken dinner plate, inscribed with line after line of undecipherable symbols. Its discovery and authentication had proved that beings who could write—everybody assumed the inscriptions were writing, though nobody had proved it—had been hanging around Mars a billion years before humans evolved on Earth.

The plaque was sitting downstairs in the middle of Town Hall right this minute, as it had been for most of the last ten years. Not a copy, which would have been sensible, but the real thing, unique in the universe so far as anybody knew, and therefore truly without price. The rationale for exposing the real thing instead of a copy was that it was one of the attractions that drew tourists to Mars, and who would steal it anyway?

1

Tonight Chin was staying late to guard it. He had better things to do, or at least other things to do. Chin was the assistant mayor of Labyrinth City, the biggest settlement on Mars—a town that needed water on a planet where what little water there was went straight from ice to vapor in the dry, thin atmosphere, a town whose people needed to breathe oxygen on a planet where atmospheric pressure was less than one percent of Earth's, and needed to stay warm on a planet where during heat waves the temperature rose to a toasty minus five degrees centigrade, a town which needed to dispose of its sewage on a planet where there were no native microorganisms to digest it.

Besides dealing with these everyday challenges to the town's infrastructure, its administrators somehow had to manage an unmanageable, unmeltable pot of residents—a third of them permanent citizens, the working-class roughnecks, with another third transient, mostly rich tourists, and a final third which floated, consisting of ivory-tower types, scientists, and Council of Worlds mouse pushers.

The pile of yellow hard copy on Dare Chin's desk would have reduced any administrator who believed in the perfectibility of humanity—as he was supposed to, being a card-carrying member of the Interplanetary Socialist Workers Party—to anger, tears, suicidal depression, or all three. The local roughnecks, with a two-to-one ratio of men to women, got drunk and cut each other up just about every weekend. The tourists daily got themselves cheated, robbed or mortally insulted. The scientists and bureaucrats, supposedly possessed of the best educations, had the morals of feral cats and spent their off hours playing spouse-, companion-, and child-swapping games.

Take the case in his wait file right now, a three-way marriage between a geologist and two hydrologists: they were breaking up because the geologist's hitch with the Terraforming Project was over, her contract hadn't been renewed, and she wanted to ship for Earth taking their daughter with her. . . . She'd borne the child, who was the product of gamete fusion between her and the other woman; the husband and legal "father" had contributed nothing genetically, but he was siding with his hydrologist colleague in the custody fight—they both had two years to run on their work contracts. Chin wished they could all go back to Strasbourg where they came from and fight it out there.

But contracts were involved, so he had to make an administrative ruling before the case could go up to the civil court on Mars Station. Meanwhile four unhappy people were spending another night together in the green-glass maze of Labyrinth City. He hoped they'd all get out of it alive. Right now there were more pressing things on his mind.

The tall blonde who was glaring at him across his desk wasn't making any of it easier. She had the thin, tough build of a Martian long timer and a net of fine lines around her eyes that indicated she spent a lot of time squinting into the distance. She was wearing the standard brown polycanvas pressure suit, its helmet slung casually from her belt. "You can't put me off tonight, Dare," she was saying, at a volume just short of a yell.

"*Any* night but tonight." He and Lydia Zeromski had been lovers for most of the last three years; that, in his experience, was about as long as a woman's patience lasted.

"Tonight," she said. "Tomorrow I'm starting a run. Do I head for your place when I get back? Or do I write you off before I leave?"

He stood up and moved toward her, his hands opening in supplication. "Lydia, nothing has changed between us. But don't try to pressure me right now. I've got a ton of work. Plus the guy downstairs to worry about.''

''That fat jerk?''

''He's got our most revered piece of scrap metal out of its case. . . .''

''And you're afraid he's going to drop it and make a dent.''

''Yeah, sure.'' Chin breathed an exasperated sigh. The Martian plaque was harder than diamond, harder than any material humans knew how to make, as everybody well knew; denting it was a nonproblem. ''Get out of here. I'll talk to you before you leave.''

''Forget it.'' She pulled her helmet over her head, a movement so practiced it was like putting on sunglasses. She paused in the doorway and gave him one last incendiary glare, but said nothing. As she turned and walked rapidly away she sealed her faceplate.

Chin could hear her footsteps rapping lightly down the hall and then going down the stairs to the ground floor. He stared into the dim, greenly lit hallway outside his office, trying to collect his thoughts.

Chin's narrow face was handsome; he had straight black hair and black eyes and a wide firm mouth, now downturned. He was a tall man, with a naturally slender build kept slim—like Lydia's—by twenty years of life at a third of a gee. It was a typical build for Martians because, while it was easy to carry extra mass at low gees, it was unnecessary and could even be dangerous to sling around a lot of extra fat and muscle.

Through the glass outer wall he noticed a lantern outside in the windswept street; the yellow glow of a patroller's hand torch wavered through the green glass like the phosphorescent organs of some benthic fish. As he watched, the light resumed its slow movement. He glanced at his watch: 20:08. Old Nutting was as regular as a cesium clock.

He went back to his desk and sat down. He leaned back in his chair, staring up through the glass ceiling at the vast shadow of the sandstone vault that arched overhead. Beyond the edge of the natural stone roof shone ten thousand stars, un-blinking—hard bright points in the Martian night.

What was to be done about Lydia? The question had plagued him for most of the three years they'd been intimate. She was younger than he was, a passionate, demanding woman. He was a man who felt older than he looked—people age slowly on Mars, because of the low gravity, provided they stay out of the ultraviolet—but for all his apparent maturity, a man still uncertain of his wants and needs. . . .

He mentally pinched himself. He had to put the personal stuff out of his mind tonight. He had to decide what to do with the information he'd recently acquired.

He pulled the yellow fax sheets from beneath the pile of other papers, where he'd hidden them when he'd heard Lydia's unexpected footsteps on the stairs. The data stared up at him. The facts were bald enough, but crucial connections were missing; Chin knew enough about evidence to know what was needed in court and what was needed to make an administrative ruling, and in the communications before him he didn't have enough of either. But there were other routes to justice.

Shortly after he'd come to Mars, years back, Chin, like a lot of other tenderfeet, had managed to get himself cheated on a work contract. Lab City had been a smaller and rougher place then, hardly more than a construction camp—not that the same kind of thing didn't still happen today—and a cheap shuttleport lawyer had given him some advice.

"Don't bother to convince me you're in the right. I'll grant you that without argument," said the lawyer, "but getting a settlement, and especially collecting on it, is something else again. So how far are you willing to go?"

"What do you mean?"

"To make them think you're crazy?"

"Crazy!"

"Crazy enough to beat somebody up. Burn something down. Zero some expensive equipment. Catch my drift?"

To Dare Chin's eventual amusement and edification, it had proved unnecessary either to sue or to carry through on his threats—so apparently he'd been willing to go far enough. As an administrator he had learned to think of this sort of paralegal strategy as the "personal approach."

The time had come to use the personal approach on Dewdney Morland. Chin left his office and descended the stairs to the ground floor.

Morland was standing in the middle of the floor under the dome, hunched over his instruments. His back was to Chin; work lights on tripods joined with the overhead spots to pinpoint the Martian plaque and Morland himself in a circle of brilliant white light. Dewdney Morland, Ph.D., had arrived on Mars a week ago, preceded by clearances from the Council of Worlds Cultural Commission. The past two evenings, starting when Town Hall closed for the night, Morland had set up his kit and worked until dawn. He had to work at night because his optical instruments were sensitive to minor vibrations, like footsteps—

"What the hell?"

—the tremor of which now caused Morland to look up and whirl around angrily.

"You! Look what you've done, Chin! Twenty minutes' recording *ruined.*"

Chin's only reply was a look of distaste bordering on contempt.

Morland was a disheveled fellow with a pasty complexion, a patchy beard, and sticky blond hair that hadn't been cut in recent months; split ends curled over the collar of his expensive tweed jacket, which had long ago sagged into shapelessness. Those bulging pockets, Chin knew, contained a pipe and a bag of shredded tobacco, the paraphernalia of a habit that people who live in controlled environments regarded as not only offensive but extraordinarily quaint.

"First that cow tromping through here and now *you*," Morland screeched. "What does it take to get it through your provincial skulls? I need absolute *stillness.*"

On the floor beside Morland's chair, Chin noted an open briefcase; from what Chin could see, it contained a few fax copies and the remains of a portable dinner. "Would you step aside, Dr. Morland?"

"What did you say?"

"Please move to one side."

"Listen, do you want me to get an order barring you from these premises while I'm working? It can be swiftly arranged, I assure you. The Council of Worlds executive building is only a few steps away."

Chin leaned forward and his features darkened. "*Move*, fat man," he bellowed, "before I break your stupid face!"

It was a convincing display of homicidal rage; Morland recoiled. "That's . . . This . . . I'm reporting this to the commission tomorrow," he choked, meanwhile dancing rapidly away from the display case. "You'll rue this, Chin. . . ."

Chin ignored him as he stepped forward to examine the plaque. It rested on a cushion of red velvet, glittering in the converging beams of light. The silvery fragment had been broken from some larger piece by a blow of unimaginable force, but nothing that had happened to it in the billion years since had left so much as a hair's-width scratch upon it. The perfect surface in which Chin now observed his own features proved that this was not a copy of metal or plastic, and when he breathed upon it and saw his cloudy breath obscure his reflection, he knew without touching it that this was no hologram. It was the real thing.

Morland was still yammering at him. "You must realize, of course," he said with all the venom he could muster, "that even the condensation of your foul breath on that surface renders everything I have done tonight utterly useless. I shall have to wait hours before . . ."

Chin straightened. "Shut up."

"I most certainly will not shut . . ."

"I've been talking to people about you, Morland. Yesterday, to the Musée de l'Homme," Chin said over Morland's breathless monologue. "The University of Arizona this morning. An hour ago, the Museum of Surviving Antiquities in New Beirut." He held the yellow faxgrams up in front of Morland's face.

Morland, for the first time since Chin had entered the hall, stopped talking and eyed the faxes warily. He did not ask to read them. "All right, Chin. I despise your primitive behavior but now at least I comprehend your pathetic excuse," he said more quietly. "I should like to remind you that penalties for libel are spelled out quite specifically in the Uniform Code of . . ."

"I'm not going to bother to tell anyone anything about you, Morland," Chin said coldly. "You're on Mars." He nodded to the nearest wall of glass. "There's not enough oxygen outside that wall worth mentioning. The temperature tonight is minus fifty cees. Our pressure tubes require constant maintenance, and every once in a while we still get failures. If that happened in your neighborhood you'd have to grab your pressure suit—you've got it with you, haven't you?'' Chin had already noted that he didn't. ''No? A lot of visitors make that mistake—sometimes their last. And even when you do have your suit with you, you can't always be sure it hasn't sprung a leak. You might want to look yours over pretty carefully when you get back to it.'' Chin nudged Morland's open briefcase with his foot, not bothering to look at it. The briefcase was big enough to hold the plaque, big enough to conceal a copy, easily big enough to hide a miniature holo projector and who knew what other clever submicro gizmos. ''I hope you hear me. I don't have any interest in libeling you. I only want to give you some expert advice.''

Chin turned his back on Morland and walked out of the hall. He waited to hear if Morland would shout after him, in threat or protest. But Morland said nothing. Perhaps the man really had gotten the message.

Lydia Zeromski needed to be alone for what she was facing, so she'd sealed her helmet and gone directly outside, into the freezing night.

Labyrinth City sprawled around her, a jumble of glass. But for the glowing pile of the Mars Interplanetary Hotel to her left, perched on the edge of the cliff, the only illumination came from dim lamps inside the pressure tubes and the night lights of darkened buildings, hundreds of little spheres of light that glowed like jellyfish behind the rippling green glass.

She paused and turned. She could see Morland clearly, inside Town Hall's central dome, lit up like a patient in an operating theater. He was bent over the plaque, apparently deep in study. High above the dome, the glow from his lights reflected from the arching sandstone that sheltered the upper town. She looked for Dare in his office; his office light was on, but she could see no movement on the second floor.

She turned away and walked until she came to the edge of the cliff. She waited there, peering into the darkness. The lower city fell away like a handful of crystals down the cliffside below her. Moving among its steep stairs and huddled houses and the ruby glow of the late-night wine houses was a single bobbing yellow lantern—Old Nutting hurrying along her rounds.

Lydia's mind was so full that she hardly saw the familiar starlit vista beyond, the huge cliffs of Noctis Labyrinthus—the Labyrinth of Night. Banded strata of red and yellow sandstone were reduced in the half light to stripes of black and gray with, occasionally, a thin edge-on layer of bright white. The white was ice, permafrost, the buried water which filled the Labyrinth with wispy sublimated clouds on the warmest of mornings, the water which made Mars habitable, upon which all its life and commerce depended.

Spires and spectacular arches of rock outlined themselves against a sky filled with hard blue stars—hundreds of spires, arrayed in ragged ranks, marching stiff-shouldered toward a horizon that should have been near but was lost in a soft haze like a Chinese ink painting, a haze of hanging microscopic dust. Lydia stood quietly, hardly moving, as the comforting wind stirred the fine sand around her.

Gradually she became aware of another figure standing and watching the sky, silhouetted against the glow of the Interplanetary.

Lydia knew the man; even masked in a pressure suit, Khalid Sayeed's tall, graceful figure was easily recognizable. He was gazing at the distant horizon, where among the stars two brighter lights gleamed.

One of the two was moving toward the eastern horizon, inching along against the fixed backdrop: that was Mars Station, swinging high enough above the planet to catch the light of the sun. The other was a wanderer too, but it moved too slowly for its movement to be obvious within a single night: that was the planet Jupiter.

Lydia thought she knew what Khalid was looking at—not at Jupiter but something far beyond that planet, far and dark and invisible but coming closer to Mars every day.

Movement caught her eye. The main lock at the entrance of the hotel opened, and for a moment a group of tourists was silhouetted against the lobby, laughing soundlessly inside the pressure tube. They milled about briefly in drunken confusion and then found an intersection that led toward the lower town. She turned away, but not before she saw the hotel manager follow them out.

Wolfgang Prott was a man Lydia loathed, an unctuous charmer who had the good sense to stay away from the local women but was rarely without a tourist lady on his arm. His romances lasted about the length of the average tour package.

It was a small town, Labyrinth City, and the people who lived here knew each other too well. They tried to laugh it off, but sometimes it was hard to do what you wanted to do or had to do, with the whole planet looking over your shoulder.

Dare Chin regained his office and keyed his commlink for patrol headquarters. He intended to take no chances—his first priority had been to let Morland know he was under surveillance, but that was only partially true; now Chin was going to try to bully or cajole the local patrollers into actually providing decent protection for the plaque until Morland was safely off the planet.

He'd tapped in two digits of the three-digit code when he heard something downstairs.

Chin left the patrol code unkeyed and walked quickly back down the hall toward the stairs. He went down the steps slowly, as silently as he could, hoping to catch Morland off guard.

Stepping into the hall from the bottom of the stairwell, he brought himself up short, surprised by what he saw. He opened his mouth to speak—

—but Dare Chin had already spoken his last words.

* * *

An hour passed. The sleepy town grew quiet. Jupiter was still bright, but Mars Station had set beyond the eastern horizon. No one was looking out over the Labyrinth when the moon Phobos crept over the rim of the town's sheltering arch, following Mars Station in its track across the sky. No one was there to see the streak of white fire that leaped from the clifftop above.

PART
1

ENTERING
THE LABYRINTH

1

In the night country there are no sure identities, no trustworthy coordinates, no breakable codes. . . .

The woman's dream was the same dream of swirling that had overcome her so often before, but she had never dreamed it in this form. Black wings were beating, beating, inches over her head; they went around like spokes in a wheel; they bore down upon her and simultaneously threatened to suck her into the center point of their turning.

In the darkness at that turning center, eyes were staring, hands were reaching, mouths were calling: *"Linda, Linda . . ."*

She thrashed and struck out, but she was mired in some viscid invisible fluid, some ethereal muck that rendered her strongest efforts feeble, her quickest motions slow.

"Linda!"

She knew that she was losing the struggle, going under—and she cried out.

The sound of her cry awakened her.

She found herself naked in hot darkness, wrapped in a clinging shroud. A man was pressing himself against her, pinning her arms against the bed, crushing her, lying across her with his own nakedness. She bucked and squirmed and cried out again.

"Linda, wake up. Please wake up." His words battered her. "It's a dream. It's only a dream."

All at once she fell limp and silent. She knew him.

And a moment later she remembered approximately where she was, on the still-accelerating ship.

"Are you all right?" he asked.

"Yes," she whispered hoarsely.

He released her wrists, lifted himself, moved his weight to crouch beside her on the bed. "Can you tell me what . . . ?"

"Don't call me Linda." Her voice was empty, drained of strength and emotion.

"I'm sorry. I was asleep. You started hitting . . ."

"Linda is dead."

In his silence, his refusal to reply, she read contradiction: no, Linda was not dead—

—but she was lost, and until she was found again she was better considered dead.

The woman peered at the man's face in the darkness, seeing him better than he could see her. To him, in the blackness, she was an immediate construct of memory, a familiar form, a warm smell, sweet textures under his hands, but to her the pinprick light on the cabin wall, gleaming red beside the commlink, was enough to lacquer his smooth-muscled skin with a faint ruddy glow. She saw his eyes gleaming in the night. The smell of him was like spiced bread, rich and comforting—

—and arousing. With the involuntary return of heat to her body came, in a rush, the full memory of the night.

They were two days out from Earth on the speeding ship, en route to Mars. They had played just-friends at first, but once they had gotten to know the ship and its crew they no longer felt awkward about being by themselves—though it took her longer than it took him to relax her innate shyness—or about taking time to be alone together. After dinner in the wardroom that evening, after the ship's clock had turned the corridor lights low, they had disappeared into her narrow cabin. The crew had taken care to pay no attention.

They had begun to pick up the fallen threads of their renewed acquaintance where they had been forced to drop them more than a week before. Here, they were alone, unrushed, unreachable, with no obligations, and with all the momentous events that hung over them held in suspension until the day, almost two weeks away, when the ship would reach its destination.

She thought she might love him. He already claimed he loved her. She loved his kind of loving: sensitive, understanding beyond even his intimate knowledge of the facts—after all, he had known her since they were children—at once intelligent and sympathetic. But his loving, his desire for love, was insistent too, and physical.

At first it had seemed as if their lovemaking would be as easy and natural as if they had never stopped being with each other, as if they had always lived together. A few minutes after they had closed the cabin door behind them, all her clothes were fallen to the floor, and all his had fallen on top of hers, and they had stretched their slim hard bodies beside each other on her narrow bunk, unmindful of the crowding.

Something she could not define was wrong. She hesitated. Responding, he paused. She felt the effort it required of him, as intensely as if she were him—what it required to restrain the hot urgency that so easily slides into mindless need. His love was before his need, but the need was strongly there. And she wanted him, too; her body had wanted his, especially and only his. . . .

When she tried to move toward him again she was seized with sudden pain. Its cause was not apparently physical; it had nothing to do with him. But it had manifested itself below the pit of her stomach—a cramping, seizing abnegation.

"I . . . I can't . . ."

"Can't?"

"I'm sorry."

"If this isn't . . . I mean, just tell me . . ."

"Something's wrong."

"Are you all right? Should I call someone?"

"No. No, stay here. Stay with me. It's better now."

He had stayed with her, eventually curving his arms and legs and the length of his body around her as she faced away from him, nestling into her as she rested in his embrace—

—while she wept silent tears. And when finally she fell asleep he stayed awake, surrounding her in her sleep.

For an hour or more black unconsciousness settled over her. He slept too, relaxing his hold on her. Then the dream started. . . .

Now she was awake again, awake and full of fear and desire. "I don't think I want you here," she said to him. "I can't be myself with you here."

He was still for a moment, unmoving. Then he swung his legs over the side of the canvas bunk and stood. "As you say—Ellen." He stooped to pick up his shirt and trousers from where they lay discarded on the floor.

"No, I . . ." Her head was spinning. "I didn't mean it that way. . . ."

"What did you mean?"

"Something . . . in me . . ." Fragments of speech fell from her lips, unconnected. She pushed herself to say what she resisted acknowledging, even to herself. "I'm afraid. . . ."

"Of them?"

"No. Yes, of course." She hesitated. "Yes, I'm afraid of them, but that's not what I meant, I meant that . . ." She forced the truth out. "I'm not human. I'm afraid I'm not human anymore. That's what I think."

He sat on the bed and reached a hand to touch her shoulder. At his electric touch she began to cry. She leaned into his chest and let his arms go around her shoulders, and she cried with sudden apprehension of the depth of her loss—the loss of her parents so long ago, the loss of herself, the loss of everyone who had tried to love her.

She cried a long time before she fell asleep for the second time. He laid her gently back on the bed, lifted and smoothed the tangled sheet, and let it settle over her. He sat beside her in the darkness, holding her hand.

They did not sleep together after that. She said little to him when they met in the small confines of the ship, and she spent her time reading obsessively, reading the files of the current case, listening and viewing and reading what the ship's library had to tell her about their destination and, having finished everything pertinent to her assignment, reading everything else the ship had in its files.

She did not ask him what he found to amuse himself. It was hard to bear his disappointment, his hurt and defensive looks.

Three nights later the dream came again. Even as she was in it she watched it as if from another persona, a newer, more hardened persona, and it seemed to her that what she was seeing was not a dream at all, but a vivid and true memory. . . .

There was a knock on the bedroom door—her bedroom was in the gray woman's house, a low brick house, prettily furnished, with a big yard and old trees, but for all its suburban charm it was inside the multiple fences of the compound in Maryland—and the knock surprised her, because the gray woman and the gray man never knocked, they just came in when they wanted to, caring nothing for what she was wearing or doing, making a point of her lack of privacy. She knew what brainwashing meant, and she knew that was part of what they had been doing, or trying to do, ever since they had taken her from her parents.

But now there was a knock. "Linda." It was her father's voice, and she could smell the warmth of him through the door.

"Daddy!" She jumped up and tried the knob—usually it was locked—and opened the door to reveal him standing in the narrow hall, small and tired, his brown tweed suit crumpled as if he hadn't taken it off for days, his black hair streaked with more gray than she remembered.

He did not move, only stared at her. "Linda, thank God you're safe," he whispered.

She threw herself into his arms. "Oh, Daddy." She surprised herself by starting to cry.

He hugged her tightly a moment in silence before he whispered, "We have to leave right now, darling."

"Can I bring . . . ?"

"No. Leave everything and come with me."

She leaned back in his arms and turned her tear-streaked face up to him. The touch and smell of him alerted her that he was afraid. She nodded yes silently and stepped away, still clinging to his hand.

He led her through the darkened house. She saw the men in the shadows—at the front door, in the kitchen hall, beside the glass doors to the back-yard—standing in brace-legged poses with pistols held high. As her father pulled her through the living room and toward the open glass doors he signaled to them, and they fell into step at their backs, covering their retreat with nervous glances.

A low black Snark crouched on the lawn, its twin rotors swinging quietly in whistling arcs, its twin turbines whispering through muffled exhausts.

Her father hesitated inside the glass door and then broke from the cover of the house and ran for the helicopter, tugging Linda after him. The men followed, moving out to flank them.

With her uncanny eyesight Linda could see in the night, could see the staring white face of her mother waiting inside the open side door of the chopper. She opened her mouth. Something was wrong. . . .

A hand yanked Linda's mother aside. A man stepped into the chopper door. Linda heard the cough of the gun muzzle and the simultaneous screech of enfilading fire from above and behind her, saw the fiery streaks of tracers overhead.

She and her father had come half the distance from the house. The man in the chopper door was directing his fire not at Linda or her father but at the men who guarded them. There was at least one attacker on the roof of the house, at least one other in the trees. Caught in the crossfire—taken by surprise—the guards were falling.

Linda's father had yanked her arm and sent her sprawling on the grass, diving and rolling after her.

But she was up and on her feet again before he came to a stop—*at the time she did not know she possessed the dense tissue knotted in her forebrain, but her separate persona, her new persona, who was watching this vivid dream, knew she possessed it; that knotted bit of brain kicked in to make the calculations and deductions; her right eye zoomed in on the man in the helicopter and saw his deliberate aim, tracked the trajectories from his automatic weapon, saw that he was carefully shooting around her, even at the risk of leaving himself exposed—* and she crossed the final few meters of lawn, under the whistling rotor blades, in a lightning sprint. Inside the chopper her mother was screaming with open mouth, but the words emerged so slowly that Linda could not hear them. The gunman turned away from his work in what seemed like slow motion, comically shocked to see Linda rushing at him.

His hesitation was his death. She caught him at the knees and knocked his weapon aside with a wrist-breaking blow, and as he twisted in a vain attempt to avoid her, he put his head in the way of a bullet from one of the wounded guards and tumbled out of the chopper, lifeless. She had already memorized his appearance; now she could forget it.

Linda thrust at the person who held her mother, not hesitating at all when she recognized the gray woman who had been her captor, but launching her fist like a piston into the woman's eye and sending her reeling back against the fuselage wall, stunned.

"Linda, behind you!" her mother shouted.

Linda spun and dived for the chopper's cockpit. She could have been floating on the moon: the scene was a frozen tableau. The man in the left seat was half out of it, twisted toward her, swinging his arm toward her at the rate of one millimeter per century; the body that slumped out of the other seat was presumably that of the legitimate pilot. Linda—in case she should ever meet him again— dispassionately recorded the usurping pilot's looks and the strange smell of him, half cologne, half adrenaline, noting calmly that she had seen him at least once before. Then she plucked the pistol—a .38 Colt Aetherweight with flash suppressor—out of his unwilling hand.

Time unfroze. She brought the pistol down with precisely aimed force against the side of his head, under his ear. He collapsed, and she yanked him out of his seat, pulling him bodily over the backrest.

She moved with the grace and sureness of an acrobat, leaping into the seat, taking hold of the controls. She shoved the throttles forward; the turbines rose in pitch and the rotors accelerated. She twisted the pitch control, and the armored machine shuddered and rose half a meter from the ground. Expertly she let it spin where it hung on the axis of its own rotor shafts, just a quarter turn, until it faced the attackers on the roof of the house, presenting those unseen gunners with a slender target. She stopped it there and squeezed the triggers of the Gatling guns.

The noise was an ear-piercing howl. Blue fire—a hundred rounds in half a second—ate off the roof of the house.

In the stark white beams from the chopper's floodlights she saw her father's body lying facedown in the grass. There were other bodies in the grass, not moving, those of the guards. She pushed the chopper's nose down and the heavy craft stuttered forward, roaring and blowing, until it was hovering almost on top of her father, its steel skids bracketing him.

She spoke aloud to the helicopter. "Snark, this is L.N. 30851005, do you acknowledge?"

"I acknowledge your command," the helicopter replied, confirming her voice pattern.

"Hold this position in three-dees," she ordered. "Rotate to cover me if necessary. Return fire if fired upon."

A handful of bullets sprayed the chopper's nose, crazing the armored cockpit glass—somewhere in the shadows to the right, there was another gunner. The Snark jerked right and its starboard Gatling gun screeched; the tree from which the bullets had been fired exploded in tatters.

There was no resumption of fire from beyond the

disintegrated tree. "Order confirmed," said the helicopter, with a machine's satisfaction.

"Hold your fire," she heard a man shout in the darkness, and she knew the voice: the gray man's, Laird's.

She jumped out of the command seat, into the cabin. "Mother, help me." Together she and her mother—a strong and slender woman, her hair as black as her husband's—wrestled the limp bodies of the hijacker-pilot and the gray woman and rolled them through the open door. The gray woman tumbled out after the man and bounced from the skid to lie motionless beside him in the grass.

"Stay back. Inside," Linda said to her mother, as she jumped out and landed lightly on both feet, flexing deeply, diving and rolling under the chopper in a continuous series of precise actions. The noise and the wind buffeted her ears, but she could separate the boom and shriek of the chopper from the shouted voices nearby.

Her father's black hair was bright with blood from a scalp wound, but he was conscious. "Can you move?" she shouted.

"My leg is broken."

"I'll pull you."

The chopper suddenly shifted where it hung in midair, and she saw shapes running at the edge of the lawn. But no bullets came out of the dark, and the Snark, following its orders to the letter, did not fire. Crouched on her knees, she hauled her father by his shoulders, and he did what he could to help, pushing at the muddy lawn with his good right leg; she saw that he had lost his shoe. For fifteen seconds she was exposed as she pulled him under the skid.

She boosted her father by his shoulders and he hopped unsteadily onto the skid. Her mother took his hands and tugged as he bent and pushed off with his right leg. He landed heavily on the floor of the chopper.

As Linda poised to jump after him she felt the blow to her hip. There was no pain, but it was as if someone had hit her and pushed her to the ground, and when she tried to jump up again, nothing happened. She felt nothing in her leg and could not move.

The Snark swiveled, but its Gatling gun stayed silent. It had not heard the bullet any more than Linda had.

Linda lay on her back, staring up into the meshing blades, seeing the white faces of her mother and father peering down at her only a meter away—*"Linda! Linda!"*—their hands outstretched.

Her mother started to climb out over edge of the door.

"Snark," Linda shouted. "Immediate evasive action. Take all necessary measures to protect your passengers."

The Snark heard her. Its searchlights went dark; its turbines instantly wrapped up to supersonic pitch and it rose screaming into the sky, rocking sideways.

Laird's shout: *"Fire! Fire! Stop them!"*

Tracers tore at the chopper and bounced from its skin and whined away from its rushing rotors. With her uncanny eyesight Linda saw her mother fall back through the open door and saw the armored door slam closed behind her, as the Snark took steps to protect its human cargo. In seconds the helicopter had vanished into the hazy night sky.

She lay on her back, alert and helpless, smelling the wet warm grass and the burned fuel and the H.E. and the blood, as figures came running out of the darkness to stand over her.

"Kill her, sir?"

"Don't be stupid. Not until we're sure her parents are dead."

"We'd better face facts, Bill," said another. "We can't just pretend that nothing's . . ."

"Don't tell me my business. Patch her up and do a good job of it. There may be inquiries."

"Bill . . ."

"It's *not* over. This can be contained."

"William . . ."

The gray man flinched, and Linda looked up ruefully at the face that pushed into the tightening circle of her consciousness, the face of the gray woman; she stood beside Laird, her long gray hair spilling in tangles, a silenced pistol in her hand. That's who had shot her, Linda realized—after Laird had told the others to hold their fire. Shot her because Linda had not taken the time, had not had the will, to kill her first.

"Why her?" Laird barked at the gray woman. "It's Nagy you should have killed, him and his wife."

"I didn't intend to kill her, William. I intended to keep her here."

The bedraggled helicopter pilot staggered into the circle of faces, his face contorted in rage. "You left her an opening! She . . ."

"Shut up," the gray man said, ignoring him, glaring at the woman. "Nagy came near to succeeding, and he's not through yet. How could you be so careless?"

"We can't simply discard her, William. She could be the greatest of us."

"No more! She resists our authority. She has always resisted it. Look at this . . . this debacle."

"She's a child. When she realizes the truth, when she really understands everything . . ."

"To resist us is to resist the Knowledge."

"William . . ."

"No more talk from any of you." He looked down at Linda with the hardest eyes she had ever seen, even in his hard face. "This one is so much

unenlightened meat. We'll put her away somewhere she can't be found. Then we'll start over.''

Seeing herself lying paralyzed on the grass, her
new persona knew that if she could free herself
from this horrible dream of reality, she would be
safe. Linda opened her mouth—*"Blake,"* she whispered. *"Blake."*

Laird looked down at her and his face twisted
into a bitter sneer.

This time when she came awake, there was no
one with her. And as she lay alone in the dark
cabin, her heart pumping, she struggled mightily
to remember what she had just been dreaming.

2

The gleaming white ship fell swiftly toward Mars, a sleek cutter emblazoned with the blue band and gold star of the Board of Space Control. It was falling tail-first toward Mars Station; its fusion torch had been extinguished at the radiation perimeter, and the ship was braking itself into parking orbit on chemical rockets alone, maintaining a steady one-gee acceleration.

Shielded against heavy radiation in every wavelength, its hull had no windows opening upon the universe. The young woman stood before the wall-sized videoplate in the wardroom, watching the view from the stern, where black Phobos slid across the pale orange disk of Mars—a moon only twenty-seven kilometers long seen against a planet only 6,000 kilometers away. "Potato-shaped" was the cliché people had used to describe Phobos for over a century, but no other phrase captured the essence of its form so succinctly: pitted, lumpy, black, Phobos could have been a fine russet spud freshly dug from Idaho's volcanic mud.

The woman who watched this intimate spectacle called herself Sparta. It was not her real name. It was her persona, the mask she showed only to herself, and Sparta was a secret name, secret from everyone but herself. To most people she was known as Ellen Troy—Inspector Troy of the Board of Space Control. Which was not her real name either. The people who knew her real name held her life in their hands, and most of them wanted to kill her.

To those who did not know her, Sparta seemed young, beautiful, intelligent, mysteriously gifted, strangely lucky. She was in fact powerful beyond casual comprehension. But to herself she seemed frail, her humanity crippled, her psyche constantly on the edge of dissolution.

Now she'd been yanked out of the normal course of her life once again—if her life could in any sense be considered normal—to be thrust without preparation into a situation which would require her complete alertness and total concentration, a peak performance that was to be demanded after two weeks of suffocating shipboard imprisonment on this cutter. Given the present alignment of the planets, an Earth-Mars crossing in two weeks was as close to instantaneous as even a Space Board cutter, the fastest class of ship in the solar system, could get . . . two weeks during which Sparta had nothing to do but study the meager information on the unsolved case that awaited her.

Her brooding was interrupted by the young man who entered the wardroom behind her. ''Phobos and Deimos,'' he said cheerfully. ''Fear and Terror. Wonderful names for moons.''

''They fit well enough,'' she said. ''The chariot horses of Mars, weren't they?''

He lifted a black eyebrow over a green eye. ''Ellen, is there really something your encyclopedic brain hasn't stored? If you want to get fussy, the god in question was Ares—the Greek war god, not the Roman. Phobos and Deimos were two of his three sons by Aphrodite, not his horses.''

''I read they were his horses, and they ate human flesh.''

"Mangled mythology. The man-eating horses—there were four, one also named Deimos but none named Phobos—belonged to Diomedes. You'll recall him from *The Iliad*."

She smiled. "How do you keep all that stuff in your head?"

"Because I love that stuff. I love *The Iliad* enough that I got through even Alexander Pope's awful translation." He smiled back at her. "A woman who calls herself Ellen Troy," he whispered, "really should read it at least once."

Blake Redfield—his real and quite public name—was one of the few who knew that her name was not Ellen Troy. He was one of the few—perhaps the only one of those who knew the truth—who did not seek to kill her for it. If at times Sparta thought she loved Blake, at other times she was afraid even of him. Or perhaps of her love for him.

Love was a subject she had been avoiding lately. "Look, you can see Phobos Base."

Bright points glistened on the edge of Phobos's biggest crater, high-rimmed Stickney, eight kilometers across. Sharply limned against the midlatitudes of Mars, Stickney was an iron-black chalice against a golden mirror. Eighty years ago the first human expedition to Mars had landed on Phobos, and for several decades the moon had served as a base for the exploration and eventual settlement of the Martian surface. "Looks like it was built yesterday," Blake said. "Hard to believe it's been deserted for half a century."

Aluminum huts and domes still stood on Stickney's far rim, undamaged, unoxidized, a time capsule of planetary exploration.

On the videoplate Phobos was already sliding away; off in the far corner of the screen Mars Station emerged from the crowded field of stars—it being the reason Phobos Base was deserted, no longer of practical use. The station was a big bottle of air that rotated fast enough to provide substantial artificial gravity on its inner surface.

They watched in silence until Mars Station blazed as bright as the sun and the black moon had dwindled to a void in the star field. Sparta turned to Blake. "What we talked about before . . . I've thought about it some more. I want you to stay on Mars Station until I've completed the investigation."

"Sorry. I won't do it."

"They know who we are. We *don't* know who *they* are."

"We know how they operate, anyway. I better than you."

"I was trained for this job," she said, her voice hardening.

"I believe my training matches yours," he said quickly, "even if it has been a bit unorthodox."

"Blake . . ."

"I'll prove it to you."

"Prove it?"

"Right now, in the gym. Hand to hand."

"What would that prove?"

"You said it yourself: we don't know who they are. So you'll have no more warning than I will. If I can beat you hand to hand, what's the logic of penning me up?"

She hesitated only an instant. "I'll meet you in the gym."

Perhaps Blake had played into her hands. The side of her that loved him had its own motivation, for she wished him to survive even if she did not. The side of her that wanted him out of her life, that wanted all things human out of her life, could dispense with him easily. But as she knotted the black belt around the rough cotton of her gi, she knew that she would have to fight him handicapped.

Was he really playing into her hands then? Or was she playing into his?

* * *

They entered the ship's tiny circular gym from opposite sides. Sparta was slight, muscular, her sandy blond hair falling straight to her jawbone, where it was chopped off in a practical cut that made no concession to fashion; the bangs above her thick brows were short enough to leave her dark blue eyes unscreened. Blake was a few centimeters taller, with broader shoulders and heavier muscles. His dark auburn hair was as straight and choppy as hers and his green eyes were as steady as hers; his Chinese-Irish face could have been unsettlingly pretty, but it was saved from perfection by a too-wide mouth and a sprinkle of freckles across his straight nose.

They bowed to each other, then straightened.

A heart's beat . . . their knees flexed, their hands came up like blades, they began warily to close. Unlike most human fighters, who tend to circle, they came straight on like animals. In combat, neither favored their right or left; any such asymmetries they had failed to train out of themselves would be betrayed only in the extremity.

At two meters distance they reached an imaginary boundary, the edge of the lethal zone. Here each could still take in the other at a glance, from head to foot, from eye to hand. Here neither could reach the other without evident preparation.

But Blake was the one with something to prove; he would have to make the first move. It was quick, a leap and a high wide-legged kick that left him vulnerable. For a flicker of time her inhibition intervened—as he had calculated and hoped.

But his kick missed her jaw.

She would not be reticent again. So quickly was she on him when he landed that he barely escaped with a sideways roll. He regained his balance and shot a hard jab at her belly, but she pivoted and chopped at his neck, connecting only with air.

The battle was truly joined. The minutes stretched to two, then five, then . . .

A shoulder roll across the rough polycanvas floor of the gym brought Sparta bounding to her feet in time to catch Blake's counterattack; despite a feint to her midriff with his left fist she easily read his intention and brushed aside his right hand as it swung toward her nose, taking his wrist. As she pivoted to take his arm down and past, she indulged in a split-second's reconsideration and realized that the move had been a setup. Here was the real assault. Just as the fingers of his left hand brushed the lapel of her gi, she let go and somersaulted backward, launching herself with a knee to his hip; his fingers closed on nothing.

Again they rolled away to opposite sides of the little gym. Again they bounced up, panting. Both were pouring sweat, nearing exhaustion. For ten minutes they'd been going at each other with all the strength and guile they could muster. He'd laid an offensive hand on her just once. She'd done little better. The ruddy patch on her cheekbone where he'd caught her with the hard edge of his palm was darkening to a bruise; his bruises, on his ribs and the outside of his left thigh, were invisible under his gi, but they would leave him limping when he cooled down.

Neither of them said a word, but no one seeing the red gleam in Sparta's eye or the knotted muscles of Blake's jaw could mistake this for friendly exercise.

It got abruptly unfriendlier when Blake pulled a knife.

In half a second he had hitched up his thick black belt and freed it from where it was strapped to the small of his back. Its diamond-filmed carbon-carbon blade was just long enough to be lethal;

standard North Continental Treaty Alliance military issue, it was a useful tool for cutting or stabbing or, in a pinch, for throwing.

He moved toward her, the knife grip snug in his right palm, its leaf-shaped blade pointed at her wishbone.

"Aren't you taking this . . . a little far?" she rasped.

"Give up?"

"Don't make me hurt you," she warned.

"Words. We've been even. Until now."

Warily he circled, lunged in a feint, recovered before her darting hand could capture his wrist, lunged again and went inside her guard, found himself snared by her leg and had to snap roll out of it, found her diving for him. He faked a retreat and then rolled into her; she overshot.

The tip of the blade ripped the cotton of her gi at waist level. He too had his inhibitions.

Before he could get to his knees she was back on her feet and coming at him. He measured the kick aimed at his head and dodged it, but her bare heel connected with his wrist instead. The knife flew out of his numbed fingers, but he got his other hand on the back of her black belt and allowed her momentum to carry him onto her back as she sprawled. His right hand was useless, but his arm went around her neck and he pulled her chin back with the crook of his elbow.

Not soon enough. One of her legs and one of her arms had escaped his pin and she was twisted sideways under him. He felt the tip of his own knife against his kidney; her long jump had brought it into her hand.

For a moment they lay like that, frozen, two battling carnivores caught in the ice.

"You could have broken my neck," she whispered.

"Just before I died, maybe," he said. He slowly relaxed his grip and rolled away from her.

Sparta sat up. She said nothing, but flipped the knife endwise to catch the tip and handed it to him handle first.

"Okay, I didn't beat you." As he took the knife he expelled his breath sharply, ballooning his cheeks. "But you didn't beat me, either. And nobody we're likely to come up against could be as good as you."

"You don't think so?" She put her hands behind her neck and gripped it with knitted fingers, rolling her head to stretch out the kinks. "What if Khalid turns out to be our man after all? You said his training was the same as yours."

"Up to a point."

"Maybe beyond it. We don't know *who* they *are*, Blake. . . ."

"Yes, yes. But I'll hold you to your promise." He gave her his hand and they helped each other stand. "I've proved I can defend myself."

"At a constant one gee. Mars gravity is a third Earth's."

He ignored her sophistry; she didn't need reminding that she'd never been to Mars either. "I didn't come all this way to sit in a tourist hotel in Labyrinth City."

"You're a civilian consultant, not a Space Board officer."

"Then I'll work the case on my own." He slipped the knife into its scabbard and settled his belt over it. "With your cooperation or without it."

"I could arrest you for interfering."

"Forget what a sap that would make of you," he said hotly, "since it was you that brought me along. Just think about how much time you'll waste trying to find me after I disappear."

Sparta said nothing. He had no idea how easy it would be for her to find him, no matter how clev-

erly he disguised himself, no matter what steps he
took to cover his trail. She could follow the touch
and smell of him, the warm tracks of him, anywhere he tried to run. That he had fought her to a
draw impressed her, for she had fought as hard as
was humanly possible. But she did not want him
to know how far she was from simply human, or
that she had not used against him the abilities that
set her apart.

Not that she was stronger or better coordinated
than he. Her muscles were smaller and her ordinary nerve impulses were no quicker than his, but
this was compensated in the normal way of things
by her smaller size and mass, her ability to move
the parts of her body faster through space in simple
obedience to the laws of physics. Weightlifters are
not good gymnasts; sumo wrestlers are not good at
karate. But between her and him it was an even
match, more even than it might have been.

Things had been done to her brain, among other
organs. The natural human brain had evolved to
its species-specific state in grasslands and open for-
ests. The ancestors of humans effortlessly per-
formed simultaneous partial differential equations,
continually matching and revising trajectories while
running alongside fleeing zebras and wildebeests
while pelting them with rocks, or swinging from
branch to branch, plucking an occasional fruit
along the way—and our relatives can still be observed doing it, in the great parks of Africa and the
Amazon. We humans retain some of this ability, if
only a shadow.

We are very good at throwing things, much better than our nearest relatives, the chimpanzees—
good at hurling spears, shooting arrows, aiming
guns, playing horseshoes, and so forth. We are almost as good at catching things. Perhaps the most
extraordinary demonstration of the human brain's
capacity to compute and match trajectories occurred

in the mid-20th century when an athlete named Mays, playing the traditional American game called baseball, positioned himself—while running as fast as he could—beneath a small white horsehide-covered sphere which, struck by an ashwood club, had been lofted into the air some hundreds of feet on an unpredictable parabola. Mays—still running, not turning around, and shortly before colliding with a wall marking the boundary of the playing field—caught the ball as it descended over his left shoulder into his glove.

Probably no natural human before Mays or since could have done that. But Sparta, if the need arose, could do the equivalent. The tiny dense knot of cells that nestled in her forebrain just a little to the side of where the Hindus place the eye of the soul was a processor that integrated trajectories and made many other kinds of calculations faster, far faster, than the brain itself. Had she made use of this knot of cells, had she switched it into her mental circuits, Sparta could have read every move Blake Redfield made before he had well started it; she could have ground his face into the mat ten seconds after their match had begun.

She had stayed human voluntarily and done her best. Which was as good as they naturally come. And Blake had done his best, which was equally good.

"Okay," she said. "You can work on your own. If you promise to keep in touch." She didn't tell him he was right, that he was probably as formidable as anything the enemy could bring against him. And if they were armed, which was likely—well, he would be too.

The look on his face was peculiar. "I promised that already."

"I know you, Blake," she said.

He leaned toward her, and as his lips parted there was a softness about his eyes and mouth, an expression almost of longing. But then a ripple of uncertainty crossed his face. His mask hardened. When he spoke he said, "I wish I could say the same."

Still sweating, they rode the cramped elevator to the command deck.

"All this is useless if anybody makes you," she said.

"Makes me what?"

"Excuse the jargon. Recognizes you on Mars Station, I mean."

"We've gone over this."

"Equally useless if you don't make it onto the regular shuttle run. I could commandeer a shuttle if I had to, but you've got to make the scheduled run or you're out of the fight."

"Give me credit for *some* brains."

"I give you credit. I don't want anything to go wrong."

"Stop worrying about me."

She watched him sidelong. "Before I met you, I didn't worry about anybody but myself."

"You worried about finding your parents," he said bluntly.

"Yes."

"And the others."

"Yes, Blake, the others. The ones who tried to kill me and who probably killed them."

"Because that's why I'm here . . ." He broke off. When his emotions got the better of him he sometimes forgot that he must always call her Ellen, if he named her at all. When he'd first met her as a child, and throughout the eight years of their growing up together, her name had been Linda. "That's what all this is about."

"No, it's simpler than that. We're here to solve two murders. We're here to recover the Martian plaque. That's all anyone needs to know."

"I think your bright-eyed and bushy-tailed, blue-eyed Space Board commander knows more already. A lot more."

She was saved a reply when the elevator door abruptly slid open. "Let's talk to the captain."

"Through the flush tubes," said the captain. Her name was Walsh, and she was maybe thirty years old, this veteran cutter pilot—old enough to have gained the experience, young enough to have retained the synapses. "We put you in a bolus bag, flush you into the station's holding tank; half an hour or so later, somebody fishes you out."

Blake paled. "You want to flush me into a tank of liquid hydrogen?"

"Deuterium slush, technically speaking."

"What keeps me from freezing? What do I breathe?"

"That's all covered. These bolus bags are supposed to be pretty good," said the captain. "Never had occasion to use one personally."

"Is there some method a bit more traditional?" Sparta asked quietly.

Walsh shook her close-cropped head. "We know there'll be spies. Every port crawls with 'em, free-lance types mostly. We know some of the spies on Mars Station, and we know they're onto what you call the traditional methods, Inspector—assuming you mean laundry bags, that kind of stuff." She shrugged. "Told me before, we could have dumped him on Phobos, picked him off on the next orbit."

"That's standard?" Sparta demanded.

The captain grinned up at her. "I just thought of it this minute. Phobos looked pretty good on this approach. Might be worth a try, don't you think?"

"You're very resourceful, Captain," she said.

Walsh relented. "I know it sounds scary, Mr. Redfield, but it works. I can't guarantee the local busybodies aren't onto it already, but at least you're not going to die in there.''

Blake let his breath out slowly. ''Thanks for the reassurance.''

''Make sure your bladder's empty when you climb into the bag. Could be a while.''

''I'll keep that in mind.''

Mars Station dominated the sky, its thick blunt cylinder turning against the stars, its axis pointing straight down; from the approaching cutter's angle the space station looked like a slowly spinning top, balanced on the sharp arc of the planet's horizon.

Newer and more comfortable than L-5, the first of the giant space settlements which orbited the Earth, but older and simpler than Venus's Port Hesperus, the crown jewel of colonies, Mars Station was a pragmatic place built from metal and glass that had been smelted from a captured asteroid, its design owing much to the Soviet engineers who had supervised its construction. The station was too close in the cutter's videoplates for those on board to see anything but the glassy expanse of the cylinder's starside end—its angled mirrors, its communications masts, its docking bays protruding from the unrotating axle like spokes from a nave.

A ring of ships floated ''at anchor'' in near space, for docking room was limited. But the Board of Space Control maintained its own high-security locks and had its own ways of moving passengers and cargo on and off its ships. The paid spies and idle watchers who continually lurked about Q sector clustered thicker whenever a Space Board ship arrived.

This time, after the docking tube had slammed shut over the cutter's main airlock, the watchers saw only one passenger emerge, a slight blond woman in Space Board blues. Inspector Ellen Troy.

3

Blake spent two hours cuddled in fetal position inside an overheated black plastic bag with an oxygen mask clamped to his face. As he was beginning to feel the first nibblings of anxiety—*do they remember I'm in here?*—something punched the side of the bag; a teleoperator arm had gripped it and was drawing it slowly through the deuterium slush in which it was immersed.

Once through the tank's locking valves, it took Blake several minutes to work himself free of the triply insulated bag. He was getting unseen help from outside. Finally he clambered sweating out of it, leaving it wobbling like a collapsed balloon in the microgravity. Blake found himself hovering inside the Q sector pumping station, surrounded by huge spherical tanks of deuterium and lithium, the precious fuels that powered the Space Board's fusion-torch ships.

"You are Mr. Redfield," announced a small, black-haired woman in Space Board uniform, who was studying him with evident distaste. "I am Inspector L. Sharansky."

Blake nodded at Sharansky, trying to be polite as he glanced curiously at the raw steel walls that surrounded him. The cavernous chamber was festooned with thick garlands of pipe and cable. Clouds of white vapor rolled through the air, condensing from tanks and pipes that flowed with liquid hydrogen. Red and yellow warning lights made the clouds glow and turned the dripping steel room into an antechamber of hell.

He returned his gaze to the inspector. She was definitely unhappy about something; her thick black brows were knitted together in a fearsome scowl.

"Very happy to meet you, Inspector Sharansky," he said.

"*Da*," she said. "These for you." She thrust a bundle of smelly clothes at him. "Please put them on now."

He was glad to comply, since he was wearing nothing at all, and if he was in hell, hell felt like it was freezing over.

It occurred to him that Sharansky's disapproval had to do with confronting a naked man; for all their political progress in the past century, the Soviets had never lost a certain puritanical streak. When he finally finished pulling on the grease-stiffened black pants and heavy black sweatshirt and black boots—no simple task in weightlessness—he oriented himself toward her and tried another smile. "They'll never see me coming on a moonless night."

"Is no moonless nights on Mars," said Sharansky.

"A joke," he said.

"No joke," she said, shaking her head vigorously.

"Right," he said, clearing his throat, "and it's not funny, either."

"Is other clothes," she said, shoving a duffle bag in his direction. He took it without comment and waited for her to make the next move. She consulted her noteplate, then held out a tiny sliver. "Is

I.D. sliver and job record. You are Canadian. Your name is Michael Mycroft.''

''No doubt I'm known as Mike,'' he said brightly.

''That is correct,'' she said, nodding briskly. She continued to consult the noteplate. ''You were dismissed from Mars Station Central Administration Bureau of Community Works. You were grade six-point-three-three plumber. . . .''

''Why?''

She glanced up. ''Why?''

''Why was I fired?''

She stared at him a moment before she said, ''Insubordination.''

He grinned. ''I'll bet you just made that up.''

She colored slightly and bent her head closer to her noteplate, peering as if she were nearsighted. ''You want to go home but have not enough credits. No one on Mars Station will hire you. You have only enough credits to get to Mars surface. If you do not get employment there . . . work shelter for you.'' She looked up then, and he suspected that she was perversely satisfied at the prospect of work shelter for *him*. ''Your passage to Labyrinth City is reserved and paid.''

''I don't know the first thing about plumbing,'' Blake said. ''Does it have something to do with pipes?''

Sharansky handed him another sliver. ''Learn from this. Contains all details of your covering story. Earpiece in shirt pocket. Learn fast, data self-erases in one hour—sliver becomes popular-music library, latest hits. Questions?''

''Uh, no point in asking . . . just steer me out of here.''

Dressed in the greasy coveralls that seemed to be the lot of workers at the bottom of the pile, even in socialist utopias, Blake followed Sharansky's directions and got himself out of Q sector without being challenged or, he hoped, observed. He had sixteen hours to catch the shuttle at the far end of the station; Sharansky had firmly suggested that he report directly to the planetside shuttle port, but he thought it would be a good idea to become as familiar with Mars Station as he could without drawing attention to himself.

He wasted no time in the starside docking area, where a grade six plumber would have had little to do, but instead headed for the living areas. He rode one of the three wide, slow escalators from the starside hub, the one marked 270 DEGREES in Russian, English, Japanese, and Arabic. He got on the thing weightless, grabbed a moving handrail, found gentle footing after a few dozen meters of descent, and walked off the telescoping steps at the bottom weighing what he would have weighed on Earth.

The ride had taken him down the long slope of faceted glass window-rings that refocused the rays of the distant sun, like the Fresnel lens of a 19th-century lighthouse turned inside out. He moved past built-up terraces where passengers lately arrived from other gravitational environments—Earth's moon, the asteroids, the surface of Mars, or any long journey through space—could spend time adjusting to heavier gee forces. Blake was already adjusted; most of the cutter's trip from Earth orbit had been at one gee, the first half accelerating, the second half decelerating.

Mars Station was simple in design but impressive in its sheer size—an entire town curled up inside a kilometer-long cylinder, so that houses and public buildings climbed up the sides and hung down from the opposite wall far overhead. Each narrow street was lined with neat, modest town houses stacked side by side, each with its patch of grass and carefully trimmed trees and flowering shrubs—

the whole lot looking like a prosperous Siberian suburb under the long summer's midnight sun, but rolled up like a map. Sunlight entered the station from the angled reflectors at both ends of the cylinder, and some visitors had likened the effect to living on a planet with two small but rapidly rotating suns.

Mars Station lacked the contrasts of sprawling L-5, lacked that station's huge farms or its raw-steel industry or the range of its living quarters, from the primitive to the opulent—nor was Mars Station as luxurious or as tasteful as Port Hesperus, with its great garden sphere. But it was home to 50,000 busy souls, half again as many people as lived on the surface of Mars itself.

Blake studied the view a few minutes, matching the reality to the maps he'd been given. The mythical Mike Mycroft had been employed in maintaining water mains and sewers; the datasliver provided by Sharansky included not only instructions on how to fix pipes, but a layout of Mars Station's water recycling system.

The principles of municipal plumbing were simple enough, and Blake thought he could be persuasive on the subject if the need arose; he was more interested in the feel of everyday life on the station. He set out on a walking tour.

His first stop was on nearby Nevski Place at the base of the escalator, at the residential hotel which was supposedly Mycroft's last address. Like many of the station's larger buildings, the two-story hotel was sided and roofed with corrugated iron streaked with a thin wash of black paint; from a distance the effect was surprisingly delicate, almost like that of plaited bamboo.

Blake walked boldly past the front door and then returned to peer into the small lobby. On his first pass he'd seen an old woman in black dozing behind the counter, snoring profoundly. With quick, quiet steps he crossed the asphalt tiling to the narrow stairs. He climbed to the second floor and quickly located what was supposed to have been Mycroft's room, which faced the building's facade. He put an ear to its thin painted iron door and heard nothing.

It took him no time to force back the latch bolt, using as a lever the stiff datasliver Sharansky had given him. That act ruined the datasliver, but he'd already absorbed what it had to teach him, and he was not interested in the album of "latest hits" into which it was soon scheduled to transmogrify.

He looked around the closet-sized room with its bunk bed, wall-mounted videoplate, iron desk, and iron chair. It occurred to him that wood is necessarily a rare commodity when the best source of raw materials is a captured asteroid. The wall hooks had nothing hanging from them. It was apparent that the local Space Board office had done their homework—it was the sort of place a lone man like Mycroft would stay, and it appeared recently vacated.

The room had a single open window. Standing at it, Blake could see down into the crowded plaza. The grand escalator was full of people descending and ascending, like angels on Jacob's ladder. Blake had never been to Russia; the potpourri at the bottom of the staircase reminded him of the tram terminal at the Manhattan end of the Fifty-ninth Street bridge, although here, in one corner of the square, a woman in a red velvet jacket was putting a dancing bear through its paces, and nearby a man was selling not bagels or franks but hot piroshkis from a wagon.

He leaned forward and peered out the window. From this angle—or to someone lying on the room's bottom bunk—the window gave a view of the huge glass rings at the starside end of the cylinder. The angle of the prisms which filled the circular "sky" had gradually adjusted so that now the incoming sunlight was halved; the blue street lights surrounding the plaza had begun to glow, and a stage-managed twilight was about to close upon the station.

Station time had been arranged to correspond to time at the prime meridian on Mars; because the normal Martian day, or sol, was twenty-four hours, thirty-nine minutes, and 35.208 seconds long, humans adjusted happily to the diurnal rhythms of Mars.

On Nevski Place, opposite his hotel window, there was a restaurant; the leafy ornamental trees of its "outdoor" patio were strung with festive colored bulbs that spelled out its name in several languages: Nevski Garden. The aroma of grilled sausages wafted to Blake, and he realized that not only was it the local dinner hour, but he had not eaten since gulping a prepackaged high-carbohydrate snack on the cutter, more than five hours ago. Surely Mike Mycroft would have been a frequent patron of that attractive place.

Then Blake noticed something else. Two men and a woman had stopped still in the crowd that swirled in front of the Nevski Garden and all three were staring up at him. One of the men pointed, and his shout carried easily across the bustle of the crowd to Blake's ears.

"It's him!"

The men and the woman started pushing their way through the crowd toward the hotel, shoving people out of their way, breaking into a run when spaces opened before them.

Blake jerked away from the window. What was going on? Three people were coming after him and they looked *mad*.

There were only two ways out that he'd noticed, the main stairs up which he'd come and the fire escape at the end of the hall. From half a block away it's hard to make subtle judgments about people you've never met, but he doubted that his pursuers were stupid, even if they were making a big mistake. They surely would split up to cover both his escape routes.

That was about all the thought he had time for. He looked out the window again. The three weren't in sight. A couple of them were probably already inside and coming up the stairs.

He threw the sash all the way up and climbed onto the windowsill. He stood there a moment looking up—the eaves were wide—and then down. He would survive a jump to the plaza below, but he could easily break an ankle. He turned around on the sill, facing the inside. Carefully he balanced himself, extending his arms and bending his knees like a diver on the edge of a high platform preparing to do a back flip. He let himself fall back—

—and a fraction of a second later jumped with all his strength.

He got his hands on the edge of the eaves. The corrugated iron dug into his palms, but he hardly noticed. He swung once, twice, his body straight as a pendulum, then up, thrusting his upper torso flat across the roof—the pitch was gentle, to match the programmed rains—and he got his right knee up, then his left, and he was on the roof and running.

He ran to the opposite end of the building, hoping to find another fire escape. No luck. There were no alleys in all of Mars Station; the sort of business that went on at the back doors of buildings on Earth—deliveries, recycling, and the like—was handled in the station's sublevels, and most buildings were widely separated. Blake saw no neighboring roofs within handy jumping distance.

In the garden behind the hotel—an L-shaped patch of grass defined by the back of the hotel and two apartment buildings—an exhaust stack thrust

up from the sublevels. With luck, he could leap
across to the ladder rungs on the side of the stack.
He hurled himself across three meters of plain air
and hit the stack hard, slipped on a rung, wrenched
his shoulder, and banged his ear against the side of
the stack—

—but he was still mobile enough to climb down.

His feet hit ground level just as the two men tumbled through the back door of the hotel. For a second they all stared at each other. Then the men
rushed him.

Blake was cornered in the little garden, hemmed
in by walls of corrugated iron. The men—young,
lean, hard, curiously slender—set on him with
flailing fists. They had more enthusiasm than style.
''Dirty scab,'' one of them hissed, just before Blake
discouraged his ardor with a savage kick to the
groin.

That one was down, writhing in pained surprise
on the ground, but the other man was a little
quicker, a little warier. Blake easily parried a couple of his vigorous light-handed blows, but—
feeling an awkward wrench in his shoulder from
his slip on the ladder—fumbled the counterattack.
Still Blake managed to roll out of the clench. He
dashed for the corner of the hotel, hoping to reach
the crowded plaza beyond.

From above, two booted feet slammed into his
wounded shoulder—the woman, the third member
of the trio, had climbed up the fire escape ladder
but had turned around when she realized he'd gotten past her, getting back down in time to jump
him as he ran under her—and he went sprawling
under her two-hundred-and-fifty-kilo weight.
Blake's bad landing slowed him, and he was on
his knees when the woman kicked him again, her
boot connecting with his ribs beneath his upraised
left arm. She was *strong* for a skinny gal! He caught
the shadow of the two men out of the corner of his

eye and tried to hurl himself away, but he was too late; he was hit from behind by something blunt and heavy.

For a second—or maybe a minute, or maybe more—everything was black with whirling purple splotches. When Blake opened his eyes, the woman was walking away, looking back at him with undisguised venom, her pale complexion flushed and her brown hair streaked with sweat, but showing no apparent inclination to continue the fight. Behind her stumbled the two men, equally angry but oddly subdued. The one Blake had kicked was trying to disguise his limp; he spat on the ground in front of Blake as he passed, but said nothing.

"You are all right?" The man helping him sit up had a huge square face, chiseled in flat strokes as if it were a sculptor's rough wooden model, deeply lined around his mouth and nose. He was wearing loose blue coveralls that like Blake's might have been washed once within the past year or so.

"What . . . oww!" A searing pain shot through Blake's side as he turned to look at the sullen trio, now arguing loudly among themselves as they disappeared into the crowd.

"You are sure you are not hurt?"

"Not really, just bruised," said Blake, gingerly feeling his ribs. The bruises were psychological, too. After his bravado performance in the gym against Ellen, he'd flunked his first real test and had needed rescue by a stranger. "Thanks for helping." He lifted himself slowly to his feet.

"Yevgeny Rostov," said the man, thrusting out a callused and grease-blackened hand. "I convince them they make big mistake."

"Mike . . . Mycroft," Blake said, holding out his own right hand, suddenly conscious of how badly it matched his cover. Not that it was a soft hand—Blake exercised himself by climbing rocks, among other pursuits—but neither was it a plumber's hand. Blake's ordinary work, which he had not paid much attention to of late, was with rare books and manuscripts. Dusty work, not greasy work. "Who did they think I was? Who are *they*?"

"They are from Mars, like me. They think you are man living in that hotel room last week, but I stay in that hotel and I tell them *nyet*, that room is empty two days now, you are not him."

"I wonder what he did to get them upset?"

"Something bad, who knows?" Yevgeny shrugged expressively. "You come with me, Mike. You don't need clinic, maybe, but you need to re-store your strength."

A few minutes later Blake and his savior were seated under a gnarled Russian olive at one of the Nevski Garden's outdoor tables, anticipating the arrival of a platter of the sausage of the day. The waiter slid a couple of foaming mugs of black beer onto the zinc tabletop and Yevgeny nodded at him, which was apparently good enough to settle the bill.

"Thanks. Next round's on me," said Blake.

Yevgeny raised his mug. "*Tovarishch*," he growled.

"Comrade." Blake raised his own. He sipped tentatively at the opaque brew and found its flavor strong but not unpleasant.

In the busy plaza nearby, most people were hur-rying home for the night. A few poor souls, possi-bly including a grade six plumber or two, were trudging to their night jobs. The inhabitants of Mars Station were less flamboyant than the hothouse crowd on Venus's Port Hesperus, their clothes and hairstyles tending toward the sensibly dull—more overalls than shorts and miniskirts—but the racial and social mix was what Blake was beginning to think of as typical of space, mostly Euro-Americans, Japanese, and Chinese, with some Arabs. Most people were young to middle-aged; there were only a few children and first-generation old-sters in evidence. But Blake knew he shouldn't generalize from his brief experience. Besides Port Hesperus, he had visited only Farside Base on the moon, and that briefly, and there were many other colonies in space, farther from the sun, where the odor of vegetable curry was more prominent than the odor of grilled meat.

"You are new to Mars Station," Yevgeny said.

"Passing through. Going to Lab City on tomor-row's shuttle," said Blake, thinking that perhaps he should have taken Inspector Sharansky's advice and gone to the shuttle dock right away.

"Thought I might take a hotel room for the night, but they ask a lot here. For what you get, I mean."

Yevgeny's thick brows lifted above his deep-set black eyes. "Not tourist, I think."

"No, looking for work."

"What kind of work?"

"What kind you got?" Blake said with a shrug. He didn't want to be too mysterious, but he hoped he could curb Yevgeny's bold curiosity.

The waiter arrived with their dinners. Blake sliced into a crisp brown sausage with enthusiasm as Yevgeny stabbed his and raised it whole toward his mouth. After a few minutes of relative silence Yevgeny emitted a satisfied belch. Blake said, "Good food."

"Pig that went into it raised here on Mars Sta-tion. Pigs are efficient. Garbage in, protein out."

"As efficient as the engineered food molds?"

Yevgeny shrugged. "You don't look like vegetar-ian to me."

Mike grinned and wiped the last drop of fat from his chin, reflecting that maybe a plumber's life on Mars Station wasn't all that bad. Already his stressed muscles were beginning to relax.

A woman came out of the restaurant and sat at

a table in the shadows beneath the wide eaves: Ellen, looking slim and confident—and, Blake couldn't help thinking, beautiful—studying a portable flatscreen. She was wearing her blue Space Board uniform. He stared at her a second longer than he should have, but she betrayed nothing.

Yevgeny was watching him. By now the fractured sun had disappeared from the glass sky, and the big man's swarthy features were illuminated only by the colorful glow from the strings of decorative bulbs. "Personal history not important, only social history," said Yevgeny with heavy affability, his eyes flickering toward Sparta, the cop in the shadows.

"Her? I'm not running from the cops, if that's what you mean."

"There is great socialist work to be done on Mars."

"The terraforming?"

"*Da*. Two centuries, maybe sooner, people will walk outside without pressure suits, breathe good air. Then water will flow on surface. Beside canals will be green fields, like in fantasies of 20th century."

"Big job," said Blake.

"Plenty to do. You find work without trouble, Mike."

"You said you live there?"

"But do liaison work here, for Pipeline Workers Guild. Guild workers employed by capitalist corporation, Noble Water Works Inc., employed by socialist government of Mars, prime agent of consortium of North Continental Treaty Alliance and Azure Dragon Mutual Prosperity Endeavor under charter from Council of Worlds." Yevgeny grunted. "In spare time am student of history. Is necessary."

"You'll be up here a while, I guess," Blake said hopefully.

"Going back tomorrow on *Mars Cricket*, same shuttle as you." Yevgeny lifted his mug and downed the bottom half of its contents with a series of muscular swallows. When he slammed the mug down on the tabletop again he said, "You stay by me, I introduce you around Lab City. Make sure you find work without trouble."

"That's great," said Blake, cursing himself. Blake, not much of a drinker, took a sip from his mug and tried to look enthusiastic. He knew now that he should have taken Sharansky's advice and kept out of sight. Unless he could find a graceful way of detaching himself from this insistently friendly character, he would arrive on Mars with his cover blown in advance.

"You know any women here, *tovarishch?*" Yevgeny asked. One woolly eyebrow arched lasciviously as he slowly swiveled his great head to watch the women passing in the plaza. He returned his gaze to Blake, and his expression sagged. "Is foolish question. I introduce you around Mars Station. Maybe you meet somebody you like, don't need hotel tonight. Now drink your beer, is good for you, plenty proteins." Yevgeny belched heartily. "Must keep in condition. Easy to go soft, on Mars."

Among the craft clustered at the station's planet-side docking hub was a sleek executive spaceplane, the *Kestrel*, flagship of Noble Water Works Inc. In the little head just forward of the tiny four-couch cabin, the *Kestrel*'s pilot was peering intently at his reflection in the mirror, using small tweezers to pluck at the fine hairs of his pale eyebrows. He was a pleasant-looking fellow whose round face was covered with confetti-sized freckles; his bright orange hair nestled in tight curls against his skull.

A warning bell sounded. The pilot reinserted the tweezers into a slot in the handle of his penknife, straightened the knot of his orange wool tie, and turned away from the mirror.

He pulled himself effortlessly through the cabin to the airlock aft and checked its panel lights. "Pressure's fine, Mr. Noble. I'm opening up."

"About time," came the answering voice on the comm speaker. "I catch you in the head again?"

"Things to do forward, sir." The pilot spun the wheel and pulled the hatch open. He floated back toward the nose of the plane as Noble emerged from the airlock. Noble sealed the airlock and followed the pilot toward the flight deck.

Noble slipped off the jacket of his dark pin-striped suit and secured it in the locker opposite the head. As the pilot strapped himself into the left seat, Noble climbed into the right. Noble was a square-built man with a sandy crewcut, his handsome face made rugged by wrinkles he'd acquired in two decades of drilling and construction on Mars.

"Did the meeting go well, sir?" The pilot, without prompting, was already running the prelaunch check.

"Yes, the laser drills and the truck parts will be offloaded today and come down to us on tomorrow's freight shuttle. The textiles and organics will have to go bonded through customs. Should be three days or so."

"That's not crowding the launch window?"

"No, it's not. It's precision timing. Rupert assures me *Doradus* will be loaded and cleared for launch on schedule."

"Well, sir, no problem then."

"No problem." Noble rearranged his silk tie under the harness. "By the way, the Space Board investigator is here. Quick trip."

"I saw the cutter starside as we came in."

"Aren't you curious?"

"Should I be?"

"She's famous. Getting to be their star. Let's

see"—he ticked off the examples on his fingers—
"solved the *Star Queen* case. Got Forster and Merck
off Venus. Saved Farside Base." Noble raised an
eyebrow. "Maybe the Martian plaque will be
next."

The look on the pilot's face was curiously mixed:
part pleasure, part something else. "Ellen Troy?"

"Right first time."

The pilot nodded and resumed his flight check.
"If you're all set for launch, sir, I'll notify traffic
control."

4

The gossamer Martian atmosphere extends much farther into space than does the air near gravid Earth; the wind began to whistle over the wings of the *Mars Cricket* soon after the shuttle left Mars Station, falling planetward. It would not stop even when the shuttle rolled to a halt on the ground, for on Mars the wind is eternal.

After what seemed a too-short trip the shuttle's tires walloped fused sand and the craft slid unimpeded across the desert floor. Sparta bent her head to peer out the tiny oval window for a first close-up peek at the landscape of Mars.

Nearby, it was an astonishing blur.

Spaceplanes and shuttles land hot on Mars. Supersonic aircraft must be wedge shaped, and even with swing-wings forward they stall easily in the thin atmosphere, despite the low gravity. So runways are narrow lines across the red sands, thirty kilometers long and aligned with the prevailing winds, with ranks of barrier nets across their ends.

Farther from the blurred runway Sparta could resolve a plain of shifting dunes stretching to the base of distant bluffs. The banded bluffs were steep and high and everywhere in shadow, except to the east, where only their tops were in sunlight; their line stretched across the horizon, glowing vibrant gold at their ragged crests, deepening to royal purple in the open shadows below. At this longitude evening was approaching, and the twilight sky was a peculiar shade of burnt orange in which pale stars were already twinkling.

Minutes passed, until at last the shuttle perceptibly slowed its headlong rush, finally braking to a smooth stop well before it needed a barrier, letting its pointed snout droop toward the ground. Its wings, carbon black when cool, still glowed orange in the Martian twilight.

A ground tractor fetched the shuttle from the runway and towed it slowly toward a distant cluster of low buildings. The freshening breeze blew wisps of pink sand across the taxiway. Except for blue runway lights and the distant green gleam of the passenger terminal, there was no hint of life in the dusty expanse. Then Sparta caught sight of figures moving across the sand, people wearing brown pressure suits, hunched against the wind. She had no idea what their business was, but in their postures she read the cold, and she shivered.

Inside the terminal the air was warm. She stepped lightly from the docking tube; she weighed no more than eighty-eight kilograms, forty pounds, and here she was strong enough to lift a desk or jump all the way across the little terminal building, which was no bigger than an ordinary magneplane station on Earth.

The building was oddly charming: it was a long barrel vault of green glass, improbably arched, its interior surface cast in intricately slick and watery designs, its streamlined outer surface polished by the wind. Iron-rich green glass was a favored building material on Mars, and low gravity permitted virtuoso feats of architecture. Unlike brick, which needs water for its manufacture (much less

cement, which needs quantities of fossil sea creatures as well), glass requires only sand and solar
energy. Even a little thickness of glass screened the
ubiquitous ultraviolet radiation that impinged on
the Martian surface. Thus an entire Martian style
had arisen, an oddly light and delicate style for a
frontier culture.

Sparta did not linger to admire the terminal
building's miniature glass cathedral. She stayed just
long enough to watch Blake and his big, boisterous
new friend Rostov walk off in the direction of the
shuttleport hive. They'd climbed aboard the *Mars
Cricket* showing every sign of intoxication; while the
Russian was belting out a soldier's colorful drinking song, Blake had been imitating a balalaika—or
so his *thrummy-drumm-drumm* noises were intended, as he'd loudly announced to the passengers.

Most unlike Blake. He wasn't a drinking man.

Shortly after she'd spotted them at the Nevski
Garden, datalink access had identified Rostov and
provided her with his resume. Yevgeny Rostov was
a high-level operative in the Interplanetary Socialist Workers Party, currently the business manager
of the Pipeline Workers Guild, Mars local 776.
Sparta wondered how Blake had managed to make
such an interesting connection in so short a time.

Unless Rostov, not Blake, had made the connection . . .

Given that Blake's cover had made him out to be
virtually indigent, the shuttleport hive was the only
place for him. Sparta, traveling expenses paid, had
a reservation at the Mars Interplanetary Hotel. She
grinned. Too bad for Blake, but he was the one
who'd wanted to work underground.

Among the two dozen shuttle passengers were a
few businessmen and engineers, but most were
gaudily coiffed and coutured tourists of the type
who could afford the money and time required for

a grand tour of the planets. Sparta followed the pack past the exchange desk to the luggage chutes.

"Direct transportation to Mars Interplanetary Hotel! Premier accommodations on Mars! Visit Phoenix Lounge! Best view of spectacular natural wonders and entertainment nightly . . . !"

A robot trolley squatted in the mouth of the main corridor, a jolly pink light revolving on the mast above its open seats, its voicer squeaking: *"Visit Ophir Room! Lavish gourmet fare! Swim in largest expanse of open water on Mars! Only three thousand dollars per night, per person, double occupancy! World Express and major bank slivers accepted! Limited number of rooms available to late registrants . . ."* by which the trolley meant that the hotel wasn't full.

The trolley repeated its spiel in Russian, Japanese, and Arabic while fumbling tourists climbed aboard. Sparta was in no hurry to arrive at the hotel. She stood by watching as the loaded robot vehicle trundled off down the slanting corridor on its rubber tires. She shouldered her duffle bag and began walking slowly along the underground corridor.

She went through two pressure locks and arrived at a curving slab of dark glass in the wall. Overhead, the shuttleport runway ended in a cliff. The corridor through which she was walking had brought her through a short tunnel to the side of that cliff—and what she saw through the clear glass of the vista point was so beautiful it brought tears to her eyes.

What she saw was the standard holocard picture of Labyrinth City, set in a tiny corner of the Labyrinth. Like any famous view, the local residents took it for granted and, in fairness, anyone no matter how aesthetically responsive would sooner or later have filed the view with the familiar—that was human nature. But at this moment it was new to Sparta.

She wiped her eyes, angry at the stab of emotion that left her feeling vulnerable. Why does a person cry, confronted with unexpected beauty? Because sudden beauty is a reminder of what we believe we have lost, whether or not we ever really had it. At least we had—before our lives got too far down the line—the potential. Here Sparta was presented with a glimpse of paradise, a perfect world that once was or might have been, but now never would be.

Overhead, Phobos was moving against the stars as slowly as if in a processional. That close dark moon was no wider than a fourth the width of Earth's moon seen from Earth, but for all its inherent blackness it was a beacon in the Martian sky. And even at its slow pace Phobos was a hustler, orbiting Mars once every seven and a half hours, rising twice each day in the west and setting in the east.

Beneath Phobos the Labyrinth's great mesas stood up steeply out of canyons so deep their bottoms were lost in shadow. On the far western rimrock, beyond a thousand baroque spires, a dust storm raged; spikes of lightning stabbed out of its rolling black clouds.

Natural spectacle was not the only thing that had arrested Sparta. Against the shoulder of the nearest mesa a frozen torrent of softly glowing green glass spilled toward the canyon's gathering shadows: Labyrinth City itself. At the head of the glass cascade were the principal buildings—the Town Hall, the local Council of Worlds executive building, the sprawling Mars Interplanetary Hotel—wind sheltered by a soaring arch of sandstone that would have swallowed all the Anasazi cliff dwellings of Mesa Verde. Below the great stone arch, arranged in precipitous terraces, were the town's shops and houses, trailing off somewhere below in hydroponic farms and livestock barns. Bottommost, glowing brighter than the town above it, was the sewage processing plant.

Sparta lingered long enough to match the sight of the Labyrinth and the city to the maps she had stored in her memory, and then turned away from the vista point and started the curving walk to the center of town.

Noctis Labyrinthus, the Labyrinth of Night, was a huge, chaotic patch of badlands—only a fraction of which was visible from any vista point—carved out millions of years ago by the catastrophic melting of subsurface permafrost. Before explorers had landed on the surface of Mars it wasn't known whether the heat needed to form the Labyrinth had been generated by the impact of a giant meteorite, by a vast volcanic outburst, or by some other mechanism. Whatever had melted the ice, the resulting torrents had flowed northward and eastward in flash floods as great as any in the history of the solar system, into the rift valley of the Valles Marineris, where they had helped sculpt the fantastic cliffs and hanging valleys of the biggest canyon on any of the known worlds—four times deeper than North America's Grand Canyon, longer than North America is wide.

When the first explorers reached the Labyrinth, they confirmed that it had formed not as the result of an instantaneous event but over tens of thousands of years—instantaneous by geological standards, perhaps, but not in terms of human life. Mars was still geologically active; deep down, and occasionally at its surface, the planet's volcanic fires still burned. Vulcanism was more common on Mars than 20th century planetologists had suspected. The first active volcano on Mars was sighted within a year of the establishment of a permanent observation base on Phobos.

The Labyrinth's volcanic heyday was over, and today it was stabler than other regions of the planet. The cliffs were still rich in water ice, which here and there lay exposed in layers. The site included some of Mars's most spectacular scenery and was only five degrees south of its equator, which made shuttle landings and takeoffs convenient and fuel conservative. Even the temperature was balmy—for Mars. Throughout its short history Labyrinth City had grown simultaneously as a scientific and administrative base and as a tourist attraction.

A fifteen-minute walk brought Sparta through the municipal tubes to the grandiose lobby of the Mars Interplanetary Hotel.

Sparta's only luggage was the carefully packed duffle bag that rested lightly on her shoulder. Her instinct was to resist the bellgirl who reached for it as she approached the desk, but the social awareness in which she'd been trained, although she'd never felt it a part of her nature, reminded her that the Mars Interplanetary wasn't exactly a youth hostel. She surrendered the duffle without resistance.

She had not been at the desk half a minute when a man approached; disguising her wariness, she turned calmly toward him as he came too close, pushing into her personal space. His blond hair was cut very short and he had skin of the peculiar burnt-orange color that comes from addiction to a tanning machine. His transparent eyebrows were lifted in a smile over his watery blue eyes, and all his yellow teeth were exposed. Sparta noted the wide gap between his upper incisors. He needed work.

He leaned even closer. ''You are Inspector Troy?''

She nodded. Sparta needed no heightened perception to smell the rademas heavy on his breath. It was a common addictive stimulant.

''Please allow me to introduce myself. I am

Wolfgang Prott, the manager of our Mars Interplanetary Hotel here.'' Prott was a tall man, wearing a shiny suit of some silklike fabric—not real,
which would have been worth a fortune—a suit
that was expensive enough to border on the flashy.
''Please call me Wolfy, everyone does, and it would
be odd if you did not.'' He held out his right hand.

His W's were V's, and as she took his moist hand
she asked, mocking his thick Swiss-German accent,
''Did you say *Volfy?* Or *Wolfy?*''

''Volfy or Volfy, it's all the same to me,'' he replied, resolutely cheerful.

Sparta wondered why she'd been rude. She was
not habitually sarcastic, not the sort to dislike people at a glance.

''I am here to extend my personal and most
hearty welcome,'' Prott continued, pushing on.
''May I present you, as a distinguished guest, with
this brochure explaining the particular luxurious
advantages of our establishment?'' He released her
hand and at the same moment thrust a folder of
press releases and publicity holos into it. ''And I
hope you will now join me in our lovely Phoenix
Lounge so that we may enjoy drinks on the house
and listen to the enchanting Kathy at the key-
boards.''

''Thank you but no, Mr. Prott,'' she said firmly.
The enchanting Kathy? The man talked like a recorded advertisement, like the hotel's robot trolley.
She realized that she was responding to more than
one layer of phoniness in Prott—some layers were
deliberate; others seemed compulsive, perhaps
psychotic. ''I will contact you later to arrange an
appointment.''

He seemed unfazed by her rejection. ''I understand, you are tired from your trip, you have many
important business matters to attend to''—making
all the polite excuses for her that she had not bothered to make for herself—''and this is not the most

proper time, but *soon*, and meanwhile be assured that our entire most efficient and friendly staff is at your disposal, and now you will excuse me, I regret that my own pressing business calls me away." With that rush of words he retreated, smiling fixedly, calling out one final, "What a pleasure to meet you!" as he disappeared into the echoing depths of the hotel lobby.

Sparta turned back to the desk clerk. The clerk—who doubtless had signaled her arrival to his boss—returned her gaze without the slightest suggestion of humor.

Her hotel room was discreetly lit and cool, featuring polished glass and slabs of picture sandstone. Glass, lava, petrified dust: the bounty of Mars . . .

She fumbled with a bundle of the local paper and put some of it into the discreetly upturned palm of the bellgirl, who promptly left.

The message diode on the bedside phonelink was blinking redly. She addressed the link verbally as she stripped off her uniform jacket. "Messageboard, this is Ellen Troy. You have a message for me?"

"Just a moment. . . ." The voice was that of a human clerk, not a robot. "Yes, Inspector Troy. Would you prefer a direct feed?"

"No. Read it, please." Why not? The staff and who knows who else had doubtless read it already.

"Dr. Khalid Sayeed of the Mars Terraforming Project called to ask if you would allow him to take you to lunch tomorrow at the Ophir Room. He will meet you at noon, if that is convenient for you. If not, his commlink access is . . ."

"Never mind." She knew Sayeed's commlink number. "Thank you," she said and keyed off. She went to the window and pulled back the drapes. Rather than the wild and austere beauty of the Labyrinth, she was looking down into a stone atrium, a forest of leggy potted palms and spidery ficus trees and, as advertised, the largest open expanse of water on Mars, the hotel's Olympic-sized swimming pool. The ''lavish gourmet fare'' of the Ophir Room was evidently served at poolside.

She studied her reflection in the room's window. Interesting. First Wolfgang Prott and now Khalid Sayeed. Neither of them knew, or should know, who Ellen Troy was, other than a Space Board inspector.

As manager of the hotel, Prott at least had an excuse—but why would Khalid put himself forward? Would Khalid be coming boldly forward to extend a greeting to the detective who'd been sent from Earth to determine his role, if any, in the disappearance of the Martian plaque and the murders of two men?

Or did Khalid know that Ellen Troy's name had once been Linda? No one alive knew that, except Blake—and some few others among the *prophetae* of the Free Spirit.

The spaceport hive was what hives are, a stack of steel honeycomb compartments, each outfitted with a hard bed, enough shelf space to fold your clothes, and an overhead videoplate you could watch while lying on your back. Blake had no intention of spending time there. After he said goodbye to Yevgeny he started prowling.

The shuttleport turned out to be a livelier place than he'd expected. The marshaling yards and motor depots for the big trucks that drove the Tharsis highway were here. This was where they transferred the off-planet goods from the freight shuttles to the truck caravans—tools and machinery, sheet metal and plastic pipe, shoes and clothes and food and medicine and all the other necessities that weren't produced on Mars. Warehouses and commissaries and shops and fuel depots were here, and barracks for workers and researchers and half the population of Labyrinth City, in fact, who referred to the glass houses on the cliffside as the ''showcase.''

If the transients who passed through the hive had little to entertain them besides the canned viddies on their 'plates, the locals had a hangout they didn't talk about much with strangers. Yevgeny had told Blake where to find it. Trudging through the drifted sand between the half-buried hangars and warehouses, Blake had been walking head down into a forty-knot breeze, and he almost missed the long narrow shed tacked onto the back of a spaceplane hangar.

A yellow spotlight illuminated a torn-off scrap of titanium aluminide which hung over the pressure-lock door, a chunk of metal only an expert could recognize as part of a rocketplane's vertical stabilizer, with a name sintered onto the metal in black carbon script: My Pain.

The name of the place was officially the Park-Your-Pain, but Yevgeny said everybody called it Porkypine, or just 'Pine.

Blake pushed through into the lock, waited for the green, and opened the inner doors. He slung his helmet back. The unique atmosphere of the place hit him in the head, a really special stink compounded of rademas, tobacco smoke, perfume, spilled beer, pressure-suit sweat, disinfectant. The noise was at rocket-test-stand level, and this was still early in the week; the synthekord was programmed for a melody like the anguished shriek of a shuttle disintegrating in the upper atmosphere, supported by a complex basso that sought to suggest the sound of the first moments after the Big Bang. No lyrics, though. Pure introspection.

Blue runway lights lit the place, helped out by a dozen surplus videoplates tuned to rolling color bars; it would have been a lot darker if the walls hadn't been sheathed in stainless steel and slag-glass. The burnt-out steel casings of penetrator rockets and spent RATO bottles hung from the ceiling.

Getting from the door to the bar was fun too, sort of the way rugby is fun. Blake wished he were invisible, but every eye in the house was staring at him. He moved as cautiously as he could, inching toward the bar. He didn't want to bump anybody's beer bottle too hard, and he didn't want to brush against any of the local women at the wrong angle—even when they looked at him the way they did. One set of problems at a time.

He made it to sanctuary. "Let me have a Pilsner," he said to the barman, whose bald scarred head had suffered at least as much damage as the torn rocketplane fin outside—in the same wreck, maybe? Well if the wreckage had anything to do with the name of the place and the fact that the owner was supposed to be a retired pilot, this guy behind the bar was so crazy-mad-looking Blake was not about to ask.

When he got his beer he tried to find a corner where he could stand out of the flow of the crowd. He kept his elbows in and his beer at chest level.

Yevgeny was supposed to meet him, having promised to do a bit of job scouting for him. Blake wasn't really all that eager to get a job, but he'd just recognized three faces, the two men and the woman from Nevski Place who'd jumped him, and he wished Yevgeny would hurry. He didn't want to have to repeat his flimsy story again. He'd dribbled out bits of the plumber business here and there, although he'd been forced to improvise, shifting the background of his employment from Mars Station to Port Hesperus.

He moved along the bar, waiting for something

to happen. The men closest to him were yelling at each other over the music.

". . . bust the PWG. They think they can make it bad enough to make us walk."

"What good does that do 'em?"

"When we get hungry they invite the STW in. We have to sign or starve." The speaker's creased and sun-blackened face seemed to belong on a much bigger man, but this was a long-time resident of Mars, with the light build of an old-timer.

His pale opponent still wore a lot of extra one-gee fat. "Noble's never gonna talk to those crooks in the STW. His ass is too tight."

"Noble's not the saint you think he is," a third guy put in.

"I didn't say he was a *saint*, I said . . ."

"Noble's the biggest capitalist on the planet. He doesn't give a damn about the PWG or the STW. He's out to bust the MTP."

"That's the dumbest theory I every heard . . ."

The beery debaters confirmed what Blake had already picked up in a couple of hours of scrounging around the shuttleport. The local Pipeline Workers Guild was under siege; the huge Space Transportation Workers union, one of the first workers' consortiums to extend its influence beyond Earth, was trying to swallow it up. According to some barstool analysts, the entrepreneurs who ran the private businesses on Mars wouldn't mind seeing the PWG, tinged as it was by old-style syndicalism, broken once and for all, even if that meant cutting a deal with the corrupt STW. Others claimed that the real aim of laissez-faire capitalists like Noble was to undermine the Mars Terraforming Project—of which Noble himself was a board member.

"What's a waterworks for?" The pale one was pressing his case. "It's for people. For houses, industry, development. And who's stopping development? The MTP . . .''

''Man, have you got it backwards! The project is developing the whole planet . . . the project is contracting with Noble for the pipeline! So what would *he* have to gain . . . ?''

''That kind of development is *too* real. The MTP measures development in centuries—and meanwhile don't disturb the fossils, all that crap. Look, friend, they say capital accumulates in the long term. Maybe, but where it comes from in the first place is short-term scams. What Noble and the rest of the honkers are looking for is a land rush. . . .''

Too much political theory in the absence of fact made Blake's head spin. He sidled further along the bar and tuned in another high-volume conversation.

''. . . a coupla' months ago they got a case of cyclines. Last month half a metric tonne of copper wire . . .''

''*Merde* . . .''

''You're not kidding. And a week before that, a crate of survey rockets.''

''Penetrators?'' The questioner was a tiny brunette whose brown hair fell in straight bangs to her heavy brows.

''Three to a crate.'' Her friend was a tall sandy blonde whose eyes shifted to catch Blakes's.

''That's in my department. How come I never heard that?'' the brunette demanded.

''Nobody reported it. I came across it in manifests and my supervisor said to keep my mouth shut. I think the company wants to keep it quiet.''

''Why?''

''So other people don't get ideas, I guess.'' The blonde studied Blake while sucking her beer and, in a gesture that was at once crude and oddly delicate, wiped her mouth with her thumb.

''Who's doing it?'' The brunette was persistent.

''I mean, what would you want with a crate of penetrators?''

''Depends on how desperate I was,'' the blonde said, still watching Blake—

—who decided it would be a good idea to sidle back the way he'd just sidled from.

''Mike! Mike Mycroft! *Tovarishch!*'' Yevgeny's baritone cut through the shouting and the whistle and mud of the snythekord music, and for an instant Blake saw every eye in the house flicking his way again.

So much for establishing an identity.

He grinned as Yevgeny plowed toward him. He hadn't figured out exactly what Yevgeny did for the union, but it was something important: a path was opening before him through the packed bodies. The big man had his right arm around a slender woman's shoulders and was crushing her affectionately against his ribs. ''Look who I brought to see you,'' Yevgeny roared, with a wink that would have done credit to Long John Silver. ''Lydia, here is my good friend I have been telling you about so much. . . .''

Big brown eyes, bold eyebrows, high cheekbones and a generous mouth, long blond hair tied in a practical knot at the nape of her neck—what was that name again?

''Mike, here is Lydia Zeromski, whose praises you have been hearing from me. We are lucky to have her with us. She is to leave tomorrow, but had delay. She will be gone soon, though.''

Actually Yevgeny had mentioned Lydia Zeromski once, while reeling off a list of currently unattached women he should keep an eye out for, but Blake knew very well who she was.

He went along with the gag. ''Nice to meet you.'' He smiled his most charming smile at Lydia and got back a stare that went straight to the back of his head.

"Sure," she said, shifting her penetrating gaze to look past him at the wall.

From Ellen's files, Blake knew that the man Lydia had supposedly been in love with was one of the victims who had been murdered two weeks earlier. It was a bit early to expect her to have recovered her cheerful disposition—even if she'd killed him herself.

"Mike, very best of news," Yevgeny said, turning back from the bar with two sweating beer bottles in his wide hands. He handed one to Lydia. "Mm," he said to Blake, meaning wait, and poured half of the other down his throat. "Ahh . . . news! You have job, my friend!"

"I have job . . . a job?"

"Grade eight mechanic, at pipeline head. Even though you are not of our union, I was able to arrange you to enter at appropriate level."

"Yevgeny, not that I'm not grateful, but I'm already a grade six plumber. A grade eight mechanic's a swabber, a gofer . . ."

"Be glad you don't have to enter as apprentice, *tovarishch*, according to strict interpretation of bylaws. Also, because I pull strings, no written exam for you. Start day after tomorrow."

"Day after *tomorrow*!?"

"Report eight in the morning at waterworks motor pool. Crummy leaves for Tharsis at eight-thirty sharp."

Blake stared at the big grinning Russian for several seconds before he found his voice. "What's a crummy?" he croaked.

"Personnel carrier," said Yevgeny. "Ten of you in back. Will be four days on road. Food is standard spacepak—well, almost. Don't worry, *tovarishch*! Is job, eh? And good job! You save much money—no place to spend it!" Yevgeny's laughter was a bark. "Have one more beer from me."

Blake looked at Lydia, who seemed to be profoundly absorbed by one of the bright senseless videoplates on the stainless steel wall. "How long does it take you, the run to the pipeline head?" he asked.

"Three days," she said, without looking at him.

"All by yourself?"

"Usually we do it in convoy. This trip I'm doing it alone."

"Doesn't anybody ever go with you?"

"Never." She turned to him. "Hardly ever. Only when the honkers make me take him."

PART
2

PEOPLE
WHO DIE
IN GLASS HOUSES

5

"Inspector Troy reporting, Lieutenant." Sparta threw a neat salute at the man behind the steel desk in the tiny cubicle.

Polanyi, the local chief, was a pudgy fellow with pale skin and an officious manner, a newcomer to his job and at most five years her senior. "Sit down, Inspector Troy."

She didn't really want to sit, but she had to let him play his role. She took the steel chair facing his desk.

He peered down at the flatscreen on his desk. "We have everything you requested, I think. Our people have been on it full time."

"You know what I really want, don't you?"

"I beg your pardon?" He looked up.

She smiled, trying to reassure him. "I want you to tell me you don't need me. Then I can go home."

His smile was thin. "I think we do need you, though. You've made quite a reputation for yourself in just the few . . ."

"Lieutenant, excuse me, but I start itching when people read my resume out loud. I think it's hives."

He seemed to relax a little. "My point is, maybe some of your famous luck will rub off." He shoved the desktop flatscreen toward her. "While you've been en route we've conducted a couple of hundred interviews, anyone who could have been in the neighborhood at the time of the robbery and murders. We even managed to account for most of the tourists." He and his people had done their work by the book, and he wanted her to know it. "The three locals we named earlier are still on the list. They had opportunity, anyway. Motive . . ."

"Let's not be too concerned about motive for now."

"I take it you're referring to the connection with the sabotage of the other Culture X materials."

"I mean that if we develop the means, the motive will follow," she said, quoting from the manual.

Lieutenant Polanyi nodded. He liked things by the book; what he didn't realize was that Sparta knew the motive behind the motive and had no intention of sharing her knowledge with Space Board functionaries like him.

"What's your unit's relationship to the local patrol force, Lieutenant?"

"The patrol force does what it can to keep the peace, and we handle anything that gets complicated."

"Such as?"

"Black market, that takes up a lot of our time. Drug smuggling is a problem. Occasionally we see contraband items of artistic, historical, or cultural value. Also there are labor questions—this so-called socialist government seems to have had difficulty adjusting to the notion of unions—but short of sabotage or financial finagling, we let the patrollers handle the brawls between the workers and the state. Or the corporations. Whichever." The state and the corporation were evidently equivalent concepts to Lieutenant Polanyi; in that, he was a typical Euro-American, a typical good soldier of the Space Board, willing to do what he was told wherever he was posted.

Sparta glanced at the graphic display on the flat-screen and slid quickly through a few screensful of data. She pushed it back to him and said, "I'll study this later." When she got some privacy she could tap the system memory and absorb what she needed in a few seconds, rather than slog through hundreds of pages of police prose. "Right now I'm still vague on the geography."

"I have a model of the crime scene right here." He took a holo unit from the shelf behind him and set it on the desk.

"Good, bring it with you. Let's look at the real place first." She stood abruptly.

Polanyi was taken by surprise, but jumped up quickly. "Sounds like a good idea," he said heartily, as if he'd been just about to suggest it himself.

They walked through the busy halls of the Council of Worlds executive building, where all the administrative functions of Mars that couldn't be handled from Mars Station were centered. They passed a courtroom and a library. Glowing signs pointed to the detention center, the clinic, the cafeteria. Through the glass walls Sparta could see people moving, talking, communing with their computers; through the thin green floors and ceilings she could see even more people.

She remembered a toy she'd played with once, a plastic maze made of stacked sheets of clear plastic; the objective was to roll a steel ball bearing around and down through the whole stack—through each of the single bearing-sized holes in each deck. She wondered how easily she could find her way down through this vertical maze at night, unless she already knew it well.

A few steps through a busy, echoing connecting tube brought them into Town Hall. All of Mars wasn't big enough to require two jails, two well-equipped clinics, two master libraries, so Labyrinth City's Town Hall held only offices.

With one exception.

She stopped inside a dome of clear green glass. People brushed by on both sides, their heels clicking on the glass floor, some wearing pressure suits, others in indoor clothes, but with their pressure-suit bags slung easily over their shoulders.

Sparta looked around, intrigued. The architecture was Palladian inspired but stretched in the vertical dimension; here again the building material was almost all glass. The glass dome was perhaps thirteen meters high and six meters across, cast in a single bell-shaped paraboloid; arches on four sides of the central dome led into vaulted corridors, also of glass, through one of which they'd just come. The other wings could vaguely be seen through the glass walls, although with the increasing thickness and distortion, it was rather like looking into deep green water. But overhead, where the thickness was minimal, the roof was transparent. The improbably high sandstone ceiling of the cave in which the upper town nestled was clearly visible.

"The glass is so clear," Sparta said, studying the dome. "I'd have thought that your infamous sand storms would have etched it to translucence."

"Martian dust isn't like Earth sand," Polanyi said. "The individual grains are more like clay particles, only a thousandth the size of typical terrestrial sand. They tend to polish the glass rather than etch it."

Her neck was still craned back. "Dust carved that arch, it looks to me."

"Maybe. Melting and freezing water did the rough work—and think how long ago. Keep in mind, most of these buildings are only about ten or twenty years old; in the long run you can polish a hole through anything."

Sparta lowered her gaze to the floor. "Not through that," she said. "Wherever it is, it hasn't been scratched."

Centered beneath the dome stood a display case capped with a hemispheroid of Xanthian crystal that mimicked the dome above it. There was nothing inside the case except a red velvet cushion and a hand-lettered cardboard sign: "Exhibition temporarily removed."

Temporarily, eh? Someone was optimistic.

She looked around at the busy foot traffic, heard the echo of voices and footsteps. "If you wouldn't mind waiting here a minute, Lieutenant."

"Well, if you . . ."

"Just for a minute," she said sharply; his hurt feelings would heal.

She walked quickly down the daylit corridor in which the other murder had taken place, looked at the pressure-lock door at its end, checked the orientation of the buildings outside.

On the way back she made a quick trip up a staircase, walked down another hall, poked her head into an office into which someone was moving new furniture. She ignored the curious stares of those around her. Senses of which they had no imagining were probing and storing in memory everything she laid eyes on.

Barely a minute had passed before she was back under the central dome with Polanyi. "Let's see the model now."

"All right, Inspector. If you'll give me a moment . . ." Polanyi fiddled with the tripod mount of the holo projector, then adjusted its beams. "Here we are." He keyed the projector. Daylight vanished, and the people around them with it. Sparta and Polanyi were invisible to each other.

Around them had formed a visually perfect reconstruction of Town Hall shortly after local patrollers had arrived on the scene of the crime. "The night of seventeen Boreal, twenty hours, eighteen minutes—that's local time in sols," said Polanyi, from somewhere in darkness, "which would correspond to fifteen September on Earth, about two A.M. UT."

The display case was open, its crystal hemisphere tilted back to expose in the crossed beams of overhead spotlights the blank cushion where for almost ten years the renowned Martian plaque had rested. Around the case stood several tripods, some with additional lights, others carrying instruments whose snouts peered at the empty cushion.

Nearby, on the floor, was an overturned chair— and a body.

"Dewdney Morland," said Polanyi.

Sparta walked forward. The whole virtual building responded to her movements; she came closer to the body of the man on the floor until it was at their feet.

"Twenty-two caliber, high-velocity uranium slug entered at the base of the skull, exited upper forehead," said Polanyi's disembodied voice. "Clean entry and exit wounds, powder burns indicating shot was fired from less than a meter away. An execution."

"Why a uranium slug?"

"Couldn't say, but it's a common load on Mars. The patrollers claim the extra mass gives stopping power at a distance in low gees. Local folklore."

"You haven't found the bullet."

"No, nor the one that killed Chin. Nor the pistol."

"The killer must have located them with a counter and picked them up," Sparta said. Uranium slugs were made from spent reactor fuel; they carried slight residual radioactivity.

She bent her attention to the victim, peering at the holographic body on the floor. Morland was a thirty-five-year-old xenoarchaeologist who had been studying the Martian plaque under high visual magnification and in various other wavelengths. He was overweight, with a scruffy blond beard that climbed his cheeks in patches and hair that hung in tangles past his collar. His clothes were expensive organics, baggy tweeds which had apparently not been recently cleaned. A pouch of tobacco had spilled on the floor by his side, and his right hand gripped a pipe.

"Rotate, please," she said.

The invisible Polanyi invisibly fingered the holo projector's controls. The projection turned slowly, the building seeming to sway with it, so that the body could be viewed from every angle. The apparently solid masses of the display pedestal and instruments slid through Sparta without tactile impression.

"Underneath too, please."

The scene tilted strangely away, and Sparta was looking up from beneath the floor at Morland's body where it lay face down.

"Not completely relaxed, but no sign of fear," she said. "The pose suggests he had no suspicion of what was about to happen."

"What do you make of that?" Polanyi's voice was distant and hollow.

"I don't know what to make of it. Maybe he was tense because of what he was seeing through his instruments." She paused. "How much do we really know about Morland?"

Sparta rarely asked rhetorical questions, but she hoped Polanyi would start thinking in less conventional directions than he'd taken so far.

What Sparta herself knew about Morland, while detailed, lacked focus. The man's archaeological reputation, a minor one, had been based on only three papers—although he'd published dozens—which attempted to deduce the nature of prehistoric tools from the marks they'd left on the artifacts they'd been used to shape. Morland had written about calendar lines scratched by Cro-Magnons on reindeer bones, about scraped ears of maize found in Anasazi garbage pits, and about masons' marks on Syrian neolithic shrines. No precise examples of the tools and methods he had posited had been found, but his arguments were persuasive and no one had disputed them. Journeyman scholarship.

Mars had been new territory for him, a leap from the study of primitive technologies on Earth to the study of an alien technology so advanced it was not understood. Although the elemental composition of the Martian plaque was known—titanium, molybdenum, aluminum, carbon, hydrogen, traces of other elements—the techniques by which these had been alloyed into a compound far harder and stronger than diamond were a mystery. Equally mysterious were the methods by which the plaque had been machined with script; this was the question Morland had been pursuing.

It was a question other researchers had studied without success. This, the hardest alloy ever discovered, had been shaped by tools harder still, if by any tools at all. Morland had convinced the Council of Worlds Cultural Commission that he could do no harm to the plaque—no problem with that, who could?—and had persuaded them that he might add some trivial details to humankind's knowledge of it.

"We've recorded his data banks," said Polanyi.

"Have another look at them," she said. "And see what else you can dig up. That's enough of Morland for now."

The building tilted and skittered under Polanyi's controlling fingers, until it was upright. Without moving, they were suddenly moving swiftly down the corridor Sparta had investigated earlier.

"The other victim . . ."

The view halted instantly—had the illusory walls had mass, they would have splintered from inertia—and there was the second body, lying on its back with arms and legs spread wide in a pool of bright blood.

"Dare Chin," said the lieutenant. "Darius Seneca Chin. One of the best liked of the original settlers of Labyrinth City."

"The assistant mayor, working late because Morland couldn't do what he needed to during business hours, and somebody had to keep an eye on him," Sparta said tonelessly.

"That's accurate."

"And where was the mayor that night?"

"The mayor's been on Earth for two months. Leadership conference, I believe."

Chin was a tall man, sparely built, with black hair and a handsome face more deeply lined than his thirty-five years would have suggested. His dark brown eyes were open; his expression was one of interested surprise, not fear. He was dressed in the practical, heavy brown canvaslike polyweave fabric favored by Martian old-timers.

"Uranium slug again?" Sparta said.

"Through the heart. This time at a distance. Tossed him eight meters."

"Not merely an executioner, then. An expert shot."

"A professional, we think," said the Lieutenant.

"Maybe. Maybe an enthusiastic amateur, a gun lover, someone with a cause." The crime had been committed for a cause, that much she knew. "He came down the stairs back there?"

"Yes, those go up to the second floor near his office. He was working on a batch of civil cases. We have his . . ."

"I'll get to it later," she said. "His office is visible from the street?"

"Yes. Old Nutting—that's the patroller who

walked by outside just a couple of minutes before the estimated time of the murders—said the whole building was dark except for Morland's work lights under the dome and Chin's office lights on the second floor. That and a few corridor lights. Anyway, she could see them both clearly, alive and well. Lydia Zeromski was with Chin. They were arguing.''

''They didn't care who saw them?''

He smiled. ''There's a saying here, Inspector: people who live in glass houses don't give a damn about stones. About privacy, that is.''

''Never?'' She was skeptical.

''They have window shades when they want them.''

Sparta knew from the reports that the patroller, a veteran near retirement, had sworn she'd seen no one else in the building except those three. From seeing the real building and its nighttime holo reconstruction, Sparta knew the patroller could easily have been wrong—someone could have been hiding motionless in the shadows; the distortion of the glass was sufficient to disguise even a human shape.

''I'd like to speak to her this afternoon.''

''The patrol office is in the executive building. You can set up a meeting on the way back to my office.''

Sparta would go through the motions, but she knew what she would learn. For one thing, Nutting's rounds were as regular as clockwork, against all accepted security practice—Nutting had fallen into laziness and a lifetime's habit, and her movements about the neighborhood had no doubt been timed by the killer in advance.

It was easy to sympathize with the old woman. Compared to a night on Mars, Antarctica is Tahiti, and normal people stayed inside if they could. Sparta could understand why the patroller—old enough to feel the cold in her bones even through her heated suit—would delay leaving the warmth of the office, would put off sealing her pressure suit to walk the cold, sandy streets of the town until the last minute. The killer had probably been waiting in one of the pressurized tubes that connected with the Town Hall until she passed.

Three minutes after the patroller passed the lighted building, alarms went off in the patrol office—hardly a hundred meters from the scene of the crime. The first alarm sounded when the Martian plaque was moved. Most of the other alarms—sniffers, movement detectors, pressure detectors in the floor, and so forth—were already disarmed in deference to Morland's work, but additional alarms went off when the outer door of the airlock at the main entrance of the building was opened before the inner door had closed, permitting a temporary pressure drop inside.

So the robber had been wearing a pressure suit too; he or she had fled the scene not through the warm corridors but through the freezing streets.

''Let's look at the airlock.''

''Not much to see, Inspector.'' Polanyi manipulated the holo controls and carried them spastically to the big bronze-rimmed doors of the main airlock—and then through the doors to the outside.

In the sand outside the airlock there were only smooth windblown rills and a few vague depressions, nothing suggesting a clear footprint. A few meters away, the entire scene faded into a black void at the edge of the holo.

''Seems there was a wind blowing.''

''A light breeze by local standards.''

Sparta peered at the holographically frozen ridges in the fine sand. Her visual capacities far exceeded the resolution of the holo recorder, so her eyes were almost useless here—as were her nose and tongue, with their capabilities for chemical analysis. The crime was two weeks past. Perhaps if she had been on the real scene, in real time . . . "You're right, Lieutenant. Not much to see."

"This is pretty much the extent of our reconstruction. We figured the killer went outside because the way back through the corridors was blocked by the patrollers responding to the first alarm. Or maybe there was an accomplice outside."

"Maybe," said Sparta. Without evidence, she did not make hypotheses.

"The local patrollers did a good job," said Polanyi, loyal to the locals he had to live with. "They responded in minutes. What you've seen is what they found. No murder weapon. No witnesses. No unusual prints or other physical evidence."

"Thanks, you can turn it off."

He did so. Instantly they were standing in the bright and busy center of Town Hall.

Ten minutes later, they were back in Polanyi's cramped and overlit office. "Now shall I run down for you the likely ones? The three with opportunity?"

"Please." Let him do his job; she would draw her conclusions later.

She already knew the Martian plaque had been taken that particular night, and not, for example, the night before or the night after, because the robbery had been timed to coincide with the destruction of the Culture X records on Venus and elsewhere throughout the inhabited solar system. Simultaneously the *prophetae* had unleashed their secret death squads in a mass attack—attempting to murder everyone who might remember the texts well enough to reconstruct them. A dozen scholars had died on Earth. Here on Mars, Dewdney Morland was the intended victim, Dare Chin only an innocent bystander.

One man, the most important of all, had been missed in this assault against the crown jewels of xenoarchaeology. Aboard Port Hesperus, Professor J. Q. R. Forster had barely survived the bombing attack on his life and was now protected by heavy Space Board security.

Polanyi was talking. Sparta reminded herself to listen.

''. . . permanent population of almost ten thousand,'' he was saying. ''At any given time there could be at most a couple of thousand tourists on the planet. We were able to account for all 438 of the registered guests at the Mars Interplanetary Hotel and the six other licensed accommodations in Labyrinth City that night. If there were other strangers in town nobody saw them, and in a town this small that's a good trick. So we concentrated on the locals.''

On the desktop videoplate a young woman's face appeared. Bold eyes, wide mouth, with blond hair tied at the nape. Despite the apparent delicacy of bone that characterized a long-term resident of the Martian surface, the woman looked competent and tough.

''This is Lydia Zeromski,'' the lieutenant said. ''A truck driver who works the pipeline run. She was Darius Chin's girlfriend—one of them, anyway—the one seen in his office a few minutes before the murders. Nobody saw her leave.''

''Her?'' Sparta was skeptical. ''She would have had to go downstairs, shoot Morland, swipe the plaque, and then turn and shoot Chin when he came to investigate.''

''Not impossible.''

''If she was after the plaque, why make a fuss first?''

''Well, if she wasn't the killer, she could have been an accomplice,'' Polanyi said stiffly.

''Lieutenant, she doesn't have a record.''

"Beaned a guy with a pipe in a bar once. He didn't press charges."

"Guns?"

"Well . . . none registered."

"Other relationships?"

"None known."

Sparta grunted. "Next."

"This man."

Zeromski was replaced on the screen by a smooth-faced man in his late thirties. His blond hair was fine and pale, almost colorless, and clipped so close to his head that his pink scalp shone through. She recognized him without trouble.

"Wolfy Prott—Wolfgang Prott, that is—the manager of the Mars Interplanetary Hotel. It's an open secret that the hotel has been the scene of illegal trading in Martian 'souvenirs'—mineral samples, fossils, even artifacts. Prott was assigned to Mars a year ago by the Interplanetary chain."

"Zurich based . . ."

"Right. Prott's been working for them about ten years—Athens, Kuwait, Cayley on the moon—first in their PR department, then in sales, then as assistant manager. This is his first stint as manager. He's got a rep as an off-hours pickup artist."

"His pattern?"

"Tourist ladies in the wine shops, rarely on his own premises—and he's mostly stayed away from local women. Maybe he's afraid of the local men."

"And he can't account for his whereabouts that night."

"Claims he was asleep in his suite in the hotel. But he was seen leaving the lobby a few minutes before the murders, wearing a pressure suit. An hour *after* the murders, he was having a nightcap with his own barkeeper."

"That alibi's so weak it's ridiculous."

"He was up to something . . . whatever it was."

"Not murder."

"Oh, but one more thing," Polanyi couldn't disguise a touch of self-satisfaction. "Wolfy's known to be an expert shot with a target pistol. There's a range in the lower level of the hotel, and he's his own best customer."

"Any of his pistols missing?"

"Well, we're not sure how many he . . ."

"Fine," she said coolly. "Who else have you got?"

This was the face she had hoped not to see, a dark and handsome face, elongated and delicate, a young man's face with deep brown eyes, crowned with black and curling hair. His lips were parted in a smile that revealed straight white teeth. He was wearing a standard pressure suit.

Alas, Polanyi had not eliminated him from the list. "Dr. Khalid Sayeed, Council of Worlds planetologist. Less than an hour before the murders, Sayeed and Morland were shouting at each other in the bar of the Interplanetary. . . ."

"Khal . . . Dr. Sayeed was *shouting?*"

"A vigorous disagreement, anyway. Something about the terraforming project. Morland went straight from the hotel to Town Hall. Sayeed claims he went to his apartment—it's near the shuttleport—but we can't corroborate that."

Sparta studied Khalid's picture intently. He was a year younger than she was, Blake's age, and she hadn't seen him since she was sixteen years old; he'd aged well, grown into a poised and confident adult.

Like Sparta and Blake, Khalid was a member of the original SPARTA, the SPecified Aptitude Resources and Training Assessment project, founded by Sparta's parents in an attempt to demonstrate that the multiple intelligences inherent in every child could be enhanced to levels the world regarded as genius. Khalid was one of SPARTA's great successes, intelligent and sophisticated, multiply talented, dedicating his career to the improvement of human welfare.

But according to Blake, Khalid was also quite possibly one of the *prophetae*. A member of the Free Spirit. A member of the deadly cult.

"If you don't mind, Lieutenant, I'll take these with me," Sparta said, withdrawing the data slivers from his videoplate.

"All yours, Inspector." He leaned back and opened his pudgy palms. "You've got what we've got. What else can I do for you? Show you the nightlife?"

"Thanks, I'll take a rain check."

Polanyi smirked. "Rain? What's that?"

6

The glass ceiling of the Ophir Room
was clouded with condensation; the
air was humid. The maître d' led
Sparta up and down steps and across
terraces among tables that overlooked
the largest open expanse of water—
very green water—on Mars. In the palm-ringed
pool half a dozen young men and women splashed
and swam, all lithe and tanned and naked. Sparta
thought they looked more like models than tourists; probably the hotel paid them to disport themselves prettily during the lunch hour, a kind of
fashion show *manqué*.

Khalid Sayeed's table was on a balcony near the
pool, screened from it by skinny palms. He rose to
greet her. He was one of those erect and graceful
men whose smile was so dazzling, whose eyes were
so arresting, that he seemed taller than his medium
height.

"Inspector Troy, thank you so much for agreeing
to see me."

She took his hand and shook it once, briefly. "Dr.
Sayeed." Her nostrils tasted his faint, pleasant
scent. Unaided memory confirmed that it was him,
the boy she had known a long time ago.

If he recognized her as the girl who had been his
schoolmate in SPARTA, he gave nothing away.

With the schooling they had shared, both were so adept in social matters—she only when she had to be, though to him, or so it had seemed to her, it had always come naturally—that neither would give anything away involuntarily.

As she sat down opposite him the rush of long-suppressed memories surfaced. . . .

Khalid, age nine, arguing theology with Nora Shannon in the playground on the roof of the New School, maintaining sweet calm in the face of the girl's increasingly desperate refusal to accept his contention that Islam had rendered Christianity irrelevant. And he finally forced Nora to retreat, if only because he had committed far more of the Koran—not to mention of Thomas Aquinas—to memory than she had of the New Testament. Whereupon he proceeded to explain why the Shi'a sect into which he'd been born was the only trustworthy repository of Islamic teaching. . . .

Khalid, age twelve, on a field trip to the Caribbean, terrifying her mother and father with a narrow escape from sharks: after ditching his pedal-powered airplane in the warm sea he had kept the sharks at bay for twenty minutes by kicking their snouts with his deck shoes. . . .

Khalid, age fifteen, conducting the Manhattan Youth Philharmonic in a crisp, energetic rendition of Mendelssohn's Italian symphony, to be hailed with wild applause which was soon followed by worldwide videolink reviews announcing the debut of a new Bernstein. . . .

"I'm scheduled for a survey flight tomorrow morning and I wanted you to have a chance to get at me before I left," he said.

The maître d' handed them elaborately printed menus, made of real paper by the feel of them, printed with real ink.

"Get at you?"

"The flight should only take about two days.

Flying on Mars is inherently unpredictable, however, and should I be delayed I didn't want you to think I was evading you.''

''If you will excuse me,'' the maître d' simpered, ''would either of you care for anything before your meal?''

''Will you have something to drink?'' Khalid asked Sparta.

She saw that he was drinking tea from a glass, Sri Lankan by its aroma. ''I'll have tea,'' she said, ''the same.''

''Very good, madame; sir, your waiter will be along in a moment.'' He glided away.

Khalid poured fragrant tea from the pot on the table into her glass. For a moment she concentrated on sipping the tea, which was flavorful but a bit too old—shipping technologies had improved in the last few centuries, but Sri Lanka was farther from Mars than from England—before returning her attention to Khalid.

''All I need from you, Dr. Sayeed, is proof that you could not possibly have killed those men or stolen the artifact. Then I'll be free to concentrate my attention elsewhere.''

''Proof?'' He didn't smile this time, except with his eyes. ''Whole schools of philosophy and mathematics have sprung up around the proposition that there is no such thing.''

''There is, however, such a thing as truth.''

''So I believe, Pontius Pilate to the contrary. And law—in the law I believe without question. I assume you've already read my statements, Inspector. And read the story of my life.''

She nodded. ''You argued with Dr. Morland here in the hotel not long before he was killed. You left shortly after he did and were not seen again until the next morning.''

''That's right. I cannot prove that I went to my apartment and watched an infovideo on the Sahara rehabilitation project, then observed evening prayers and went to sleep. But that is the truth."

"You live alone, Dr. Sayeed?"

"Yes."

"But you are married."

"My wife lives in Paris with her parents, not to mention with numerous aunts, uncles, siblings, and cousins. As you perhaps already know." An odd expression, half teasing, half wistful, bent his curving brows, but was quickly gone. "But do you know that I have never met my wife? She is fourteen years old."

Sparta did know it. When she'd known him before, Khalid's family had been poor; he had been enabled to attend SPARTA on a grant from a society of wealthy do-gooders who called themselves the Tappers. Khalid's brilliant performance in SPARTA had drawn the attention of his powerful relatives. His subsequent marriage, by arrangement—without a word of prior consultation with him—was a great honor, a sign that Khalid might one day be named imam of the Sayeedis by his great-uncle, the khan.

Sparta said, "Your apartment is near the spaceport."

"Yes, on Kirov Place in the MTP complex."

"The building is not directly connected to any civic pressure tube. When you are outside your home you habitually have your pressure suit with you." She tilted her head to indicate the brown canvas bag in the chair beside him.

"All Martians do so as a matter of course. Where's yours?"

"In my room."

"I would advise you to adopt our custom quickly," he said. "All this"—he waved at the trees, the pool, the glass roof dripping with condensation—"is an illusion; it can vanish in an instant. The reality is freezing thin carbon dioxide.

Say a rock were to fall from the cave arch over our heads . . ."

"I'll take your advice." And she meant it; just thinking about the possibilities, she regretted her carelessness. But that was not a fact to be shared with him. "Your building . . . it has three units, each with a separate entrance. Yours is on the second floor, reached by an outside stair."

"Well, you *have* done your homework this morning. Do you know why I chose that apartment?"

"For its view, I assume."

"In fact that's a good part of the reason." He leaned back in his chair and sipped his tea. "When followers of Islam first embarked into space, Inspector, there arose the problem of determining the *qibla*, the direction of prayer, which as you know is toward the Kaaba in the Great Mosque of Mecca. The times for prayer can be decided locally, but the position of Mecca—which at a sufficient distance is coincident with the position of Earth, of course—is in constant relative motion. So we orthodox carry these." He set down his tea glass and brought a flat round object from his pocket, the size of a large pocket watch but much thinner. He laid it on the table. "Mine is a copy, about one-quarter size, of a rather unusual 14th-century astrolabe made by the astronomer Ibn al-Sarraj of Aleppo."

The astrolabe consisted of a thin stack of incised bronze disks, inscribed in Arabic. The topmost was a net of spherical coordinates, a rete. Tiny scratches and irregularities revealed that the piece had been made by hand.

She looked at it with interest, studying it more closely than human eyes permitted, although no one would have suspected that her glance was anything more than casual . . . for the brain is a flexible organ: it can be trained to suppress or ignore double exposures, as users of old-fashioned monocular microscopes well knew. Like those ancients,

Sparta could focus closely on any small or distant object with her macrozoom right eye with both eyes open, and without betraying herself by squinting.

"An expensive copy."

"It is functional," Khalid said. "It can actually be used as an astrolabe in the northern latitudes of Earth—or with suitable conversions, even on Mars, I suppose—but its principal operations are carried out by a microminiature inertial guidance system." He rotated the tiny astrolabe with his fingers until a bronze pointer fastened to its center pivot had risen above the curving equator of the rete. "My spiritual compass. No matter where I go, or where the Earth wanders, the alidade points to Mecca."

"A beautiful device," she remarked, without expression. "What does it have to do with your choice of an apartment near the shuttleport?"

"Simply that my little room faces sky through some two hundred degrees of arc. Thus the *qibla* is rarely in the direction of a blank wall." He looked up. "Ah, here we are . . ."

The waiter arrived, with timing so precise it might have been rehearsed. Khalid smiled; his uninsistent charm was as glassy as the table between them. The presentation of the astrolabe, which he now repocketed, had been a fascinating diversion from which Sparta had learned nothing germane to her case.

Khalid led the waiter though a recitation of the specials—roast goat stuffed with garlic and prunes, all grown on Mars Station, and poached salmon, fresh by freight shuttle from the hold of the freighter *Doradus*, recently arrived in orbit—and details of the preparation of several of the more elaborate items on the menu.

When Sparta asked for a green salad, Khalid reacted as if this were not only normal but in fact an exceedingly rational choice; but as for himself, the salmon was too tempting.

The waiter left. Sparta said, "Tell me about your argument with Morland, Dr. Sayeed."

His smile thinned. "I'll give you the bare bones. I trust you'll flesh them out from your own sources."

"I have plenty of time."

"Some background, then." He sipped his tea and made a show of considering his words. "Xenoarchaeologists and xenopaleontologists have a difficult task," he began. "The Martian atmosphere was once rich in water vapor; the Martian desert once flowed with liquid water . . . as in fact it still does, several times a year, in a few low places where exposed ice hasn't sublimed and the atmospheric pressure is just sufficient to keep water from evaporating instantly. But these are scattered, evanescent episodes. A billion years ago, or more, things were different. The atmosphere was thicker, the climate of Mars was mild, conditions were stable long enough—just—for the appearance and rapid evolution of life. Thus today we find fossils of living creatures. And thus the much rarer evidence that Mars was visited, perhaps only briefly, by an ancient intelligent race. No scrap of these most precious of treasures must escape our attention."

He paused for further contemplation. "The task of the xenologists is not only difficult but noble," he resumed, "the task of preserving the past. On the other hand"—the fingers of his right hand opened like a flower—"in the future Mars will again be a living paradise. Even without human intervention—given the passage of another billion years."

When she did not react to his dramatic assertion, he went on. "The period of precession of Mars's orbit around the sun and of its poles suggests that every couple of billion years or so Mars becomes warm enough for icecaps and the permafrost to melt and for liquid water to collect on the surface. The Mars Terraforming Project has been charged with accelerating this natural cycle. To do so we must increase the density of the atmosphere and enrich it with water vapor. At some point the greenhouse effect will take over and begin to raise atmospheric temperatures, one consequence of which will be to increase atmospheric pressure even more. Once the positive feedback is established, the plentiful water resources now locked up will melt and flow freely across the open desert, without instantly evaporating. True plants will survive in the open. The plants will excrete oxygen; meanwhile a much greater supply of oxygen will be released from the rocks by seeded bacteria. Eventually we Martians will not have to worry about keeping our pressure suits handy.''

She was sure he'd given this speech often, and his oratory was rousing. But she said only, ''You were telling me about your argument with Morland.''

He nodded. ''Mars is dead and has been for a billion years. But because there was life here once, the xenoarchaeologists and xenopaleontologists and xenobiologists—*xeno-* is a prefix that seems to apply only to previously Earthbound disciplines; there are no xenophysicists or xenochemists—these xeno-optimists would like to believe that indigenous life survives to this day. Somewhere. Somehow. I understand their passion. I would like to believe so too,'' he said, his expressive fingers drumming the green glass, ''but I don't. That was the gist of my disagreement with Dr. Morland.''

''You don't seem the sort of man to get into a shouting match over theories,'' she said.

''There was nothing abstract about our argument. Liquid water is the key to everything I have described. In the past there have been many schemes: to melt the north polar icecap by spreading it with dark earth to absorb solar radiation, or by engineering especially dark lichens or algae to achieve the same thing. Or by using nuclear reactors, dozens of them, perhaps hundreds or thousands of them. Other ideas. Any of these methods *might* work, but it would be centuries before the partial pressure of atmospheric water vapor would rise to significant levels. Schemes to melt the permafrost have been even more outlandish, including the subterranean detonation of nuclear devices by the thousands—an idea motivated less by concern for Mars, I think, than by the desperation of Euro-Americans to rid themselves of the antique weapons with which they once threatened each other. All of these plans have serious drawbacks."

"They all seem hard on the planet," she observed.

"*Unnaturally* hard on the planet," he said. "But there is a way to speed up the natural Martian cycle of water and drought using only natural means. These means would also be hard on the planet. But at least they would be consistent with its ecological history."

This time when he paused she cooperated, supplying him with the question he was fishing for. "And what would those be?"

"Cometary bombardment," he said eagerly. "Comets are mostly ice. During the early history of Mars—and the other inner planets—swarms of comets fell, bringing water and carbon and organic molecules. Eventually the intensity of the swarms decreased, starting a billion years ago. But we can engineer a new bombardment. We can steer comets. In fact, Inspector, we're planning to steer one now."

"A comet to hit Mars?"

He nodded. "A test case, but if it works, the water will not be wasted. It will briefly flow over the surface of the Tharsis plateau before evaporating in the atmosphere—a greater injection of water vapor than fifty years' slow melting of the polar cap.''

''When will this test be completed?''

''Not for several years. Our first candidate comet is still beyond the orbit of Jupiter.'' He smiled. ''As far away as it is, it is already encountering resistance from hot air.''

She almost laughed. ''I see. . . .''

''That's what Morland and I argued about, Inspector, not abstract theory but the specifics of Project Waterfall. He was opposed to it in any form; he went so far as to compare it to that odious nuclear-bomb scheme I mentioned. Of course he was quite drunk at the time.''

''Drunk?''

''He'd been in the Phoenix Lounge for two or three hours, I'm told. I often have dinner here, Inspector—an indulgence, but I allow myself only a few indulgences. As I was leaving I encountered Morland coming out of the lounge. It was . . . the only adequate word is 'assault' . . . he assaulted me with his crude sarcasms.''

''Why did he attack you?''

Khalid lifted a wagging finger, paraphrasing his late opponent: ''Cometary impacts may preserve polar caps, but they dig large holes; something could be lost, some pocket of tenacious bacteria, some precious artifact.'' His palm opened upward, conceding the point. ''He couched these objections in language I don't care to repeat.''

''Had you met before? How did he know you?''

''We had met, briefly, at a reception that Wolfy—Mr. Prott, the manager of the hotel—held for him a week earlier. Thereafter I would gladly have stayed out of his way. Morland was a flamboyant character, but in his opposition to the project he was not unlike others in the xeno-professions. He found me as offensive professionally as I found him personally."

"What's your role in Project Waterfall, Dr. Sayeed?"

"To put it concisely, it was my idea."

The waiter arrived, bearing an iron tray. He slid their plates in front of them.

For the next few minutes neither Khalid nor Sparta spoke; she was busy absorbing the odd textures of the space-station–grown lettuce. He relished his salmon.

When the meal was finished there was an awkward silence that neither seemed eager to break. For Sparta it was a delicate moment, and she found herself uncertain how to handle it. "You should know, Dr. Sayeed, that you are a principal suspect in the murders of Morland and Chin."

"I had thought so, but thanks for confirming it."

"You can't stage-manage your own interrogation, you know. You can't walk cleanly away. There are too many unanswered questions."

He didn't argue or protest his innocence or try to explain himself. He only watched her, evidently weighing his options. "For my own sake, I'd like you to get to the bottom of this. If I could delay my trip, I would. But it would be dangerous—at this time of year the weather grows worse every day."

"Don't worry, Doctor. I'll be waiting for you when you get back. No matter how long you're gone."

He leaned toward her, his dark eyes filled with serious purpose. "In the interests of both of us, then: if you want to continue our discussion, come with me. I promise you will learn more than you imagine."

Here it was, the crux of the meeting, the real goal of his stage-managing.

"I'll consider it," she said.

"Call the MTP office when you've decided. If the answer is yes, I'll meet you in the lobby at five-thirty tomorrow morning," he said. "Wear your pressure suit." Abruptly he stood. "If you will excuse me . . . the account is already settled. I have to leave." He turned and walked away.

She watched him go. His long, deliberate stride seemed more suited to the desert than to a hotel restaurant.

With the pistol on full automatic she fired a full clip into the paper target twenty meters away. The roar of the gun was continuous in the long stone room, its muzzle flash a single strobing flare. Spurts of sand leaped from the bullet trap against the back wall; shreds of paper fluttered lazily down from the target.

She lowered the gun and cleared the chamber, then stepped away from the line and pushed the headset back from her ears.

The range director lifted his own ear protectors from his head and set them on the bench. "Well, let's see the bad news." He was a burly man in whites, with the hotel's insignia on his close-fitting tee-shirt. He punched a button and the target traveled slowly along its guide wire until it came to the line.

He unclipped the paper target and studied it in silence, then looked up at Sparta with sour suspicion knitting his thick black brows. "Fair shooting."

He handed her the target. A hole the size of a dime had been punched out of the center.

"Beginner's luck," she said.

"You're trying to hustle me, Inspector. You've shot on Mars before." He nodded at the target. " 'Course you did miss once"—there was one other hole in the paper, a hole the diameter of a single bullet, outside the outer ring in the lower right-hand corner; Sparta's first shot had missed the bull's-eye—"Still, I wouldn't mind taping this on my office wall. Inspire the other amateurs."

"That's a nice compliment, but I'd better decline." She handed him the target pistol, handle first. "Thanks for letting me try out."

"Go ahead, use another clip. The hotel can afford it."

"No, I don't want to get a sore wrist—these uranium slugs pack a wallop."

"Don't do anything for you except make the pistol harder to control." He took the gun and set it aside for cleaning. "Goes against the natural advantage you've got here, a lighter weapon with the same punch."

"Why does Mr. Prott use them? He's an excellent shot, I'm told."

"He's not as hopeless as some." He hesitated. "Never knew him to use uranium slugs, though. Doesn't mean he didn't."

"Who does?"

"Not many who use this range; this is for guests of the hotel, and maybe a few of the local business types. That guy that got killed tried them once."

"Morland?"

"Yes. A real S.O.B., but after he practiced awhile he got so he could hit the back wall."

"He'd never shot before?"

"Not with a pistol. Not on Mars. I think Prott sicced him on me to give the guy something to do. Keep him out of the bar. Tell you, with his mouth I was tempted to shoot him myself."

Sparta looked at him straight-faced. "And you don't care who knows it, do you?"

He shrugged. "So arrest me."

"Too bad. A whole roomful of witnesses puts you elsewhere on the night of the crime."

The man's round, sour face widened in a grin. "Yeah, those guys out at the 'Pine are great, aren't they? They'd say anything to keep a friend out of trouble."

7

Phobos was sliding across the stars and Deimos was a bright distant spark when Blake left his cubicle at the hive.

The Noble Water Works motor pool was half a kilometer away through dark windblown alleys. Blake moved swiftly through the shadows until he reached the edge of the shuttleport complex. His target for tonight faced open desert.

Fifty meters away, a clutch of liquid-hydrogen tanks bulged from the sand like half-buried ostrich eggs. He dashed across the exposed sand to their shadow. Crouched in the darkness, he peered at the fenced and floodlit marshaling yard. He'd cased the motor pool earlier in the day, but had decided not to show his face to anyone in the yard until he was supposed to report for work.

Outdoors on Mars one did not have to worry about sniffers, either chemical or biological—a guard or two perhaps, but there weren't going to be any dogs around. Chain-link fences, floodlights, remote cameras, maybe pressure sensors and movement detectors . . . at best, the security would be primitive. And if freight depots were raided as often as the scuttlebutt at the 'Pine had it, even the guards weren't going to be too alert. Someone on the inside was inviting the thefts.

The vehicles in the yard were ranked behind a double line of fences. A row of huge marstrucks squatted like beetles. Rovers and utility tractors huddled around the trucks as if seeking shelter from the wind. The vehicles Blake was looking for, the personnel carriers that Yevgeny had called crummies, were parked together in the shadow of a building that looked like a fueling shed; the crummies resembled military APCs, armored personnel carriers—steel boxes on treads—although there was no war on this planet. None declared, anyway.

Blake hunkered down in the lee of the liquid hydrogen tank and cogitated. APCs. Three of them. He could disable them one by one, but it would take most of the night, and if all three were found to have crippling mechanical defects at the same time, that might rouse a bit of suspicion.

Better an accident that took them all out at once. Plus a few other vehicles along with them, and maybe some miscellaneous machinery thrown in. Blake tried to suppress the incipient thrill: he loved to blow things up, even though he knew he shouldn't. So he only did it when he had a good excuse.

He peered up at the shell of the liquid hydrogen tank. A big Noble Water Works corporate symbol was painted on its side. Some distance away was a stack of slimmer tanks, requiring less pressurization: liquid oxygen. Liquid hydrogen and liquid oxygen, derived by electrically dissociating water-ice mined by the company, fueled the big gas turbines that powered the marstrucks. Hydrogen plus oxygen. Highly efficient. Highly energetic.

The pipes from the bulging tanks ran on pylons above the sand, left exposed for easy maintenance, and high enough to bridge the traffic in the yard. A couple of meters up, the pylons were braceleted with razor-sharp accordion wire to discourage climbers. With some effort Blake could have gotten around the wire, but his expert eye had earlier located an easier entrance to the yard.

Blake slipped across twenty meters of open sand to a salient of the chain-link fence. He paused in a cone of shadow, hidden from two angled floodlights by the bulk of a clumsily placed transformer. Clumsily placed or expertly placed? Blake almost laughed to see the often-cut, often-spliced square of wire fencing in front of him. Others had been here before him. Great thieves—not to mention everyday thieves, even company thieves—think alike.

Blake reached into the patch pocket of his pressure suit and withdrew his "tool kit." Improvisation was his way of life, and on his travels around the shuttleport he had accumulated a handy set of tools just by keeping his eyes open and his fingers nimble.

He used an induction sensor he had rescued from orphanhood to make sure no current was running through the patched wire; then he swiftly reopened the fence with a pair of lever-wrench pliers, out to him on long-term loan. He was through the outer fence in no time and almost as swiftly through the inner fence.

In the yard, yellow windblown dust glistened in the haphazard floodlighting, which could hardly have provided better cover for intruders if it had been designed for that purpose; lanes of black shadow connected one squatting vehicular hulk to another.

As he had predicted, there were pressure sensors scattered across the yard, but their placement was obvious and their sensitivity was necessarily low; a few thrown handfuls of dust and rock offset the tremors of his footsteps. It was like slow-motion dancing through a minefield, with all the mines lying on the surface.

The movement detectors depended on lasers and would be set off if the brightness of the reflected beam varied from the reference setting. For Blake's purposes many of the beams were conveniently obstructed by carelessly parked trucks or by empty fuel dewars and other equipment. Blake moved cautiously among the metal giants in the yard, hugging the big treads of the marstrucks.

He was about to cross between two rovers when he saw a red thread of beam set to trip him; it was betrayed by a sparkle of drifting dust a half meter away.

The unobstructed beam was looking straight into the night beyond the fence. Blake peered at its focus point; a small red dot came and went as the fence links blew back and forth in the wind. Blake took a shiny, nickel-plated socket wrench from his pocket and gingerly inserted it into the beam path; he was poised to run. There was no alarm; he cautiously twisted the wrench, reflecting the beam to another part of the fence. Careful of the movement detectors, he walked around the beam, rotating the beam as he went. When he was past, he pulled his makeshift reflector out of the way.

Still no alarm. He let his breath out slowly.

Nothing to it.

The videoplates in the guard station were ranked in a semicircle around the security chief's desk. The picture on each screen slowly panned back and forth across a different sector of the deserted marshaling yard.

"Nothing yet?" Yevgeny Rostov was standing behind the security chief, his massive arms folded over his chest, a scowl on his saturnine face.

"You can see as good as me, Yev. The board's all green and the viddie on the 'plates ain't switched channels."

"So many holes you've left in security, he could walk in and out again and you would never know."

The security chief leaned back easily in his ergonomic chair. The size of his rear end suggested how much time he spent in it. "No call to be slingin' around lost insults."

"Not lost, *unfounded*," Rostov grumbled. "Baseless. Without foundation. We are speaking English, yes?"

"Unfound, yeah, and besides, if I was that bad at my job, the company woulda fired me by now."

Yevgeny made a noise in his throat, rather like a hard-starting engine.

"Anyway, what makes you so sure this guy's gonna show up tonight? He didn't last night."

"He never lifted wrench in his life—so I do not think he wants to go to pipeline, where he would have to work. Tonight is his last chance or he will have no excuse."

"Why couldn't he just call in sick or somethin'?"

"And bring note from mother? Don't be stupid. I tell you, this man is *professional*." Yevgeny turned away and looked through the glass windows of the guard tower into the empty yard.

Blake was under the main pipe bridge now, precariously shielded from surveillance by a steel stanchion. The pipes from the big storage tanks were directed into the fueling shed, where the portable dewars were loaded. A videocam mounted on the corner of the fueling shed panned slowly toward him. He eased back into the shadow of a marstruck's giant tread until the camera had scanned his position. Blake noted that the coaxial feed that ran from the camera down the side of the shed was rhythmically swinging in the steady breeze, inaudibly slapping against the wall's crude glass bricks.

That loose cable, now . . . it certainly looked overdue to wear through. . . . And if it were to wear through high enough, the wind might carry the length of it across a big shunt valve inside that wire cage beside the fueling shed. And if that shunt valve had an internal leak and unfortunately happened to contain an explosive mix of hydrogen and oxygen . . .

When the camera was looking the other way, Blake did his step and shuffle across a few meters of exposed dust, reaching the shelter of the fueling shed. There he discovered a bonus; the exterior communications terminal through which the camera lines led also contained the connecting circuitry for the pressure sensors. Three snips of his pliers and a bit of hasty splicing disarmed the detectors all at once. Again he poised himself to run—

—but he didn't have to; he'd wired it right the first time.

He left the video cameras functioning.

The door to the unpressurized shed swung easily on its hinges. He went inside, into a pea-green semidarkness illuminated by the reflected glow of floodlights above. They were aimed outward, into the yard.

The routing shunts and valves were arranged in banks against the wall, big steel manifolds of pipe, a tangle of tubes as extravagant as an octopus orgy.

On Mars, liquid hydrogen and liquid oxygen remain liquid only in containment, so for Blake's purposes the fluids would have to be mixed inside the pipes. His recently acquired book knowledge of space-station municipal plumbing had not addressed fueling manifolds, but extrapolation was easy enough by visual inspection. And some of the handles were painted red.

It took most of his strength to turn the red-painted wheels; these particular valves weren't reset often. Then he turned them back.

Outside again, waiting in the shadow of the doorway for the camera to look the other way . . . he wriggled on his belly to the cage around the shunt valve. More wire work, for none of the thieves who had passed this way before him—and passed frequently, at that—had had reason to cut through *this* fence. Once inside it, he twisted a wheel this way, another wheel that way . . . these wheels turned a lot easier. He got quick results. Leaning his helmet against the pipe, he could hear the hiss of mixing gases.

He climbed back through the hole in the fence and studied the videocam's loose coaxial cable. In the low gravity it was a simple matter to mount the rough wall to the roof line, keeping himself close enough beneath the camera's angle of depression to be effectively invisible.

He meant not to have the falling cable trigger his bomb while he was clinging to the building next to it. Which meant he must cut to within a few strands of wire, which would wear through in the time it took him to escape but in less time than it took anyone responding to the malfunction to appear on the scene.

This cut had to be precise. He used his black knife. Three strands of bare wire glistened in the night.

Then he half slid, half fell down the wall of the shed. It wasn't an elegant dismount, but he knew the ground now, knew where to duck and jump. Any half-decent starlight security camera would have witnessed his odd solo ballet, out there among the shadows of the trucks and crummies.

A single red light lit up on the board.

"He is *here!*" Yevgeny shouted. "Where is that sector? Send guards there now."

"Calm down, Yev, they're already scramblin'. He's not inside yet, not by a long shot. We'll get the guy while he's still climbin' through the fence."

On the monitoring videoplates, the figures of two armed guards ran in the improbably long strides of one-third gravity toward the salient of the perimeter fence.

"Coulda told you he'd try to get in through there," the security director said.

"Yes? How could you have told me *that?*" Yevgeny roared.

"Oh, instinct, I guess you'd call it." The fat man lolled back in his chair and grinned. "Yeah, instinct. Plus my years of exper . . ."

One of the video monitors went dark at that moment, and simultaneously the night sky outside the windows turned a brilliant white orange. The security chief was so relaxed that when he tried to straighten up, his sudden movement caused him to fall backward out of his chair. Yevgeny dived for his pressure-suit bag as the double-plate windows bulged inward.

The shock wave and tremor almost shattered the building's pressure lock, but it held. So did the windows, luckily for the security chief and Yevgeny Rostov.

A brilliant ball of orange rose like a Japanese lantern into the night sky over the motor pool. A fountain of white flame spewed after it, a steady torch burning brighter than the gas burn-off that once lit the Texas oilfields.

Blake sat in the shelter of one of the big hydrogen tanks that was emptying its contents to fuel the spectacle.

Good show. Jolly good. He just couldn't keep himself from grinning.

Sirens are useless in the atmosphere of Mars; the call went out through the commlinks and alarm circuits.

None of the guests in the Mars Interplanetary Hotel could hear the alarms or see the display, invisible from the hotel, so none were disturbed by the incident—none but one.

Sparta woke, *listening.* . . .

She heard the frantic song in the wires, the tremor of footsteps and the rumble of vehicle treads. She heard voices through the walls: *An accident at the shuttleport, a big fire, something blew up . . .*

She groaned. That Blake.

Dammit, if he was tearing up the neighborhood again, he was on his own. This time she wasn't lifting a finger to protect him from the law.

PART
3

ACROSS
THE FREEZING SANDS

8

Half buried in drifting dust, the Terraforming Project's hangar at the shuttleport was almost invisible against the sea of dunes beyond. The wind slithered over it as if over a huge airfoil, tugging the groundbound building gently skyward.

Inside, the hangar was an immense vault of steel covering an expanse of glass tile. So gentle was the curve of the arch that the roof seemed low, yet in the center its slender, unsupported steel beams stretched thirty meters above the floor. Through panels of green glass in the roof the morning sun penetrated the interior gloom with diffuse shafts of light.

A dozen huge and spidery black marsplanes were clustered on the floor, like a nest of daddy longlegs. Khalid and Sparta crossed the floor toward the nearest.

"This is how we get around. These are a bit like the bush planes of 20th-century Alaska." Khalid's voice was thin over the commlink. Their pressure suits were sealed; the wide hangar doors were closed but not sealed against the Martian atmosphere.

"We live on a small planet, half the diameter of Earth, but it's not as small as it might seem. Oceans take up three quarters of Earth's surface, so Mars has virtually the same land area." He ducked under a narrow black wing as long as a football field; the wingtips drooped to rest on the hangar floor. The plane's slender tail fins, mounted on delicate booms, reached almost to the ceiling behind it. "Try to imagine Asia, Africa, Europe, the Americas, Australia, Antarctica, the major islands, all as one continent, all as one cold, dry, dusty desert—and in all this desert there are only five roads. Even to call them roads is a courtesy."

Sparta contemplated the marsplane whose wings now shadowed them and thought that it didn't look at all like one of the old bush planes of Earth. It was graceful. Not graceful like a dart, as a spaceplane or supersonic shuttle was graceful, but graceful like a sea bird. The wings had narrow chords and were bent a little forward, then swept gently back, with a thick foil designed for maximum lift at minimum velocity. It was a craft made for soaring.

Khalid opened the bubble hatch of the small fuselage, which was slung beneath and forward of the long wings. "We need wings this long to get lift in the thin atmosphere, but with carbon fiber it's easy to build giants. Material strength here is effectively two and a half times what it would be on Earth."

At Khalid's direction Sparta settled herself into the aft seat and pulled the harness over her pressure suit. "I see wings and tail booms and this little pod I'm sitting in, but what does this thing use for engines?" she asked.

"Weather." He bent to inspect her harness. "Plus RATO bottles to get us up if local wind conditions aren't favorable. Once aloft, we're a glider."

"Just a glider?"

"Yes, just a glider."

She thought she'd said it coolly enough, but from his chuckle, he'd caught her apprehension.

"The first explorers powered unmanned planes something like these using microwave beams: the antennas were in the wings, and onboard electric motors turned big propellors." He finished checking her harness. His approving glance told her she'd done it right the first time. "The microwave system wasn't efficient—the beams were sometimes blocked by dust, for one thing—and in the long run it proved unnecessary. Once there were enough satellites in orbit, the whole weather system became the engine for a fleet of planes."

He went forward and climbed up into the pilot's seat. "These days, satellites communicate directly with the plane's flight-control computers. The plane always knows exactly where it is and the best way to get where it wants to go." He buckled his harness and tightened its straps. "We never fly in a straight line, not for long, but there's no danger of getting lost or stranded."

"There is no such thing as 'no danger,' Dr. Sayeed."

"Dust storms can be a problem, as I indicated yesterday. Especially if they come up fast and grow too wide to go around and too high to climb over." He pulled the canopy down over them. "It doesn't happen often, but these planes are designed for that contingency. When it does happen we land and dig in."

"You said the storm season is approaching?"

He turned to look at her over the high back of his seat, his hand resting on a canopy latch. "Still time to get out," he said.

"Even if I wanted to, Dr. Sayeed, I'm far too interested to back out now."

He nodded and snapped the latches shut. He turned his attention to the controls. The marsplane had a small console-mounted joystick but no pedals, for the plane had no ailerons, flaps, rudders, or elevators; subtle movements of the stick were sufficient to flex the wings and tails in a sophisticated version of the wing-warping technique invented by the Wright brothers.

Manual control was in fact only an override mechanism. Once the marsplane had a destination entered into its computer it was happy to fly there by itself. If the pilot preferred eye-beam mode, the marsplane's computer would readily accommodate—one could steer simply by looking where one wanted to go.

A cluster of graphic screens displayed instrument summaries, but the pilot's principal aid was a false-color holographic projection of the atmosphere. The hologram was constructed from onboard and satellite weather data, and as Khalid now demonstrated by switching on the projector, it completely surrounded them. No matter which way they looked, the atmosphere outside the plane seemed as tangible as multicolored smoke. Even here inside the hangar, small eddies were visible as intricate pastel spirals.

"Tower, this is TP Five," Khalid said. "We're ready for rollout."

"Roger, Five," said the tower's disembodied voice. "You've got good weather, prevailing winds light steady at thirty knots out of the east-northeast. We'll open the doors and hook you to the catapult."

Sparta looked around curiously from her high perch in the clear canopy. Pressure-suited ground crew appeared out of the hangar's gloom, one coming to the nose and two moving to opposite sides of the plane. They took hold of the distant wingtips—the ends of the wings were so far away that they dwindled to pencil points from her point of view—and lifted them from the floor. The ground crew began walking the plane toward the hangar doors. Only a belly wheel beneath the fuselage was touching the tile.

It seemed incongruous that three tiny humans could manhandle such an enormous contraption, but on Mars the whole plane, passengers and all, weighed about half what an antique Volkswagen weighed on Earth.

Meanwhile the inner hangar doors were rolling back. The hangar was equipped with a primitive kind of airlock, not an airlock so much as a wind-lock; the space between the wide inner and outer doors was just enough to accommodate the craft's short fore-to-aft length. When the marsplane had been rolled into the area, the inner doors rolled shut behind it, protecting the planes inside from the gusty wind.

The outer doors slowly opened, unveiling the morning landscape of the shuttleport, the wide, wind-carved valley with its flanking cliffs. The great glider shuddered and creaked as the ''light breeze'' tried to lift it. Seen from the cockpit, thick pink garlands of atmosphere, coiled like the clouds of Jupiter, writhed in the computer's holographic projection. The ground crew threw their diminutive weight on the wings. Sparta sensed the constant, instantaneous adjustments of the control surfaces which kept the plane, little more than a big ungainly kite, from flipping sideways and smashing to bits.

One of the ground crew fastened the hook and cable of a gas catapult to a hardpoint on the bottom of the fuselage; in the catapult launch system Sparta recognized more technology borrowed from the Wright brothers. Khalid commlinked the controller—''Ready''—and then turned to look over his shoulder at Sparta. ''Here we go.''

The acceleration was gentle and quick. As the catapult drew the craft down the short track into the wind, the plane's agile wings and tail fins kept it pointed true until it was free of the ground. Then, suddenly, they were skimming the dunes.

Khalid quickly found an updraft over a light-colored patch of dunes in the middle of the valley. They began to ascend in a wide spiral, rising rapidly enough to feel it in the pits of their stomachs.

"The satellite net reports there's a steady north-easterly windstream at seven thousand meters," he said. "That's enough to give us clearance if we find ourselves heading down the Valles."

As the huge plane wheeled and banked, Sparta peered out of its bubble canopy, fascinated. Through the false holographic atmosphere she could see a faulted, cratered landscape falling away beneath her, a crisply intricate topography of tawny buttes and golden sands. A haze of frozen fog hung in the depths of the canyons of the Labyrinth. Overhead, the sky was rosy pink, streaked with wisps of ice-crystal cloud.

Off to the west the Labyrinth of Night was filling with the morning's orange light. Far to the east, the Valles Marineris widened and deepened as it dwindled toward the distant horizon. At its deepest the system of canyons descended to astonishing depths, with a vertical drop of six kilometers from plateau to valley floor, but from above true perspective was lost, and the land seemed to flatten as the plane swiftly mounted to catch the jetstream.

Morning on Mars . . .

"Checking in. The name's Mycroft."
"What the hell do *you* want?"
"New hire. Grade seven mechanic."
The phonelinks chortled continuously in rhythm with the constant hissing of the airlock, as busy men and women passed in and out of the dispatch office.

"Look, bud, you can see we're kinda occupied around here."

INFOPAK
TECHNICAL
BLUEPRINTS

On the following pages are computer-generated diagrams representing some of the structures and engineering found in *Venus Prime:*

Pages 2–5:   *Marstruck* Open terrain heavy transport tractor—overview; cutaway perspective; cab/tractor overview; wireframe overview cutaway; undercarriage components; turbines.

Pages 6–8:   *Town Hall, Labyrinth City* Architecture—glass weld integrity scan; wireframe overview; plan view; components—cast glass, carbon filament, ceramics.

Pages 9–12: *Marsplane* Climate-driven geo-flex controlled long-range sailplane— canopy false color atmospheric display; cockpit module; perspective of cockpit; rato schematic, ratomount, geo-flex control; rocket assisted take-off; canopy display, cockpit overview, tail section.

Page 16:   *Mars* Topographical section— surface approximation.

2

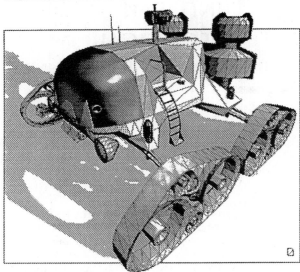

MARSTRUCK
Open Terrain Heavy Transport Tractor H₂O₂ Turbine Engines

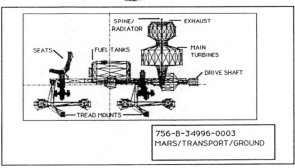

756-B-34996-0003
MARS/TRANSPORT/GROUND

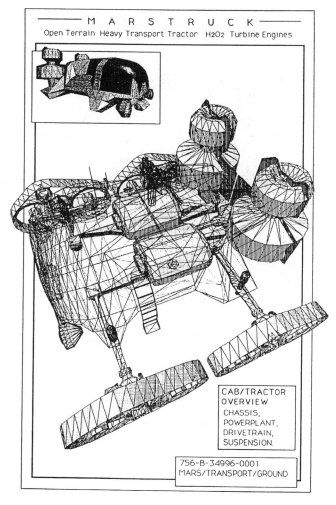

M A R S T R U C K

Open Terrain Heavy Transport Tractor H2O2 Turbine Engines

CAB/TRACTOR
OVERVIEW
CHASSIS,
POWERPLANT,
DRIVETRAIN,
SUSPENSION.

756-B-34996-0001
MARS/TRANSPORT/GROUND

M A R S T R U C K

Open Terrain Heavy Transport Tractor H2O2 Turbine

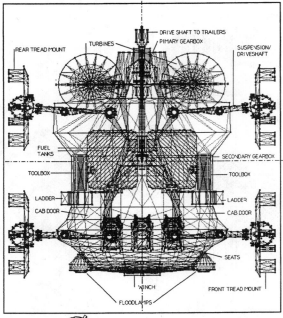

DRIVE SHAFT TO TRAILERS
PIMARY GEARBOX
TURBINES
SUSPENSION/
DRIVESHAFT
REAR TREAD MOUNT
FUEL TANKS
SECONDARY GEARBOX
TOOLBOX
TOOLBOX
LADDER
LADDER
CAB DOOR
CAB DOOR
SEATS
WINCH
FRONT TREAD MOUNT
FLOODLAMPS

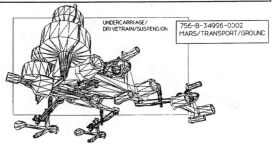

UNDERCARRIAGE/
DRIVETRAIN/SUSPENSION

756-B-34996-0002
MARS/TRANSPORT/GROUND

5

5

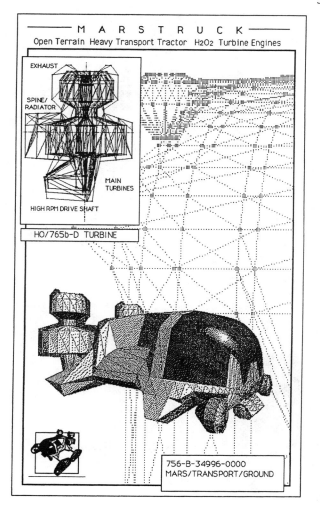

M A R S T R U C K
Open Terrain Heavy Transport Tractor H2O2 Turbine Engines

EXHAUST

SPINE/
RADIATOR

MAIN
TURBINES

HIGH RPM DRIVE SHAFT

HO/765b-D TURBINE

756-B-34996-0000
MARS/TRANSPORT/GROUND

6

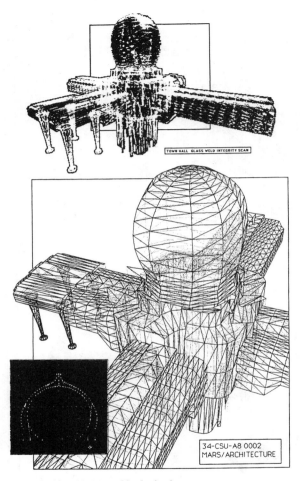

TOWN HALL GLASS WELD INTEGRITY SCAN

34-CSU-A8 0002
MARS/ARCHITECTURE

TOWN HALL

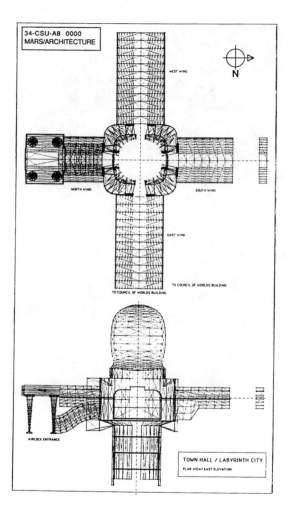

34-CSU-A8 0000
MARS/ARCHITECTURE

N

WEST WING

NORTH WING

SOUTH WING

EAST WING

TO COUNCIL OF WORLDS BUILDING

TO COUNCIL OF WORLDS BUILDING

AIRLOCK ENTRANCE

TOWN HALL / LABYRINTH CITY
PLAN VIEW/ EAST ELEVATION

8

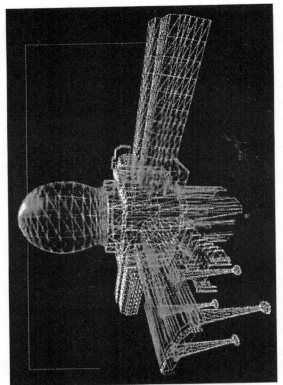

TOWN HALL/
LABYRINTH CITY

CAST GLASS
CARBON FILAMENT
CERAMICS

34-CSU-A8 0001
MARS/ARCHITECTURE

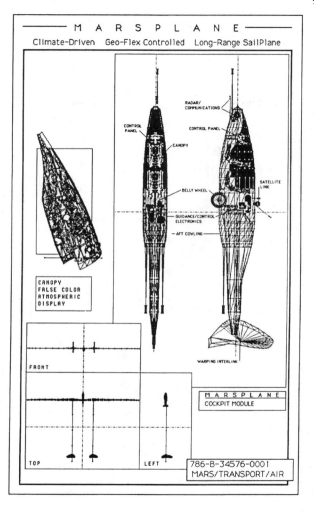

MARSPLANE
Climate-Driven   Geo-Flex Controlled   Long-Range SailPlane

RADAR/
COMMUNICATIONS

CONTROL
PANEL

CONTROL PANEL

CANOPY

SATELLITE
LINK

BELLY WHEEL

GUIDANCE/CONTROL
ELECTRONICS

AFT COWLING

WARPING INTERLINK

CANOPY
FALSE COLOR
ATMOSPHERIC
DISPLAY

FRONT

TOP

LEFT

MARSPLANE
COCKPIT MODULE

786-B-34576-0001
MARS/TRANSPORT/AIR

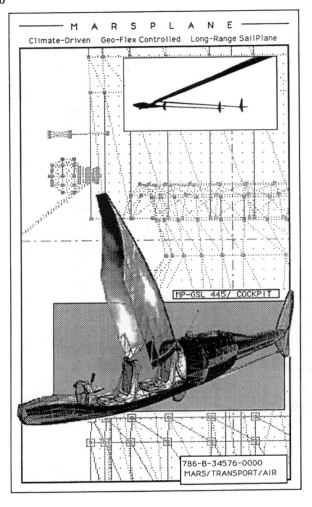

MARSPLANE

Climate-Driven Geo-Flex Controlled Long-Range SailPlane

MP-GSL 445/ COCKPIT

786-B-34576-0000
MARS/TRANSPORT/AIR

⸺M A R S P L A N E⸺
Climate-Driven Geo-Flex Controlled Long-Range SailPlane

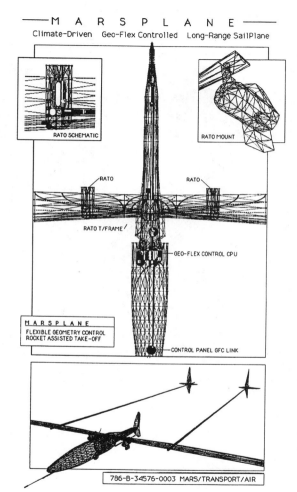

RATO SCHEMATIC

RATO MOUNT

RATO

RATO

RATO T/FRAME

GEO-FLEX CONTROL CPU

M A R S P L A N E
FLEXIBLE GEOMETRY CONTROL
ROCKET ASSISTED TAKE-OFF

CONTROL PANEL GFC LINK

786-B-34576-0003 MARS/TRANSPORT/AIR

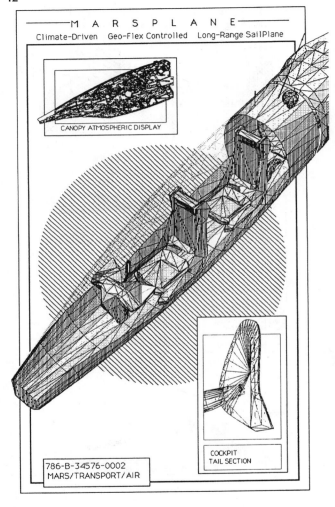

M A R S P L A N E

Climate-Driven   Geo-Flex Controlled   Long-Range SailPlane

CANOPY ATMOSPHERIC DISPLAY

COCKPIT
TAIL SECTION

786-B-34576-0002
MARS/TRANSPORT/AIR

13

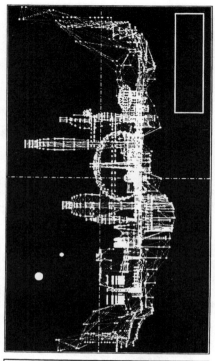

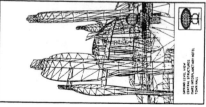

GROUND LEVEL VIEW
CENTRAL STRUCTURES
MARS INTERPLANETARY HOTEL
TOWN HALL

LABYRINTH
CITY

OVERVIEW OF
MAIN STRUCTURES

34-6569-A 0000
MARS/ARCHITECTURE

LABYRINTH CITY

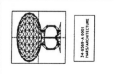

34-6569-A 0001
MARS/ARCHITECTURE

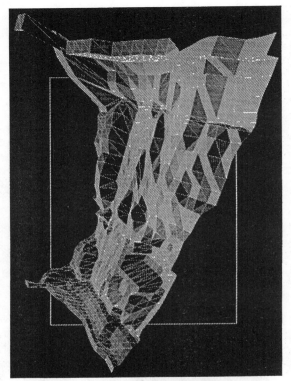

TOPO SECTION
098/77

SURFACE APPROXIMATION
MCKIBBEN GRID

34-6569-A 0002
MARS/ARCHITECTURE

"Yevgeny Rostov said I was to be here by eight-thirty today and they'd put me on a crummy to the pipeline head."

"Rostov?" The fat clerk's manners improved at the mention of Yevgeny's name. "Who'd you say you was?"

"My name's Mycroft. Don't mind telling you I'm glad to get this job. God knows I been lookin'. Up on the station they . . ."

"Can it, pal. I get all the soap opera I want on the viddie." The clerk tapped a greasy keyboard and consulted a flatscreen on which, days or weeks ago, someone had spilled coffee. "Yeah, Mycroft, you're on the manifest. Says you're a grade *eight*." The computer excreted a yellow cardboard hard copy. "Here's your job ticket." He handed it to Blake. "But you're outta luck, Mycroft. No crummy today."

"Why not?"

"Because they all friggin' blew up, that's why." The lard-slick clerk showed his rotten teeth and broke into squeaky giggles.

"They what?"

"Little industrial accident—that's what they're callin' it. All the personnel carriers are indefinitely outta commission. Doesn't mean you don't have a job at the line head, Mycroft. Just means you gotta get there on your own."

"When's the next trip?"

"Depends how long it takes to get new crummies down here. You happen to know the slow-freighter time from Earth these days?"

Blake stared at him. "Slow freighter . . . ? Oh, I see what you mean . . ."

"Maybe you can talk some trucker into givin' you a ride. But them drivers usually want plenty. Whaddya got to offer?"

Blake shook his head and turned away, dejected.

But when, entering the airlock, he paused to seal his helmet, he allowed himself a private smile.

The marsplane found the jet stream and raced northeastward, in the direction of distant Cydonia. Khalid's remarks were as neutral as a tour guide's. "Lunae Lacus—the so called Lake of the Moon—is a depression north of here where the atmospheric pressure is high enough for water—should it ever get above freezing—to stay liquid. That's one reason it's been designated ground zero for Project Waterfall. Our route will skirt the Candor region. If the winds aloft hold steady, we'll be paralleling the truck route from Labyrinth City north to the pipeline head."

"Are we going all the way to the Lacus?"

"No, we're resurveying an area just ahead of the pipeline. We could easily reach Lunae Lacus within a sol if we wanted to—our ground speed right now is over five hundred kilometers per hour—but if we went that far, with present weather conditions we'd probably have to circle the entire planet to get back."

"How far's the pipeline?"

"About three thousand kilometers."

"So we could get there in six hours at this speed."

"At this altitude, yes. But when we drop to make the sensor runs we'll lose ground speed. We'll spend most of our time on this trip working our way back, moving across the wind at low altitude. Could be two or three days. We've got plenty of time to talk." He laughed. "Maybe Candor will inspire us."

She laughed dryly. "If Candor inspires you, Dr. Sayeed, then tell me why you really wanted me with you on this flight."

"So that we *could* talk," he replied instantly. "Talk openly. The hotel is a sieve of information.

Name any group or individual with an interest in your investigation, and you can bet they have a recording of our luncheon conversation."

"It wouldn't surprise me if you had made your own recording," she said. Sparta herself recorded everything that interested her in her memory; she needed no machinery to do it for her. "And this plane's black box is recording what we say now. Why should either of us be concerned?"

"I want to warn you."

"Of what?"

"I think someone is trying to kill you."

There was no hint of melodrama or insincerity in his voice, but her flesh tingled. "Who and why?"

"I don't know who. I hear things."

"*From* whom?"

"Nothing specific, and perhaps I'm reading in meaning where none exists. Prott has made some remarks . . ."

"What remarks?"

"To the effect that he hopes you watch your back."

"You think he wants to kill me?"

"No . . . I don't think so. I don't know. As for the why, now that I've met you I would guess that it has something to do with your identity." He turned to look at her over his shoulder. "Your holos didn't give you away, but as soon as I saw you yesterday, Linda . . ."

"You mustn't call me that," she said.

"If you prefer—"

"The record of this portion of the flight will be destroyed," she said. It was an order.

"Fine. But it isn't only me. I doubt that any of us who were in SPARTA could fail to recognize you."

For a moment she said nothing. She remembered that Blake too had recognized her easily, that day in Manhattan—from a city block away. Had SPARTA formed a bond among its members that neither Sparta's cosmetic surgery nor her acting could disguise?

"Are you transmitting now?"

"Only telemetry."

"Khalid, do you understand why we must erase this conversation?"

"Yes, and I'll help you. I'll use side channels to fill the hole with background—the wind on the wings, cockpit noises. Chances are, nobody will listen to the black box anyway, and if they do they won't notice, unless they already know what they're looking for."

"They tried to kill me, Khalid. They tried to kill my parents."

"We heard your parents died in a helicopter crash."

"Maybe. I didn't see their bodies. I've never met anyone who did, and I've spent a lot of time looking."

"You mean they're *still* trying to kill you? Who are they?"

"I'm in this plane because I hope to prove that you aren't one of them."

He jerked around to look at her. "Me?"

Again his surprise seemed genuine. If he had not really recognized her, though, if instead he had known all along who she was, then there was no mystical SPARTA bond, and he was one of the *prophetae* and an accomplished liar.

"Yes, you. Ten years ago, Jack Noble was one of your sponsors to the SPARTA project. Did you know that? And he's on the board of the Mars Terraforming Project."

"What does that have to do with your situation?"

"I have evidence that he's one of them. No proof, only suggestive evidence. The group that sponsored you, the Tappers, has ties to the *prophetae* of the Free Spirit. And I do know that it's because of SPARTA that the Free Spirit wanted my parents out of the way.''

Khalid was turned around in his seat, watching her intently, letting the plane fly itself.

''And that they want *me* out of the way,'' she said—

—and then she screamed. The pain that went through her head originated in the middle of her spine and shot upward. Suddenly her torso was on fire from her belly up, and the fire was spreading to her rigid, trembling arms, which thrust themselves outward of their own accord. Her hands curved into hooks as if to seize the ether.

Sparta began to tremble. Her teeth chattered and her eyes rolled up in her head until only the whites showed between her trembling lashes. Thirty seconds later she collapsed.

9

A skinny black shadow tumbled pell-mell from the sky. Contending winds, invisible in the clear pink sky, tossed the stricken plane first one way and then another across the wrinkled desert that rapidly rose to swallow it. The marsplane's slender wings fluttered and twisted and bent back on themselves so far it seemed they would crumple and snap.

Radar, satellite radiolink, holo projection, on-board computers, even the commlink—everything had failed at once. Without computers to continuously warp and trim its control surfaces, the marsplane flew no better than a torn scrap of paper.

In the lurching cockpit Khalid tapped switches and tweaked potentiometers as calmly as he could while being tossed from side to side in his harness. What had been thick colored air all around him, the construction of the holo projector, was now a view of real sky and sand and rock swirling sickeningly across the plastic arc of the canopy.

Auxiliary power from shielded batteries came back on-line. The control computers had lost the flight destination program and many of their other functions; Khalid had to remind the amnesiac electronics that their primary job was to keep the plane upright and aloft. Another minute passed as he worked at the programs.

Finally the plane recovered from its violent and irregular plummet.

The scarp of an awesome cliff rose before them, black with basalt, red with rusty iron. The plane flew straight toward it, undeviating. With fatalistic calm, Khalid watched the impenetrable barrier approach.

The plane was seeking an updraft. Finally it found one, a dozen meters from the vertical rise of rock. As swiftly as it had fallen the plane mounted, but its long wings brushed the cliff twice before it reached the rim and won through to free air. Khalid took control of the craft then and flew it by joystick.

Auxiliary power had failed to salvage the guidance instrumentation. The radar altimeter remained out of commission, and Khalid had no communication with satellites in space or with any ground station. From the displays, he judged that the onboard inertial systems were fried. He switched off the snowy screens.

He eased back on the stick and headed the low-flying glider back in what he judged was the direction of Labyrinth City. It was the only plan he had, the only sensible thing to do. He was hundreds of kilometers from his target, but tiny as the city was it had a wider cross-section than any other inhabited place on Mars.

Each time the plane climbed too high, it would lose ground-measured distance; it was essential to stay out of the opposing winds aloft. The jetstream had already blown them so far in an hour that they would need a day of jibing around buttes and mesas, across canyons and dune fields, to regain the Labyrinth.

With the plane under his control, Khalid took the time to peer around his seatback. Sparta lolled in her harness, her head thrown back from the last violent swoop of the plane. Her face was ashen; her forehead was dewed with perspiration. Yet her breath came evenly, and the pulsing vein in her throat showed that her heartbeat was strong and steady.

He turned his attention back to the controls.

For two hours the plane flew on without incident, entering the huge plain of Tharsis. Khalid had memorized the map of Mars; from thousands of hours aloft he could match much of it to the territory. He could read the windsign in the sand below, spot dust devils spinning like dervishes twenty kilometers away; he could find the updrafts he needed to stay airborne.

What he could not do without instruments was see over the horizon.

The marsplane soared along a line of steep cinder cones, their fresh and iridescent black lava dusted with orange sand. The cone at the end of the line was the newest and highest; as the plane banked around its shoulder, an endless dune field opened to the southwest.

When Khalid saw what was out there he whispered, ''God is good.''

A boiling duststorm was crawling across Tharsis, spreading wings of dust from north to south as far as Khalid could see. Its towering front bristled with dry lightning in a phalanx of glittering spears.

Wheeling the marsplane back toward the saddle between the two nearest cinder cones, Khalid dove for the ground. He pulled up in time for the plane to skim the steepening slope. He hit switches on the console and the wing sprouted dozens of upright spoilers. At stall angle the plane was hardly a meter above the slag; it lost forward speed and gently grounded itself.

Khalid slapped his harness release, threw up the canopy, and jumped out. Reaching up under the plane's wingroots, he threw a series of locking bolts and pulled the left wing free of the fuselage. He ran to the left tail boom attachment and released its latches, laying the boom and its vertical fin flat against the ground.

He ran on to the wingtip. A slender fiber lanyard was coiled in a recessed pocket at the wingtip. Khalid pulled it out. He took a long piton from the thigh pocket of his pressure suit and clipped it to the lanyard. From the same pocket he took a steel tool like an ice axe and pounded the piton into firm lava.

More lanyards were concealed at intervals along the leading and trailing edges of the wing and along the tail boom. Working his way back toward the fuselage, Khalid nailed the disassembled left side of the marsplane to the ground. By the time he had repeated the process on the right side of the plane, the sky beyond the saddle was dark with smoking columns of dust.

His final task was to lash the fuselage pod to the ground. When it was secure he climbed back in and jerked the canopy down. He had to pull it hard in the teeth of the howling wind.

He looked at Sparta. She was still breathing, still unconscious. The pain had eased from her sleeping face. He faced front again. Inside the rattling cockpit he watched the rolling storm loom over them like an oncoming tank tread over an ant.

And suddenly it was on them, streaking toward them like a live thing, swallowing them whole. A scurrying stream of soft dust hissed over the canopy. Seconds later the air was dark, made visible again by suspended matter that hid more than it revealed, a murky scab-colored brown through which Khalid could see no more than a meter or two.

The plane's detached wings trembled against the ground. No moving atmosphere could get beneath them, and before long their surfaces were obscured by writhing snakes of dust.

Khalid imagined that the atmosphere was alive with wriggling creatures, with newts and minnows of blowing dust, with anacondas of dust.

He dug in the pocket of his pressure suit and pulled out his astrolabe. Its electronics no longer functioned. The alidade no longer pointed to Earth. Nevertheless, he had a general notion of the direction of his birth planet.

It was time to pray.

Night. Blue lights and stainless steel at the Park-Your-Pain: Blake screamed at Lydia over the howling synthekord. "I don't know whether you remember me, but . . ."

"Yeah, I remember."

". . . we met the other night. My name's . . . oh, you remember?"

"You're Mycroft. What do you want?"

"Listen, remember Yevgeny said he got me a job at the line head? Well, I really need the job, but they say they're not running the crummies because of some accident. I've got the job, but I need a ride."

She looked at him, incredulous. "You want a ride to the line head?"

"Yeah. I know you said you never take passengers, but if you knew what it meant to me . . ."

"Wait here," she said. "I have to talk to somebody."

"I'll pay you. I mean, I can't pay you right now, but I'd be willing . . ."

"Shut up, will you?" Her irritation was real enough to make him back away. "I'll be back in a minute."

He watched her elbow her way through the crowd. He could barely see her between the bobbing heads, back there in the blue shadows, yelling into her commlink.

A minute passed. She came back. "Know anything about trucks?"

"Not much. I'm a plumber."

"Sure you are. I guess that'll have to do."

"You'll take me?"

"That's what I just said."

"When do we start?"

"Dawn."

"Great! Thanks, Lydia. Can I buy you a . . . ?"

"No," she said, cutting him off. "I'll see you tomorrow. Do me a favor and get lost until then."

Khalid roused himself from a troubled sleep. It took him a moment to realize what was missing: he'd grown used to the buffeting of the wind, but it had fallen to a gentle shiver.

Outside the canopy the last stars were fading and the sky was warming to dawn. He turned and shook Sparta's shoulder, but she was deep in sleep.

He raised the canopy and got out. It took him longer to put the plane back together than it had taken to tear it apart, especially when it came to reattaching the right wing, for with the left wing and boom in place the fuselage was canted over to the left. But a hinge and winch arrangement was built into the wing yoke, and before long the whole huge glider was reassembled and the dust shaken from its wings.

He left only the wingtip lanyards pinned to the ground.

In the cockpit, Khalid set the arming switches for the takeoff-assist rockets. His preflight check was almost casual, perhaps because there weren't any instruments left to worry about. With his left hand he yanked the hydraulic lever that released the wingtips; then, gripping the stick with his right hand, he hit the RATO trigger.

When nothing happened, he went through the preset again and tried once more. Still nothing happened.

The plane stirred in the breeze, eager to rise. Without a lift to altitude it could soon tear itself to pieces on the ground.

Khalid released his harness, swung the canopy up, and jumped to the ground for the third time. He checked the RATO canisters slung beneath the wings. No mechanical problems, and he hadn't expected any. The marsplane had been crippled by a general and catastrophic electrical failure, destroying every electronic system except the multiply-redundant aerodynamic controls and their shielded batteries.

He went to an access panel in the fuselage and pried it open. There was nothing obviously wrong with the massed circuitry inside, but a foreign object was lodged in the autopilot comparator: a stainless steel ball, discolored to a strange purplish-green that suggested intense heat. He plucked the sphere out of the crevice into which it had been wedged and shoved it into the thigh pocket of his suit.

After a moment's thought, Khalid, working more deliberately this time, took the plane apart again and again nailed it to the ground. When this was done he leaned into the cockpit, left his tools and remaining pitons on the seat, and dug into the net bags hanging against the thin walls. He scooped up a little less than half the plane's emergency ration, of food and water and stuffed the food tubes into his pockets.

He studied Sparta's face one last time. There were one or two things he could try, but none that seemed worth the risk. He left her there, in a coma, and after he had sealed the canopy over her he walked into the desert.

10

This time when Blake showed up at the dispatch office, everybody was quietly busy. Even the fat clerk seemed to be shuffling his numbers with great attention to duty.

"I got a ride, like you said," Blake said.

"That right?" The clerk didn't look at him.

"With Lydia Zeromski. Where do I find her?"

The clerk pointed through the big window that overlooked the yard. A truck was leaving the loading area, its turbines blowing blue flame into the orange dawn.

Blake walked through wisps of dust in the raking light, past the blasted fueling shed. The damage was impressive—the twisted remains of the manifold where the explosion had occurred loomed overhead like a plate of spaghetti frozen in midtoss—but the blackened and gutted crummies had been dragged to one side, pipes had been rerouted, and the yard was back in operation.

As he approached Lydia's truck he caught the scream of its turbines through his helmet, even in the thin atmosphere.

In daylight a marstruck was an even more imposing piece of machinery than at night—part tractor, part caterpillar, part train. The turbines were mounted behind the cab, big gas-expansion turbines fueled and oxidized from smoking dewars of liquid hydrogen and oxygen, so that the tractor was almost as big as a locomotive. The two cargo beds behind it were covered with fiberglass cowlings to minimize wind resistance, although nearby trailers were uncovered—Blake knew from hanging out at the Porkypine that there was a debate among the drivers as to whether trailer cowlings were more efficient as streamlining or as windfoils to lift the whole rig off the ground; being an independent lot, the drivers rigged their trucks to personal specs.

Despite their size, there was something spidery about the marstrucks. The treads were steel mesh, not clanking metal plates, and they were mounted away from the body on struts that seemed too narrow to bear the weight. The cargo trailers were long, built like bridges, and looked too fragile for their wide loads.

All this was an Earthman's illusion. Blake had yet to get used to a planet where things weighed a third of what they appeared and structures were effectively two and a half times as strong.

Lydia's marstruck was pretty much standard issue, with all its cowlings in place, its paint bright and its chrome polished, and only her name on the door of the cab, in blue and white script painted like flames, to indicate the rig was hers. Blake clambered lightly over the treads on the passenger side and banged on the door of the bubble cab. Lydia looked up from the console, raised a cautioning hand, and then unsealed the door. Blake climbed in.

The inside of the bubble cab was neat and clean, undecorated except for a 19th-century crucifix of polished black wood that hung above the dashboard. Behind the seats was the opening to the fairly spacious sleeping box, veiled with feminine lace.

Lydia checked the dash lights that indicated the cab was sealed and then popped the air bottles. The cab pressurized. When the board went full green, she pulled open her helmet. Blake did the same.

"You're late," she said. "I've been sitting here burning gas."

"Sorry. I thought you said dawn."

"The sun's been up five minutes, Mycroft. Work on your timing."

"Okay, sure."

She threw the levers and the treads began to roll.

The road out of the shuttleport was the longest highway on Mars. Fifteen minutes after setting out upon it, the last sign of human life—save for the rutted dusty tracks themselves—had disappeared behind them in the thin light of the Martian dawn. The desert crossed by this often-invisible web of ruts was the biggest and driest and deadest in the solar system. Except for the wrecks of other vehicles abandoned along the way, there would be no other sign of life until they reached the camp at the pipeline head, 3,000 kilometers to the northeast.

Blake looked through the bubble glass, fascinated. *Nothing* lived here. Not so much as a blackened ocotillo was rooted in the powdery soil; not so much as a horned lizard or a vinegaroon crouched under the desiccated rocks. Everywhere the landforms, down to the smallest rill, were covered with fine dust deposited by the global windstorms that cloaked the entire planet every few years. There was a reason Mars was called the dirtiest planet in the solar system.

As the small bright sun rose higher on his right and the woman doing the driving indicated that she was determined to keep her eyes on the road and her mouth shut, Blake began to face the superlatives: driest, deadest, dirtiest, widest. A dirt road long enough to cross Australia.

Better to be stranded in the Sahel in midsummer, better to be abandoned in Antarctica in midwinter, than to be lost on Mars.

The marstruck bounded over the sand like a running cat, legs stretched, belly to the earth. Wonderful how the human mind adjusts; what was terrifying becomes routine, what was ecstatic becomes dull. The truck's speed at first astonished Blake, but he soon grew to think of it as normal.

The truck raced along the lonely road, following the shifting ruts in the sand but guided by satellite. The ruts were an immediate but untrustworthy trace; the road was there even when they blew away, for in reality the road was only a line on a map, and the map was in computer memory. One copy of the map was in the marstruck's own inertial guidance system; another copy was in computers on Mars Station, which tracked everything that moved on the planet's surface through its net of sensors—as long as the lines of communication were open.

In that sense this lonely road was not so lonely. It was in intimate contact with thousands of machines and people, on the planet and in orbit around it. A nice thought—which the unfolding landscape subtly denied.

Soon after leaving the environs of Labyrinth City the road began its descent and crossing of the western provinces of the Valles Marineris, and Blake faced that ragged planetary scar for the first time.

To those who have not seen it the Valles Marineris cannot be described. Earthbound analogies are too feeble, but Blake struggled to relate what he saw to what he had experienced before, to images from his youthful summer on the Mogollon Rim and from those other summers touring the North American west—climbing down the North Rim of the Grand Canyon or the slopes of Denali in summer, crossing the Salt River or the Scablands, coming into Zion from the east, dropping into Panamint Valley from the west, rolling down the Phantom Canyon behind Pikes Peak, winding down Grapevine Canyon into Death Valley . . . there was no easy comparison, no real comparison.

There is a path on Earth—it cannot be called a road—known as the Golden Stair, which descends into the Maze of the western Canyonlands of Utah, near the confluence of the Colorado and the Green rivers; desert aficionados call it the Golden Slide. Built as a mining road, hacked from the ringing rock of stark perpendicular mesas and the slick sides of wind-carved grabens, the sheer slippery slide has claimed many an ATV and even the lives of a few walkers.

The highway into the Valles Marineris was worse. Seconds after Lydia unhesitatingly pushed the speeding marstruck over the edge of the cliff, Blake looked upon the deepest canyon he had ever seen. In the depths of it the distant banded cliffs were lost in blue haze. He could not see ground over the dashboard, and in that instant he was convinced that Lydia was committing suicide and taking him with her, driving straight into thin Martian air.

When a moment later his heart started again, he found that there was still rock beneath the treads and he could even see the road by leaning his forehead toward the glass of the bubble. What he saw was almost as bad as what he had imagined.

The angle of attack was twice what it would have been on Earth, the angle of a playground slide rather than that of even the steepest roadgrade. Blake strained to persuade himself that this made sense—things fall more slowly on Mars, don't they?—but he kept worrying about a diminished coefficient of friction and wondering about side-sway as the truck whipped around these roller-coaster corners. Inertia concerned itself with mass, not weight, wasn't that true? So what was to keep the whole hurtling pile of pipe from flying into space?

"Lydia, do you always . . . ?"

"Shut up. This is tricky."

Now that was comforting . . .

He did shut up, trying to convince himself that she knew what she was doing. Really there was no question about it, he reasoned; not only did she know what she was doing, she'd done it scores of times before.

Tell that to your stomach, Mycroft. . . .

The truck's speed wasn't as great as it seemed to Blake, nor was the road quite as narrow or steep, and Lydia was driving with more caution, leaving more margin for error, and employing far more experience than a naive off-worlder could know. Nevertheless, the big truck was rolling down a cliff of sheer slickrock a kilometer high.

There were more cliffs below it.

When at last Blake managed to persuade himself he would not die, he began to appreciate the scenery.

For the next five hours they descended without incident, down a series of rock terraces three kilometers high from plateau to valley floor.

Reaching bottom, the truck sped across a field of dunes that spread randomly across the crumbling banks of ancient superimposed gullies. Then it began slowly climbing another cliff as high as the one they had come down.

Going up, Blake could see the road without leaning forward, but seeing it, seeing that narrow, uneven track, was almost worse than hoping something unseen but substantial was under the treads. The red rock wall was on his side of the cab now, and when he looked at Lydia all he saw was the dazzling pink sky beyond her, silhouetting her stern profile.

They reached the top of the hogback ridge while the sun was still high. Lydia stopped the truck in the only flat place on the ridge, the middle of the road itself, and powered the turbines down.

In silence they ate their lunches—shrink-wrapped sandwiches and apples, grown in the greenhouses of Labyrinth City—and took turns visiting the pressurized privy behind the cab, reached through the little tunnel beneath the sleeping box.

Lydia revved up the turbines and they moved on. The road crossed the hogback and descended at a frightening pitch. Before long they came to a place where the road seemed to run straight forward off the cliff. Blake stared at the rapidly approaching edge in horror—there must be some trick to this, but he could not see it.

"What happened to the road? Landslide?"

"Later," she said. She kept the truck rolling, right to the end of the road. Far below them the wrinkled and scarred valley floor stretched away under serrated cliffs.

Lydia flicked on the dashboard videoplate that showed the view behind the aft trailer. Now he saw it: the narrow road continued on down behind them. They had passed the branch point, like the fork of a wishbone; there was no room on the cliff for even a rover to turn around.

"We back down this stretch," said Lydia.

"How do you . . . ?"

She looked at him contemptuously. "We're built that way, Mycroft. The trailer treads are steerable. The computer does the work. I just aim."

She just aims, Blake thought, by looking into a videoplate—steering forward while moving backward. He found a little wisp of cirrus cloud high in the sky and studied it intently as the marstruck crept slowly backward.

Within a few minutes the road ended at another cliff. Lydia kept backing up until the view in the videoplate was of empty air and distant cliffs. By then, the next switchback had revealed itself in front of them. She put the treads in forward and the truck lurched ahead. Blake felt the tension gradually drain out of his neck and shoulders.

Three more times they had to back down stretches of road with no turnarounds. Blake felt almost blithe about the last one.

This time the terraced cliffs and talus slopes descended deeper into the Valles than they had before. When Lydia and Blake reached the floor of the mighty chasm it was all in shadow, though the sky overhead was still bright.

They drove on an hour past sunset, their floodlights picking out the route through high dunes and scattered boulders. When they reached the edge of a geologically new lava flow—its edges of frozen splattered magma were still as sharp as broken glass, despite years, perhaps decades, of sandblasting—Lydia stopped the truck.

''I'm getting tired. We'll spend the night here. Do you want chili and onions or dragon stew?''

''What's dragon stew?''

''Textured protein and vegetables, Asian style.''

Not too exciting, but chili and onions in a confined space with a person who really didn't want to know him all that well . . . hm. ''Dragon stew sounds great.''

She reached into the food locker, dug out a couple of plastic packages, and tossed him one. He detached the fork and spoon from its cover, unzipped the self-heating package, waited ten seconds for the dinner to heat itself, and then dug in.

They ate dinner in silence, the same way they had eaten lunch.

Midway through the bland meal Blake snuck a look at the taciturn woman who had now driven fifteen hours with only one break and had said perhaps a couple of hundred words in that time. Her most succinct statement, shortly after he'd launched himself upon what he thought was going to be a cheerful process of getting-to-know-you, was "I don't want to talk."

Now Lydia was staring straight ahead into the starlit night, just as she had been for the whole long day. Her eyes were still fixed on the road.

Blake settled back into the cushioned seat, easing his safety straps. Things weren't working as he'd planned. His scheme had been to get Lydia alone, to befriend her and gain her confidence, and then to learn what had really happened between her and Darius Chin on the night of the murders.

The name Darius Chin had never come up. Blake hadn't even had a chance to indicate that he knew about the murders. If she were innocent—even if she weren't—her grief and loss might have kept her from reaching out to anyone. Certainly she would find it hard to express her feelings to a stranger.

Something nagged him. She'd agreed to give him a lift, but now he was beginning to wonder why. It wasn't because he'd charmed her into wanting his company, that was plain enough.

Had that been Yevgeny she'd talked to in the 'Pine? Was this just a favor to Rostov? If so, Blake's trashing of the motor pool may have been unnecessary, even wanton . . .

Lydia threw the plastic debris from her dinner into the waste bin. She shoved a loose strand of blond hair out of her eyes and unlatched her harness. She climbed over the middle seat, up into the sleeping box.

"Here's a pillow," she said, tossing one down. "Sleeping sitting up's not bad in this gravity. Not for somebody from Earth.'' She yanked her lace curtains closed.

So much for good night.

Midnight. Mars Station was high in the sky.

Khalid trudged across an expanse of wind-scoured quartz sand that glittered blue-white under the stars. The plain of whiteness extended all the way to the horizon, like the dry salt bed of an ancient sea. Blue silhouettes of distant buttes and mesas raised themselves against the sky.

Khalid had enough food and water for two days—not very tasty food and not easy to eat, since he had to suck it through a valve in his faceplate, but high enough in energy content to keep him going. His heaviest burden was the oxygen generator on his back, a unit that made it possible for someone in a pressure suit to walk around in the open without carrying bottled air. The heart of the generator was biomechanical, a culture of tailored enzymes that broke carbon dioxide from the Martian atmosphere into oxygen and carbon, a sort of artificial forest in a backpack.

But the reaction needed input from batteries. Khalid estimated he had less than two days' charge remaining in his. He could never walk to Labyrinth City in two days, and he had never planned to. He was walking toward an easier landmark.

As he walked across the crusty plain of quartz he entertained himself with mathematical exercises. How many square kilometers of desert were there in the Tharsis Plateau? Draw a diagonal across that expanse, label it the pipeline road. . . .

He consulted his astrolabe and checked the stars. The thing had been made for Earth, but surely there were coordinate transformations one could perform . . . a sphere is a sphere whether it's called Earth or Mars, and Khalid knew his approximate position, his longitude and latitude, on this one. The position of the stars was the same for both.

But his mind kept wandering. Was there a rational relationship between so-many-kilometers-of-sand-dunes squared and the volume of lava in the cone of Mount Ascraeus? He doubted it, but if he let his mind drift a little farther out into the glassy night, he might discover one . . .

Long before the sun rose above the awesome cliffs the marstruck was climbing the rim of the Valles Marineris, winding its way out of the colossal valley through one of its head-eroded dry tributaries, climbing the final kilometers across sliding slopes of talus before at last gaining the open desert of the Tharsis Plateau.

Once across the Valles, Lydia and Blake had truly begun their trip. Ahead of them stretched more than 2,500 kilometers of meteorite-blasted sand, scarred with ancient lava flows, pitted with sinkholes, faulted with slumping permafrost. They journeyed into the wilderness together, a man and a woman who had nothing to say to each other.

11

What satellite sensors could not know with certainty was the condition of the ground beneath the visible surface of Mars. And so, two days out, driving blind in a windstorm, the track having already vanished in the blowing dust, the marstruck plunged into an enormous sinkhole of decayed permafrost.

The tractor went straight in and automatically decoupled from the trailers behind it, leaving the first of the two flatbeds dangling half over the edge of the hole, its cargo of pipe threatening to spill forward. Meanwhile, nimble as a gymnast, the big computer-stabilized tractor had landed on an uneven ledge of ice with its forward treads. Lydia and Blake found themselves staring down from their safety harness into depths of dirty ice.

The dashboard lit up yellow in front of her, and Lydia hit the switches that powered the turbines down and put the tractor's systems on battery.

''We've got a problem,'' she said.

''If you say so.''

For the first time in two days she looked him in the eye, both of them hanging there in their harnesses, and he thought she came very close to smiling.

* * *

They sealed their pressure suits and climbed out of the cab and up the sides of the slanted tractor to the edge of the hole. The wind at the surface wasn't quite strong enough to knock them off their feet. They couldn't see each other very well in the blowing dust, but they had the commlink between their suits, and Lydia was good at giving orders.

"Forward tool locker, your side. Slide the shackle left and down. Inside on the left you'll find a dozen rock bolts, about a meter long. Yellow barrels with red tags."

"I see 'em."

"Take out three. Mount one forward of the sinkhole on your side. I'll do the same on mine. Then we'll put two out to the sides and two aft. Try to find good rock, sandstone. Otherwise, sound ice."

"Will do." Blake was as good at following orders as Lydia was at giving them, particularly when they made excellent sense.

They found solid rock forward of the tractor, and prepared to sink the explosive anchors.

"Have you used these?" she asked.

"Looks easy."

"Easy to blow your head off."

"I'll be careful." He ripped off the tag, pulled the pin, and stepped away. Seconds later the recoilless charge spewed fire and sank the steel shaft deep into the stone.

On her side of the truck Lydia was doing the same. With the forward bolts in place, they looked for dependable anchorage to the sides and rear. They had to go farther for it, but when they found good rock they were still within range of the truck's winch cables.

"What's the plan?" Blake asked.

"Cable sling. We're going to lift the whole thing out of the hole till it's hanging on the cables, then let it pull itself forward on the cables until it gets its treads on the ground. Computer knows this trick pretty well—we've done it a few times already—it will keep the tension adjusted.''

"All by itself?''

"More or less. I ride with the truck. You stand clear, in case.''

With all cables payed out and taut, the four winches began to wrap in synchrony. Lydia was leaning half her body out of the cab, checking the tension on the lines. The front of the big tractor came up slowly until the whole mass of it was suspended over the sinkhole on a net of fine cables. Then the tractor began to inch its way across the open pit, trembling toward the edge.

Suddenly and silently the left rear cable anchor let go, like a broken guitar string—what had looked liked good rock holding its anchor was fractured. For a moment Blake thought maybe it wouldn't matter, because the tractor already had its front treads half on the dirt and the three good lines that were left could carry the tractor's mass.

But the loose cable whipped into the jury-rigged lashing of the pipe load on the first flatbed and sliced through it, and the pipe came loose and spilled slowly into the hole. The enormous mass of it cut through two of the remaining cables.

Things fall a little slower on Mars and even the inevitable comes on a like a flood of molasses. Standing-by where he was there was nothing Blake could to do stop the tumbling rack of pipe, but he had time to leap onto the front right tread and reach up to the door of the bubble cab even as Lydia tried to get through it. He grabbed her outstretched arm and held on as she came out. Just before the sliding pipes sliced the cab door off, the two of them made the desperate leap to high ground.

They lay there in the blowing dust, face down

and side by side. Their suits still had pressure. Neither of them was hurt.

"*Now* we've got a problem," he said.

"Very funny."

But it was still pretty much a routine problem. They spent some hours winching the loose pipe out of the hole and stacking it back on the flatbed. They rerigged the tractor, and on the second try the cable scheme worked; the tractor climbed back onto solid ground.

It wasn't until the day was ending and the Martian sun was setting in the western desert that they got the whole outfit reloaded and recinched, and got the detached cab door patched with big olive-drab splotches of quicksetting polymer and put back on its hinges. It was nightfall by the time Lydia pronounced the rig ready to roll.

"Now?"

"Don't be silly, Mycroft, I'm not a masochist. What do you want for dinner, chili and onions or, let's see here . . . chili and onions?"

"Who does the shopping for these trips?" he asked.

"Chili and onions it is," she said, tossing him a plastic tray. They pulled the tabs and for a few minutes they ate in silence.

"You came through on that," she said while she ate. It wasn't thanks, exactly, but it was an acknowledgment.

"Self-interest," he said. "Without you, I'd be stuck."

"No you wouldn't. The whole planet knows where we are. I don't think you did it just to save your skin."

"So I'm a bleeding heart."

"Sure." She looked at him with eyes full of doubt and suspicion. "What do you want from me, Mycroft?"

''What I've got—a ride.''

''And what?''

''I don't know. Maybe an idea of what I've gotten myself into. What's it like here? On Mars, I mean. You're an old-timer by Martian standards. Excuse me, not *old*. I meant . . .''

''I'm not old, but I'm a bitch, Mycroft. So's life on Mars. It's worth living anyway. We're building a whole planet out of dead sand. Even the bosses are taking a chance.''

''The bosses? You mean like Noble?''

''Oh, they've got their stashes back on Earth if things go wrong—still, they're taking their chances along with the rest of us.''

''Doesn't sound like a good union member talking,'' he said.

''What union you in?'' she asked sharply.

''Yours,'' he said, ''thanks to Yevgeny.''

''Right enough. In this local we like people who play our game our way. We get rid of the ones who don't.''

What was that about? ''I like Yevgeny.''

''Yeah? Well, I love him,'' she said passionately. ''Even though he's an ugly big S.O.B., I love him for what he's done.''

''Love?''

She looked at him with eyes that were red-rimmed with fatigue. ''Not that kind.''

''You loved Darius Chin, didn't you?''

Lydia's expression hardened.

''. . . I mean, that's what I've heard around,'' he finished lamely.

Lydia threw the remains of her dinner in the disposal chute and turned to climb into the sleeping box. ''Tomorrow we'll make up for lost time,'' she said.

She climbed into the box without looking at him. A second later the spare pillow dropped lazily toward him through the lace curtains.

* * *

Darkness.

Somewhere in the freezing dark Sparta was sleeping. Her head throbbed with waves of pain, pain that brought whirling, spinning, spiraling patterns of dark color to her vision and a high-pitched ringing to her ears. Something shadowy and desperate flitted by in the sucking spirals, something rich in meaning that continually escaped her because she could not concentrate.

She could not concentrate because of the pain.

Worse than the pain in her head was the pain in her belly. Her diaphragm was a band of fire, clenching her abdomen. Her dreams filled with blood now, and with wet, staring eyes and glistening textures that could have been fur or hair or scales or feathers. She clawed helplessly at her rib cage, unable to reach the gnawing creature within.

She screamed, and screamed again. . . .

12

Hard light poured into Sparta's eyes, glistening like the tracks of daylight meteors across the pink sky. It was morning. The light was from the far yellow sun. The meteor tracks were tiny scratches in the plastic canopy of the marsplane.

She was half sitting, held erect by her harness, and her head was resting awkwardly on her shoulder. She raised it—it felt like a cannon ball on the wilted stalk of her neck—but while the cramped muscles of her shoulders protested, she found that much of the pain in her head had been dream pain. The burning in her stomach had subsided until it was not much worse than the aftermath of a spicy dinner. Difference was, she was hungry.

She moved her head cautiously, taking in her surroundings, looking at the canopy under which she sat, perched wingless on a sand-dusted lava slope. She was alone. The instrument screens were cold and dead, and the position of the sun in the clear sky told her no more than that it was morning somewhere on Mars.

A note, written with ballpoint on a scrap of checklist, was stuck in back of the seat frame in front of her.

"We have no communications and are lost to

searchers. I am walking in the direction of the nearest habitation. I pray that you recover soon. Your only hope is to stay with the plane. God will be good to us.'' Khalid hadn't bothered to sign it.

Sparta released her harness straps and gingerly flexed her wrists and elbows and knees. Physically she was undamaged, it seemed. She was stiff and her lower back was aching, but her headache had subsided to nothing worse than an irritable sensitivity to light.

She tried the instruments. As many switches and combinations of switches as she tried, she could get only succotash from the screens.

She checked to see that her pressure suit was sealed. She hit the rugged switches that controlled the air pumps; they at least were still functioning. The plane's apparent electrical failure wasn't total. Maybe some of its other critical systems were still operative.

When the cockpit was evacuated she moved to lift the canopy, but as she did so the pain in her belly came back. Gasping, she fell back. She left the canopy sealed and undisturbed.

She knew intimately the place of the pain, the locality of the layered sheets of polymer battery that had been grafted beneath her diaphragm, the place from which they sent surges of electrical power to the oscillator surgically implanted in her breastbone and the superconducting ceramics that coated the bones of her arms.

Like some biological creatures—but unlike humans—she was sensitive to the electromagnetic spectrum from the near infrared into the ultraviolet. Like a few other species of naturally evolved living things—but unlike humans—she was sensitive to electric and magnetic fields of much higher and lower frequencies, and of almost vanishingly weak fluxes.

Unlike any natural creature, she could transmit and receive modulated beams of radio frequency.

Whether this peculiar and artificial power, foreign to her body and unwanted—not asked for or agreed to by her, and put into her at a time she could not even bring to memory—had now been permanently destroyed, she did not know. All she knew was her terrible pain.

She tried to reconstruct what must have happened. At first she remembered only soaring above the endless desert. Khalid had said something that had disturbed her . . .

. . . that he *knew* her, that was it. And something else—that someone was trying to kill her . . .

And then the pain.

She did not have the one benefit radio could have conferred in her present desperate situation. A brief burst of targeted microwaves, however faint, would have appeared as a small, bright blip in the sensor field of an orbiting satellite, pinpointing the exact position of the downed marsplane. She had been deprived of the ability to make such a blip, and she did not think that was by chance.

From what she had seen it appeared that the marsplane must have been crippled by a powerful broad-frequency pulse that had fried the onboard sensors and computers—and at the same time had ruptured Sparta's only nonbiological function. Until she inspected the plane she would not know whether the source of the pulse had been onboard or beamed from outside. Nor would she know whether it had been planted and triggered by a person unknown or by Khalid himself.

Why had Khalid taken the plane apart? To keep it from being destroyed by the wind. Why would he bother, if he only wanted to kill her? Because, of course, a tragic accident must seem perfectly accidental.

She lay back in her harness and concentrated on

the fire under her heart, trying to dispel it by *entering* it. But too soon the pain overwhelmed her conscious mind, and she slipped back into fitful sleep and lurid dreams.

Swirling signs tantalized her with elusive meaning . . .

Midday. Lydia Zeromski's marstruck drove north.

To the west a huge shield volcano, Ascraeus, rose from Tharsis into the Martian stratosphere. On Earth nobody would have noticed it, not from this angle; one can stand on the side of Mauna Loa, the largest volcanic mass on Earth, and not notice anything more impressive than nearby trees and rolling hills and a mildly tilted plain, so gentle is its slope. Here on Mars the much bigger volcano made its presence known only by the lava flows and raveling arroyos at the hem of its skirt.

Lydia had reassumed her customary taciturnity. The morning had passed in silence except for the now-familiar whine of the turbines, transmitted through the truck frame. Blake sat on his side of the cab, brooding.

There were no more cards in his deck. He'd tried charm. He'd tried competence—gone so far as to save her life, probably—but nothing was going to make her loosen up. Lydia Zeromski was a tough cookie.

Blake slouched in his harness listening to the hissing turbines and the grab and scurry of the treads against the sand. He'd assimilated some novel sensations on this trip. He'd slowly learned the different feel of rock and lava and sand and desert quicksand and rotten permafrost, each texture translating itself into subtle superimpositions of vibration as they passed beneath the traveling treads. Now he became aware of something new—

—a rhythmic heave and rumble quite out of synchronization with the rhythms of the treads.

"What's that?" he said, turning to Lydia. For the first time he saw fear in her eyes.

"Flash flood," she said. She sealed her pressure helmet.

Without prompting he did the same. A flash flood on Mars? Unheard of, but obviously it was nothing fantastic to her.

She leaned on the throttles. The big rig leaped ahead.

They were crossing a wide alluvial fan at the base of the distant volcano, a thin spreading sheet of pebbles and boulders sorted by weight, of terraced sand and packed conglomerate cut through and exposed by intermittent floods of liquid water. Blake, trusting the texts he'd hastily absorbed during his journey to Mars, had placidly assumed these water-carved features to be a billion years old. Looking out the cab of the speeding truck, he now acknowledged what he'd seen but not believed: the sharply sliced contours of fresh erosion.

The huge rig was plunging and wallowing dangerously through the sand, slamming into boulders and spraying gravel from beneath its treads. Lydia had never driven with such abandon.

"We're not going to make it," she said.

"What do you mean?"

"We can't get to high ground. If we can just get to an island, at least . . ."

"Lydia, how can there be a *flood* here?"

"Volcano. Outgassing melts the permafrost into a slurry and it rolls down any available channel. We're in the middle of a big one." She glanced up from the wheel. "Listen, Mycroft, when I say jump, you jump. Grab a couple of rock bolts and winch cables and get as far forward as you can. Don't worry about good rock, you won't find any in this gravel, just get out front a hundred meters or so and shoot the bolts as deep as they'll go. Tie off. Cross your fingers they hold.''

''That bad?''

She didn't answer.

She found the midstream island she was looking for a few moments later and pushed the truck up and over its shallow bank. Then she swerved the whole rig around to face upchannel, into the approaching deluge.

''Jump!''

As the truck skidded to a halt he jumped and ran. A second later she was out of her side of the cab and running out parallel lines. He found an enormous basalt boulder and figured that it was worth more than a steel bolt sunk into gravel, so he looped the winch cable around it. He planted two more bolts and tied off the cables.

By now he could feel the ground vibrating under his boots like the magic fingers in a cheap hive bed. He looked upstream.

''Oh, damn.''

A seven-meter wall of slush the color and consistency of melted chocolate ice cream was bearing down the channel, carrying whole boulders with it. He turned and ran for the truck. Lydia was ahead of him. He saw her climb in and struggle to secure the damaged door on her side of the cab, then reach across to his. Nice of her to open it for him.

He jumped nimbly up and over the tread and pulled the door handle. It was struck.

He pulled again. ''It's stuck,'' he yelled over the suitcomm. ''Get it from in there, will you?''

Through his helmet, through the truck's bubble dome, through her sealed helmet, through layers of reflection he saw her white and determined face, set in a mask. She did not move to help him.

''Lydia, the door's stuck! Let me inside!'' The wall of mud was coming at him like a miniature flood in a cheap viddie, shot in slow motion. This was no miniature. Billows of steam poured from the improbably high crest of the wave—hot water from the melted permafrost was vaporizing instantly as it was exposed to the dry, thin atmosphere.

"Who are you working for, Mycroft?" Lydia asked.

"What? Lydia . . . !"

Her voice was husky and low, but it sounded plenty loud enough in his suitcomm. "We've known about you for months, Mycroft. Are you just a company fink? Or are you one of the STW's bully boys?"

"What the hell are you talking about?"

"You want inside this truck, fink? Tell me who you work for."

"Lydia, I don't have anything *to do* with the company or the STW."

"Yevgeny was waiting for you in the yard, Mycroft—he thought you were going to blow up the yard so they wouldn't send you to the pipeline. But it seems you *do* want to go to the pipeline. What we want to know now is why."

Blake looked at the steaming face of the flood, its tumbling wings now spilling around the banks of the shallow braided channels that flanked the midstream island, carving new miniature cliffs in the sand as it came. The agonizing slowness with which it approached was almost more horrible than the onrush of an earthly flood.

"Lydia, all I wanted was a ride to the line head. With you—you in particular."

"You admit you sabotaged the yard?"

"I'll explain. Let me inside."

The first gooey surf was breaking over the island's prow.

"I figure thirty more seconds, maybe less," she said. "Explain first." She ignored the flood, staring at him implacably.

HIDE AND SEEK 161

He thought about it for a couple seconds and couldn't think of anything more that he had to lose. "My name's Blake Redfield," he said. "I'm working for the Space Board on the murders of Morland and Chin. I needed to get close to you, to find out about you."

"You think I'm a murderer?" Her astonishment seemed genuine.

"No, I don't think that, but you can prove me wrong in about fifteen seconds."

"They think *I* killed Dare?"

"You had opportunity, Lydia. You had to be a suspect, and somebody had to check you out. I volunteered."

She still stared at him through layers of reflecting plastic.

"Lydia . . ."

"Relax, whatever-your-name-is. You're not going to die." Still she made no move toward the door of the cab. Keeping her eyes on his, she tilted her chin upstream, toward the approaching flood.

What had been an enormous wall of water a minute ago was now a low-running slurry. It reached the marstruck as Blake watched; wavelets of semisolid slush lapped over the treads and dirtied his boots, but they carried no more force, and before the flood had run the length of the truck it had subsided into a smooth layer of fine ash and dirt. For a while the hot mush, like a pyroclastic flow on Earth, had sustained itself on steam; now all the moisture which had lubricated the flow had evaporated and nothing was left but a deep layer of those fine particles which covered so much of the dry surface of Mars.

Blake looked at Lydia. "Great timing."

"I improvised. Believe it or not, I wouldn't have left you out there to die, even if you were a fink. And maybe you are." She opened her own side of the cab and climbed out. "Help me pull up the stakes."

It took effort to dig down through the compacted layers of new gravel and ash and uproot the cable anchors, but in a few minutes they had done the work and were back in the cab.

The turbines rose to a scream. The marstruck floundered on across the desert.

Lydia lapsed into her characteristic meditation, fixing her eyes on the horizon of the endlessly unfolding landscape. She looked at Blake only once, a few minutes after they had resumed their journey across the alluvial fan. "What did you say your name was?"

He told her. When she said nothing more, he lapsed into his own reverie. He watched the sand hills slide by and thought about how badly he'd botched this assignment he'd insisted on giving himself. Botched it right from the beginning. The reasons for everything that had happened to him since he'd become Mike Mycroft were suddenly obvious.

He knew why he'd been attacked outside Mycroft's hotel on Mars Station and how Yevgeny had gotten rid of his attackers so swiftly—they were Yevgeny's own people, and he'd told them he wanted this Mycroft character to himself. That's why Yevgeny had befriended him, gotten him a job, waited for him in the marshaling yard. Yevgeny had set him up.

They'd known about Mycroft for months, Lydia had said. Which meant that Michael Mycroft *was* a species of fink—a false identity the Mars Station office of the Space Board had used once or twice too often.

Just before they climbed out of the channeled terrain and moved on into the higher desert, they passed the blackened skeleton of a marstruck which had not made it across these alluvial sands.

Looking at its twisted, ragged frame, half buried in sand, Blake wondered if Lydia really would have let him inside had the flood not dissipated itself too soon. Or was she waiting for a better chance to stage the perfect accident?

Sparta hung above the still point of the turning world.
She was a sun hawk, her eyes ten times sharper than any human's, her ears tuned to the farthest, faintest cry.

There was a bare tree in the desert, and around it the world turned. The world was a desert of drifting sand and plains of smooth, bare stone.

Her sharp eyes saw shapes carved deeply into the barren sandstone, carved so deeply that the shadows in them, pooled there by the low sun, were like ink on the page. Her sharp ears heard the cry from the tree.

Her hawk wings sifted the air and she descended, curious to see more.

The outward form of the shape on the tree was human, a girl not quite grown to womanhood, hanging from the branches of the dead tree. They had nailed her to the tree with splintered bones—arm bones and thigh bones. Her belly was split from breast bone to navel and the cavity was empty, dark, and red.

In her oval face her brows were wide ink strokes above eyes of liquid brown. Her unwashed brown hair hung in lank strands against her pale cheeks. She turned her liquid eyes to hold fast Sparta's gaze with her own.

> *I ween that I hung on the windy tree.*
> *Hung there for nights full nine;*
> *With the spear I was wounded, and offered I was*
> *To Othin, myself to myself.*
> *On the tree that none may ever know*
> *What root beneath it runs. . . .*

The voice was not that of a Norse god but that of a woman, rich and deep—not that of the girl on the tree, but of a woman of years and knowledge.

I took up the runes, shrieking I took them. . . .

The face upturned to her twisted and melted. The eyes of the face flared with light, and when the flare subsided the eyes were pale, the thin lips were full and parted, and the dark hair had lightened to the color of sand.

*Then began I to thrive and wisdom to get
   I grew and well I was;
Each word led me on to another word.
Each deed to another deed.*

Now the girl's belly wound had closed in a purple scar, but she had aged and was still aging with her pain. Her eyes speared Sparta with their light.

Sparta, full of fear, felt for the wind with her wingtips, found it, and rose into the pink sky. The runes were all around below her, carved in the polished desert stone. If she could stop the world from spinning long enough, she could read them . . .

She mounted higher, making the painful climb—
—to consciousness. She was in the cockpit of the marsplane. She was alone. The sun had dropped low in the west, and moving upward past it was the crisp thin crescent of Phobos.

The moon Fear.

Sparta lay motionless for a moment, not denying her fear but acknowledging it, acknowledging the likelihood of her approaching death. She let the fear of death wash through her.

When she had accepted it she let it drain away. Then at last she could turn to the business of life.

She tried the switches of the air pumps and found that they still worked. But she had already evacuated the air from the canopy—why had she forgotten?—and her suit was still sealed. This time, when she reached to release the canopy locks, the pain in her belly was only a twinge.

She stumbled out upon the steep slope of ash. The wind was steady from the west at twenty kilometers an hour. She noted the way the plane's wings had been detached from the fuselage, the way everything had been neatly pinned to the ground.

The plan and layout of the marsplane were evident. She had no doubt that she could reassemble it—it had been designed that way. But before she did anything, she needed to find out what had gone wrong. She went to the instrument access panel in the fuselage and opened it.

Her darting macrozoom eye traced the visual outlines of the devastation inside, the fused microconnections of invisibly fine solid circuitry.

An electromagnetic "pulse bomb," a surge generator like one she'd seen only once before—in a Board of Space Control class on sabotage—had been lodged in the autopilot comparator. It wasn't there now, but Sparta could picture it clearly.

It would have been a steel ball about the size of a lime; greenish-blue discoloration after detonation would have made the sour-fruit comparison even more apt. Before detonation it would have contained a microscopic sphere of frozen hydrogen isotopes, tritium and deuterium, surrounded by larger spheres of liquid nitrogen, liquid lithium, high explosives, and insulators, all under immense pressure. Triggered by an external signal, the explosives would have crushed the hydrogen isotopes, creating thermonuclear fusion—a microscopic H-bomb. The products of the miniature blast would have radiated outward, some ions at a much higher rate than others, and even though the actual force of the blast wouldn't have been enough even to rupture the superstrong steel casing, the radiation, moving at different velocities and spreading apart like the sound of a handclap in a culvert, would have produced a sort of electronic whistler, an electromagnetic pulse strong enough to fry all the unshielded circuits in the vicinity.

It was the kind of specialized and hideously expensive device that required the capacities of a rich institution: a powerful corporation, a big union, a whole nation, or a group—such as the Free Spirit—more resourceful, if less visible, than any of these.

Khalid must have taken the gadget with him.

The plane's ruined circuits couldn't be fixed, only replaced, and the marsplane didn't carry that kind of spare part. Sparta closed the access panel.

She leaned against the fragile fuselage and watched the languidly sinking sun. Maybe Khalid was telling the truth. His advice to stay with the plane may have been well meant. Nothing necessarily ruled against him; he may have removed the pulse bomb to give it to the patrollers.

Still, with the best intentions, he could die in the desert.

And if he did not have the best intentions, he might save himself and see to it that no one found her for weeks.

Common sense said she had to leave this place immediately.

Methodically she rooted the pitons out of the sand ash and recoiled and repacked the lanyards, leaving only the wingtips anchored. She reassembled the huge plane, piece by piece.

A few minutes later the whole immense and fragile assembly was trembling in the wind, pinned to the ground by its wingtips.

There were hydraulic linkages from the pilot's seat to the wingtip lanyards, the designers having anticipated that in some situations sophisticated electronic systems would be wholly inappropriate.

With the right wind, Sparta could pull the pins and let the plane rise, even without rocket assist.

She'd never flown one of these craft; until a couple of days ago, she'd never set foot on Mars. Right now there was a twenty-kilometer crosswind, not the ideal circumstance for an unpowered launch. But she had a knack for this sort of thing.

The sun had just set when she released the right wingtip. Simultaneously she leaned on the stick. The right wing lifted and the whole marsplane immediately pivoted backward on its tethered left wingtip, skimming centimeters above the slope. Half a second later, a little before the plane was head-on to the wind, Sparta released the left lanyard and leaned right on the stick. The plane quivered, tried to stay aloft—the left wingtip sank again and bounced—then rose confidently and glided slowly downslope, its line of flight falling and curving over the saddle of the dark cinder cones.

Sailplanes rarely sail at night, when the cool, dense atmosphere is falling groundward, but Sparta knew that there would be bright patches of sand in the desert that would give up their heat in rising columns some hours beyond the setting of the sun. She would have no trouble finding them. Her infrared vision, swamped in broad daylight, was at its best in darkness; she needed no holographic projection to see the atmosphere at night.

The barely visible landscape of the Tharsis Plateau was rendered in shades of midnight blue and starlight silver. Overhead, shining Phobos moved against the stars, casting deep shadows from the slopes of the desert buttes and dunes. To Sparta's eyes there was more to the scene: the desert glowed with shades of red as the rocks and sand gave back the day's heat at different rates. Revealed by their relative warmth, spirals of rich maroon slowly twisted in the dark blue atmosphere over the night landscape—escalating funnels on which the mars-plane could hitch a ride.

She skimmed the plane over the dunes and caught the nearest of the updrafts. Soon the plane was wheeling high above the desert and Sparta was searching her eidetic memory, trying to match the remembered map to the remembered territory, seeking the airy thread that would lead her to Labyrinth City.

13

A warning light glowed yellow inside Khalid's helmet, telling him his batteries were low, but he did not see it. Half the night he had slept in dreamless exhaustion while the cold wind sent trickles of sand to cover him like a comforter.

Weariness had overtaken Khalid, and he had curled himself into the shelter of a steep dune face. He knew even as he'd succumbed to sleep that he was risking the last of his precious reserves, but in the long run a human can no more do without rest than without air.

The last thing he'd done was to make sure he was lying with his face toward the east. For it would surely take the full light of the rising sun to wake him.

When it rose the sun was small, low in the east, and climbing fast. The undulating surface of the sand in front of the speeding marstruck was as smooth and sensuous as a discarded kimono of yellow silk, with folds as high as the hills. Since before dawn Lydia's marstruck had been racing across this dune field, the largest expanse of dunes Blake had ever seen or imagined.

There were tread tracks across the sand, rising

and falling over the waves, and they were a remarkable palimpsest, for as faint as they were they were still visible in the slanting light. Only the persistently reapplied imprimatur of passing vehicles could have frustrated the erasing wind.

Sixteen hours away, across the endless dunes, was the pipeline camp. They would drive all day and well into the night, reaching it when the stars were bright and the moons danced in the sky.

Lydia squinted at the road. With the sun low, every little ripple was a line of brightness and shadow. She had long since resumed her taciturn silence.

Blake's eyes were fastened on the horizon instead of the road, and he saw the apparition first.

"Good God, do you see that?" he whispered.

She slowed the truck and looked where he pointed.

It was a human figure, a man by his size and build, trudging the faint track far ahead of them, oblivious to their approach. He was frail and bent, a dark stick-puppet moving with painful speed toward God-knew-where.

Blake and Lydia sealed their suits and Lydia pumped the cab to vacuum. She sent the truck careening over the sand. Even before she drew alongside the walking figure she knew who he was. She knew his stance and gait.

She skidded the truck to a halt beside him. Gaunt and parched, the man stared up at Blake.

Blake stared back. "Khalid!"

Khalid must have heard him through his commlink, but he was too dazed or dry throated to reply. He only stared.

Lydia had her door open and was already out of the cab and running. Blake jumped down to join her.

"Battery light says he's got maybe two hours' charge," Lydia said to Blake.

"By God, he was lucky."

They lifted the frail and dehydrated man over the treads and into the cab. A minute later, Lydia had the cab resealed and repressurized. While Blake supported Khalid, she lifted the helmet from his head.

Khalid had fixed his dark gaze on Blake.

"Khalid, do you recognize me?"

"Blake," Khalid said, in a whisper so faint it was little more than an exhalation. Then his long-lashed eyes closed and his head lolled.

"He needs water," Lydia said. She reached for the emergency tube on the dash. She put it to Khalid's lips.

Khalid sputtered and choked, and then began to suck greedily. Water dribbled down his stubbled chin.

When he finally released the tube, Blake asked, "What happened?"

"Blake"—his fingers feebly grasped at Blake's chest—"Linda is out there."

"Linda? You mean . . . ?"

"Yes. The plane was sabotaged. This." His fingers scrabbled at his thigh pocket, and Blake helped him open the flap. Khalid pulled out a steel sphere that appeared to have been burned to discoloration.

"What is it?"

"Don't know. Fried the electronics. She's still out there."

"How far?"

Khalid paused before he answered. "Two days' walk. Maybe one hundred kilometers, a hundred and twenty at most. Southeast. I'll lead you."

"What about the emergency beacon?" Lydia demanded.

"No good," Khalid whispered.

"Lydia . . ."

"Out there, a miss is as good as eternity," Lydia said.

"You can't refuse to help!"

"I'm not refusing help," she said angrily. "I'll radio satellite search. Meanwhile the camp can send out search parties."

"Tell them to track *us*," Blake said. "We've got plenty of fuel. We can unhitch the trailers and make good time. Even if we don't get to her first, we can narrow the search."

Lydia studied Blake across the body of Khalid, who had leaned back against the seat between them and closed his eyes. "This man's not out of danger, you know," she said. "Who is this Linda? Is she more important than him? Who is she to you?"

"That's not her name," Blake said uncomfortably. "Her name is Ellen Troy. She's an inspector with the Space Board. She's in charge of investigating the murders."

"Yes . . . Ellen," Khalid whispered. "Something happened to her . . ."

"Why was she with you?" Lydia asked him.

He gazed at her. "Because she thought I did it."

Lydia's mouth tightened, but then some knot of inner resistance unraveled. She looked up at Blake. "How are we going to find her?"

Khalid fumbled in the patch pocket again and brought out his miniature astrolabe. "God will guide us."

"What's that thing?"

He attempted a feeble smile. "Its inertial guidance doesn't work anymore, but with . . . suitable coordinate transformations . . . it's still an astrolabe."

All night Sparta had followed the wind. Phobos was sliding toward the east as the sun climbed to meet it. The low, fast Martian moon crossed the sun more often than Earth's bigger and more distant companion, but there was rarely anyone in the narrow shadow path of Phobos across the planet's surface to observe the transit.

As Sparta guided the marsplane higher into the morning's warming atmosphere she saw the shadow of Phobos passing to the north, a slanted column of darkness in the dust-glistening sky. On the rippled plane of the dune field below, the twenty-seven-kilometer-long blob of shadow crawled eastward like a giant black amoeba.

Soon Sparta was well to the south and west of the moving moon shadow. She never saw the microscopic speck in the dunes that was the speeding marstruck, and the riders in the truck never saw the lazily circling plane that carried the woman they were hoping to rescue.

All day long Lydia drove fast and easily across the trackless dunes, aiming the tractor on the heading Khalid had specified along a snaking path that avoided the sharpest ridge crests but, where there was no alternative, plunging without hesitation down the shadowed slipfaces. Freed of its loaded trailers, the big tractor was an agile dune buggy.

Khalid, restored by water and food and clean air, was in the sleeping box—sleeping through it all. Lydia heard nothing from him until almost nightfall. Then suddenly he poked his head through her lace curtains and demanded that she stop the truck.

"It is time to pray," he told them.

Lydia, remarkably fresh and alert, or perhaps just running on caffeine—already she was brewing a fresh reservoir in the maker under the console—watched from the bubble as Khalid walked fifty meters into the barren dunes, spread a square of light polyfiber cloth on the sand, and kneeled to prostrate himself in the approximate direction of an invisible Mecca. The wind whipped the cloth around his knees and blew streamers of dust over his bowed back.

"How can you keep going like this?" Blake asked huskily. Bleary and cramped, he shook himself awake from where he had dozed off in his harness, sitting on the other side of the cab. He peered through the plastic bubble at Khalid, out there bowing to the sand.

"If either of you guys could drive I wouldn't *have* to keep going. Meanwhile the change of routine keeps me awake." She nodded toward Khalid. "He seems serious about his religion."

"Has been ever since I first knew him."

"When was that?"

"We were nine."

"He seems to like you," she said.

"I like him," he said.

"So how come this mutual woman friend of yours thinks he's a murderer?"

"She hopes it isn't true. So do I."

"Maybe I don't know Khalid as well as you two, but I've seen him around for a few years now, and I can't imagine the very serious Doctor Sayeed killing anybody. Not in cold blood, anyway."

"I can't either. But like you say, he's religious. Religion can take weird forms. And make people do weird things."

"If he did it, why is he trying to save her life?"

He brooded on that before he said, "Let's see if she's alive."

"Want some coffee?"

"Thanks." He took the steaming cup she handed him. "Who do *you* think killed them, Lydia?"

"The way you ask sounds like you don't think I'd give a lot to know. Well, I would."

"You've been a cool customer."

"Yeah?" She looked at him over the rim of her coffee mug. "With you, maybe." Khalid had vouched for Blake, and Lydia had had time to think about what that meant. She sipped at her coffee for a few moments before she began to talk.

"Dare and I were here with the first bunch of regulars, the first people to really settle here. None of the explorers and scientists before us had ever stayed more than a few months. We were rough-necks, like most of the others—we worked on wildcat wells all over the permafrost regions, helped map the hydrology of Mars. And we helped build Lab City.

"We cursed and fought and got drunk a lot, the first years. Everybody did. So it took Dare and me a while to realize we were in love. There aren't that many couples among the old-timers, you know. There used to be a lot more men than women, and a lot of the women hooked up with guys they didn't like much just to get away from a bunch of others they didn't like at all. When more people came in later, most of the early matches broke up. Some of the women discovered they liked freedom best."

"Doesn't Mars have some natives?"

"Twenty-three kids born on Mars, at last count," Lydia said. "Not exactly a population explosion, and what's it been, ten years now? I'm not saying there aren't good marriages, good companion-ships, just that they're pretty rare. But so is jeal-ousy."

"Jealousy is rare? That's not the impression I got—the guys in the 'Pine looked ready to take my head off if I looked cross-eyed at a woman."

"You're not one of us," Lydia said simply. "A stranger has to watch his step. Or her step—same goes for a strange woman. Besides, we all thought you were a fink."

"*All* of you?"

"Just about everybody in the Porkypine had you pegged for trouble, even if they weren't sure what kind. We weren't wrong, either."

"I'm not admitting anything." He nodded toward Khalid, who had gotten to his feet and was making his way back to the cab. "Not in front of a witness, anyway."

Lydia smiled. "Neither would I. They don't pay you enough to cover the damage you did."

Khalid's voice sounded over the suitcomms. "You two seem to be having a lively conversation for this late hour." He waited outside the truck while Lydia pumped the air down.

"We were talking about an explosion in the motor pool fueling depot a couple of days ago," said Lydia. "Destroyed some vehicles."

"Oh?"

Blake could see Khalid outside the cab, eyeing him knowingly through his faceplate. Blake cleared his throat. "There seems to be an odd notion that I had something to do with it."

The cab door popped on Blake's side and Khalid climbed in, maneuvering past Blake's legs.

As he settled himself into his harness Khalid smiled, his perfect teeth gleaming in his dark face. "Remember what fun we had, Blake, that summer in Arizona? Smearing our faces with black shoe polish and blowing things up?"

"Let's not bore Lydia with tales of our school days, buddy," said Blake.

"I'm far from bored," she said.

"We'll give you the gruesome details later." Inside his helmet, Blake had turned pink with embarrassment.

All three ran out of words. Lydia revved the big turbines and threw the tread motors into gear. The truck rolled.

Khalid coughed and said, "I didn't intend to interrupt . . ."

"Yes, please finish what you were saying, Lydia," Blake said. "About what happened . . ." When he ran out of words again, Khalid gave him an inquiring glance. ''. . . the night the plaque was stolen.''

Lydia looked at Khalid. ''I was saying that Dare and I were in love. That was pretty obvious to everybody, wasn't it, Khalid?''

He nodded judiciously.

But she caught his reticence, his hesitation. ''Okay. Maybe not so obvious. The truth was that I always loved him more than he loved me,'' she said. ''He was an independent guy, a lonely guy, and I knew him well enough to know that I couldn't do more than put a patch on what ailed him.'' She fell silent, choosing her words. ''But as long as he needed me at all, I put up with it. But in the last week or so before . . . he was murdered . . . it was different. He started avoiding everybody. He was edgy all the time. I took it personally. Because I was insecure, I guess. Anyway, I knew he was working late—he'd been working late every night since that creep Morland showed up—so I went to see him at work. I suppose I had some stupid idea that I was going to give him an ultimatum. As if either of us had a choice . . .''

She was quiet even longer this time. Meanwhile the air pressure in the cab was back to Earth normal. She opened her faceplate, and the men did the same. When she didn't resume her story, Blake finally broke the silence. ''What happened?''

''Dare didn't want to talk. He apologized for the way he'd been acting, said he'd talk to me later but he couldn't right then. There was something about the other guy, Morland. He talked as if something about the guy wasn't right. Anyway, he practically threw me out.''

''And you went?''

''Sure, what else? I sealed up and went outside. I hung around Town Hall awhile, but I couldn't see Dare inside.'' She looked at Khalid and almost said something, but changed her mind. Did he know she'd seen him that night, at that moment?

Lydia sighed. "Anyway, I went out to the port and drank a lot of beer at the 'Pine. I'd been there half an hour or so when somebody told me the news."

"Do you remember what Dare Chin had against Morland?"

"No. He wouldn't say." She stared out at the packed dunes, crosslit by the setting sun. "I'd better concentrate on my driving."

Blake nodded. The turbines rose another octave in pitch and the tractor leaped ahead, charging the dunes.

Khalid turned thoughtfully to Blake. "Do you know anything about this man Morland?"

"Not a thing, except the official resume. I don't even know what he looks like."

"He was an unpleasant person. An arrogant and insincere character. He had a taste for the high life. A heavy drinker."

"Is that prejudice talking, Khalid?"

"You know me better. I have no objection to the moderate use of alcohol, although I do not use it myself. Morland, however, was an addict. And something else, my friend . . ."

"Yes?"

"I am not convinced that Morland was really the expert on Culture X that he pretended to be. He played his role with great panache—indeed made a spectacle of it. . . ."

"His role?"

"The role of a typical xenoarchaeologist concerned for the preservation of the natural treasures of Mars. Yet when I made reference to certain specific finds—anything that did not directly concern the Martian plaque—his replies were vague."

"You think he wasn't an archaeologist?"

"He was an archaeologist, but his interest in Culture X was superficial. Or so it seemed to me."

"A new interest for him, perhaps."

"Perhaps," said Khalid. "Do you know what killed him?"

"Sure, it's common knowledge, isn't it? He was shot."

"With . . . ?"

"A target pistol, a twenty-two."

"Did you know that Morland bragged of being an excellent pistol shot?"

"Interesting. Does Ellen know that?"

"Our conversation was interrupted. . . ." Khalid paused and abruptly changed the subject. "How far away are we from the target area?" he asked Lydia.

"From the estimated position you gave us, we're still fifty kilometers away," she said. "You can read it on the screens."

"She's already been out there two days," Blake said.

"She'll be all right, Blake," Khalid said.

"I wish I was as much of an optimist as you."

"If she regained consciousness, she'll be all right."

Maybe she *was* all right. They wouldn't know right away.

Under moonlight, Blake and Khalid stood on the saddle between the lava cones. The wind had been light all day. Sparta's footprints, and the depressions where the wings and fuselage had rested, were still visible in the sand-dusted ash.

"She is an ingenious person," said Khalid.

"Lucky, too," said Blake.

"I'm sure she will be safe."

They avoided each other's gaze as they trudged back to the tractor. Lydia had kept the turbines turning.

PART
4

PROTT'S
LAST CHIP

14

Noon in Labyrinth City. The sun was high and the wind was strong out of the west.

The lost marsplane sailed in gracefully and kissed the sandy runway. It rolled a few meters to a stop in front of the Terraforming Project's hangar. Within moments, ground crew in pressure suits were swarming over it. Sparta pointed at her helmet and shook her head to indicate she had no radio communication. The hangar's outer doors slowly opened and the crew dragged the plane out of the wind.

Inside, Sparta climbed from the cockpit and ran in loping strides across the expanse of hangar floor. Inside the lock of the ready room, she yanked her faceplate open.

"Khalid is somewhere in the desert," she said to the startled operations officer behind the counter. "We've got to go after him—he's been out for more than three days. I'll show you where he left the plane."

"Dr. Sayeed is safe, Inspector," the ops officer replied, relaxing a bit. She said, "He was picked up yesterday by a marstruck going to the pipeline head. He told us what happened."

"So he did find help," Sparta murmured.

"The people in the truck went looking for you and found that you'd already left."

Sparta took a moment to pull her helmet all the way off. "Frankly, I didn't think he could make it."

"You did the right thing. But if we were in the habit of giving out medals, Khalid would get one. We'll just throw him a party when he gets back." The woman smiled at Sparta. "You're invited."

"Thanks. Accepted with pleasure."

The officer had been studying Sparta intently. "We've heard stories about your luck, Inspector Troy. What you did, most of us would have said was impossible—over two thousand kilometers without holo, without radio link, without even a compass—and three days ago you'd never flown one of these things at all."

Sparta shrugged. "I've got a knack for machines," she said huskily.

"Some knack. A knack for navigation, too."

"No, just a good memory. I've been studying maps of Mars for the last two weeks."

"I've been studying maps of Mars most of my adult life. I couldn't have done what you did."

"Don't underestimate yourself," Sparta said irritably. "It's amazing what you can do when you have to—look at Khalid." She fiddled with her suit straps. "Well—I've got rather pressing business. Do you need me here?"

A clerk who had been staring at her in admiring awe now suddenly guffawed. The ops officer grinned and pointed at a flatscreen. "See all the blanks on that incident report? If I let you go before they're all filled in, the locals are liable to arrest *me.*"

Sparta sighed. "All right."

The pressure lock had been constantly popping and sighing; the hangar office was crowded with mechanics and other men and women from the ground crew who were eager to get a look at the luckiest woman on three planets.

"What's the damage assessment?" the ops officer asked one of the men who'd just entered.

"Every unshielded electronic system in the thing is fried, like Dr. Sayeed reported," the man replied. "I've never seen anything like it."

"Dr. Sayeed said he found something in the autopilot," the ops officer told Sparta. "A steel sphere about thirty millimeters in diameter. He took it with him."

"It's a pulse bomb," Sparta said.

"What's a pulse bomb?"

"A very expensive device designed to do just exactly what it did—destroy microcircuitry. Somebody wanted the plane to disappear off the screens, to lose itself in the desert and never be seen again." And that somebody knows how I'm made and wanted to give me a severe tummy ache, she thought, but she kept it to herself.

"So, this blank that says 'cause of incident'—what do I put in there? Sabotage?"

"Yes."

"Mr. Prott has been trying to reach you for two days," said the breathless young man at the hotel desk.

"Really?" Sparta thought that a bit odd. "I've been away."

"He hopes you will join him for dinner. Perhaps tonight?"

Sparta needed to see Prott, too, but dinner? Her stomach leaped. The fire in her belly was banked but not dead. "Tonight will be fine."

"At six-thirty? Mr. Prott will meet you in the Phoenix Lounge for an aperitif."

She was too weary to argue. What she needed above all was sleep. "All right."

* * *

She pulled the drapes closed and turned off the lights. She stripped off her pressure suit and all her clothes and fell facedown onto the soft bed. Within seconds she was unconscious.

Two hours later she forced herself awake. Dazed and groggy, she dressed herself in her one of her two outfits of civilian clothes. They did not soften her appearance. While she had yet to go into battle in real armor, the yellow net stuff the Space Board issued in case of a fire fight, her slick black pants, tight black top, and high-collared shiny white tunic were armor enough for the social world; they broadcast a blunt message: *noli me tangere*.

As she sealed the seam of her tunic, the fire under her breastbone seared her again, so severely that she cried out and stumbled to the bed. Within half a minute she knew she could not ignore the persistent attack. She leaned over and reached for the bedside commlink. "I need to talk to somebody at the hospital."

The ruptured structures in her abdomen were poisoning her. Whatever the risk to her safety, she had to get help from outside.

"You say this was tissue replacement for trauma?" The doctor was peering at a three-dimensional graphic reproduction of Sparta's guts, concentrating his attention on the dense layers of foreign material spread beneath her diaphragm.

"That's what I told you, didn't I?" Sparta had spent a lot of time in clinics and hospitals, and although they were hardly the torture chambers they'd been a mere century before, she hated them.

"What sort of trauma?"

"I was in a 'ped accident ten years ago. I was sixteen. A drunk driver ran me into a light pole."

"Your abdomen was punctured?"

"I don't know that. All I know for sure is that some of my ribs were crushed."

''Yeah. You've got a big staple right in your sternum. Not exactly elegant work, but at least it doesn't show.''

Sparta grunted. Maybe she wasn't the nicest patient a doctor might wish for, but this young doctor needed to brush up on his bedside manner, and as for the staple in her sternum, it was elegant enough considered as a microwave oscillator, which is what it really was.

''Well, I don't know what the hell these people had in mind, but whatever it was it wasn't such a bright idea,'' said the doctor. ''That stuff is deteriorating. Your pH is so low it's practically falling off the scale—no wonder you're complaining of stomach aches.''

''What can you do?''

''Best thing would be to excise it. We can replace it with modern tissue grafts, if you really need them. Probably you don't. I'd guess your abdominal structures have already healed themselves. In fact you look in damn good shape except for that foreign gook in there.''

''No operation,'' she said. ''I don't have the time.''

''I'm telling you what you're going to have to face sooner or later. For now we can give you local implants to balance the pH.''

''Good, let's do it.''

''But I want you back here within two days. You've got a complex internal environment. I don't feel comfortable letting it go unattended.''

''Whatever you say.''

The procedure to insert the subcutaneous implants took ten minutes. When it was over Sparta shivered as she closed her tunic. She tightened the plastic sheath of her jacket around her torso and left the clinic, feeling an irrational attack of loneliness.

Irrational, or merely submerged? As she walked

along the wide, green-glass pressure tube that led to the hotel she tried to bring to consciousness a thought, a feeling, that was playing at the edge of her mind.

There was no doubt her implanted polymer batteries were ruptured; she'd been able to interpret the scan with less confusion than the doctor, who didn't know what he was seeing. The structures were not natural tissue; they would not heal themselves; they were long dead, long gone. They had never been truly alive.

She should have the stuff removed, as the doctor urged. Those gooey battery implants were part of what she resented most about what had been done to her; they were part of what made her other than human, a prisoner of what others had wanted to do with her body.

But lately she had begun to master the arcane power they conferred upon her, the ability to beam radio signals within a wide band of frequencies, which she could use—among other things—to control remote machinery. Action at a distance. Some part of her wanted not to remove the batteries but to have them repaired, replaced.

She was unsettled to recognize this temptation in herself—instead of resentment, a *desire*—to be more than human. Some controlling, power-seeking part of her did not wish to relinquish the ability to command the material world by fiat, by merely taking thought.

But at the cost of her humanity itself?

This was not the time for these thoughts. She snugged her plastic armor about her and walked faster toward the hotel.

"Mr. Prott? I'm afraid he's not here just yet. "I'll be happy to show you to a table."

She looked the place over. The far wall was a sweep of hardened glass looking out upon the

Labyrinth, its otherwise sublime view spoiled by reflections. To her right was a long glass bar and glass tables, lighting the customers greenly from below. To the left, in a corner under spotlights, a woman with stiff black hair sat at a synthekord keyboard, crooning smoky old favorites in a fetchingly hoarse voice. The enchanting Kathy.

"All right," said Sparta.

The waiter took her to a glowing glass table for two with a good view of the entertainment and the scenery. When he asked what she wanted to drink she said water.

She endured the cool and curious glances of the other patrons while she waited for Prott. Approximately every two minutes the waiter reappeared, inquiring if she would care for something else. A drink from the bar? A glass of wine? Another glass of water, perhaps? Would she like to see the hors d'oeuvres tray? Nothing, mademoiselle? You are sure? Certainly . . .

Ten minutes passed this way, and the next time a waiter descended on her she asked for a housephone link. The waiter brought it and Sparta keyed the number of Prott's office.

Prott's robot answered and offered to take a message. She keyed off. Next she keyed Prott's suite of rooms in the hotel. Another recording machine answered. She keyed off.

Prott was not the sort to put a guest in the spotlight and then embarrass her. That could be bad for the hotel's image. If Prott were anything like the ambitious and slightly paranoid middle manager he appeared to be, unpleasantness would be the very last thing he would wish on *anybody* in his vicinity.

"Excuse me, I've left something in my room. When Mr. Prott arrives, please tell him I'll be back within a few moments."

''But of course, mademoiselle.'' The steward who heard this bowed deeply. Sparta did not miss the amused contempt that lurked behind his carefully neutral mask.

She was past the simple lock of Prott's outer office in as much time it took for her to sense its magnetic fields.

She did not turn on the light. The flatscreen on his assistant's desk still glowed faintly from the day's use, warm in the infrared. No normal eye would have noticed the glow, but Sparta's read the last image readily. Nothing of interest, only a routine manifest of rooms and reservations. She had already ransacked the hotel's computer, of which this unit was a terminal.

No one had been in the room for half an hour or more. There were no glowing footprints on the floor, no glowing handprints on the walls.

She *listened* . . .

The air ducts and the solid walls brought her the gossip and complaints of the hotel's staff, the murmurs and cries and bored chatter of its guests, the rattle and thrum of its mechanical innards; she clearly heard the whisper of the outside wind.

She sniffed the air, analyzing the chemical traces that lingered: strongest was the alcohol and perfume of Prott's cologne, but through the air vents she could smell kitchen grease, burned coffee, germicide, soap, cleaning fluid, stale booze, tobacco smoke—the concentrated essence of hotel.

And faint within it, a subtler essence. Something tugged at the edge of her consciousness, a presence, distant but menacing. . . .

Sparta reached for the door of Prott's inner office. The lock was disguised as a standard magnetic type with an alphanumeric pad identical to the lock on the outer office. But the alphanumerics were dummies; the lock was actually keyed to its programmer's fingerprints in the infrared. Only a precise pattern of warm and cool fingerprint ridges on the pad, *his* fingerprints, would open the lock.

Sparta did not have Prott's fingerprints in her memory, but she had the means to reconstruct them.

Every human touch is unique; the skin secretes a mixture of oils and acids that ultimately depends on the genetic makeup of the individual—shared only in the case of identical twins or other clones. Sparta's senses of touch and smell, combined with the processes of her artificial neural structures, analyzed Prott's unique chemical fingerprints and produced a mental map of the whorls and spirals of his most recent touch on the pads—two fingers and the side of a thumb.

Reproducing the prints was trickier. It needed warmth, precision, and speed. No human could wield a tool freehand with the precision required to draw another human's fingerprint to exact scale, but Sparta was not quite human. The dense soul's eye beneath her forehead was orders of magnitude more capacious than the control computers of the world's most sophisticated industrial robots.

And for warmth she needed only her own hand wrapped around a steel paperclip. Heating it in her palm, she used the curve of the clip as a stylus to reproduce Prott's latent prints with lithographic accuracy, laying the copies lightly and swiftly on top of the originals. Then gentle pressure . . .

The lock clicked open. The door to Prott's inner office slowly swung back. She stepped through. The pressure from the inner office to the outer office was positive, and she felt the cool outward flow of air. The fine hairs rose on her scalp.

She stepped inside. The pressure-sealed door slowly closed itself behind her.

Sparta did not need enhanced analytical faculties to detect the difference in the atmosphere; anyone who had ever been near a slaughterhouse would have known it. Anyone who had been in a shooting gallery would have recognized the smell of burned powder.

Prott's body was on the floor behind his desk. He'd been dead for perhaps half an hour. The heat had long retreated from his limbs, leaving them blue in the darkness, but in Sparta's eerie eyesight the core of his head and his torso still glowed like banked fires.

She knelt carefully beside the body, not touching it—but breathing deeply, looking, *listening.* . . .

When he was killed he had been sitting in his enameled desk chair, which had fallen backward and to the side. There was a neat round hole centered above his eyes and a much larger hole in the back of his skull.

Prott's head lay twisted to one side in a pool of blood, which was congealing on the gray industrial carpet. The expression on his face could not be read, for the bullet had triggered a reflex that had left the unfortunate Prott, so careful of his looks, cross-eyed.

Sparta glanced up. There was a crater in the sandstone wall behind Prott's desk. The polished stone was marred with a splash of drying blood, at the level of a seated man's head.

She stood and leaned close to the hole chipped in the wall. Zeroing in, she could see microscopic flecks of soft metal gleaming in the rock matrix. The spent bullet had not embedded itself but had fallen to the floor, where the murderer had retrieved it, for otherwise Sparta would have had no trouble locating it. The faint odor of oxidized lead and copper wrote their simple formulas across the screen of her consciousness.

Sparta crossed to the door and touched the light switch. Soft yellow room light came from scallop-shell glass sconces near the ceiling.

Prott's office was large and lavish, furnished with

dark leather furniture—a couch as big as a bed, deep armchairs—with low side tables of polished basalt slabs. On the floor in one corner a full-bellied alabaster jar held an arrangement of imported dried plants. There was only one picture, an inane oil in desaturated colors, contrived so as to not look too much like anything. Maybe it was a landscape. Whatever. It was visual Muzak.

The room gave no hint of a real personality; the decor was high-priced, soulless industrial design by the same firm which had done the interior of the entire stone-and-glass hotel. The books and chips in evidence were restricted to business journals, biographies of successful entrepreneurs, inspirational tracts on management. . . .

Inset into the sandstone wall near the couch was a liquor shelf, glinting glassily of brown and red and green. None of the bottles seemed to have been opened recently. The adjacent crystal glasses showed a fine haze of room dust; when Sparta looked closely, she saw no recent fingerprints. Prott was prepared to entertain business guests, but apparently he had not lately had the opportunity.

Sparta looked around the room, *felt* for it.

It was too featureless. Too much the dressed set.

She had yet to begin a serious search for clues to the identity of the killer. What already bothered her was that she did not know the real identity of the victim.

She had the records which had been beamed to her while she'd been en route to Mars, of course, but like Prott's office they were too sterile, the sanitized resume of a middle manager's rise through the ranks of an interplanetary hotel chain.

How convenient. And how frustrating. The man who lay dead on the carpeted floor was surely a competent hotel manager, but also, according to the testimony of the local police, he was a lecher and an expert pistol shot. Sparta's own sense of him suggested that he was a man on the edge of a psychotic break.

Yet his resume showed the smooth curve of an undistinguished and unmarred career.

There was no such person as Wolfgang Prott. Not the Wolfgang Prott of record.

Sparta went to the tiny flatscreen on Prott's desk. From beneath her fingernails, polymer-insert spines unsheathed themselves like cat's claws; she inserted them directly into the computer's I/O ports as if she were inserting skeleton keys into an old-fashioned door lock.

But like the unit on his secretary's desk, Prott's machine was no more than a terminal of the hotel's master computer. Seconds later, she had learned everything it had to offer, which was nothing new.

There were drawers in Prott's desk, locked with standard I.D. sliverports. Her PIN spines slid into them and the drawers sprang open. Inside, beside the usual paraphernalia—stationery, tacks, rubber bands, pens, clear tape—were neatly indexed racks of RAM slivers.

After building a block against outside eavesdroppers, she used his own terminal to play the slivers, one at a time; it took more time to load and unload them than to suck their contents dry. Once again she was impressed by the sheer banality of Prott's milieu. The slivers in these locked drawers were records relating solely to business: phonelink directories, personnel records, credit checks on hotel guests, his personal financial records. From the evidence, his employees and guests were ordinary, fallible human beings. His only visible personal income was from his salary, and he had invested what he could afford of that, with only mixed success.

For a borderline psychotic, Prott had been a remarkably discreet and well-organized man. Even a good man. He hadn't wanted the details of his employees' private lives stored on the master computer, where any talkative clerk could soon spread rumors about who used what chemicals, who slept with whom, who owed money to whom, so he'd kept these and other sensitive matters on separate chips, locked in his desk.

Sparta rather respected him for that, even as it further roused her suspicions. Nothing in these files was truly revealing of Prott or of anyone associated with him.

There had to be more. Hidden not in his office but in his private suite, perhaps. But Prott's suite was visited daily by maids and accessible to any determined guest in the hotel—it would be a much less secure locus than this, his inner sanctum, where even the unused glasses on the bar testified that no one ever came except his assistant and the janitor.

No, this was the place. Prott's murderer had not used stealth or force to enter it; the lock had not been wiped clean, and only Prott's touch was upon it. The murderer had walked through an open door, done the work without touching anything, then left and let the door quietly close itself.

Sparta moved more quickly now, searching the room with all her heightened senses. There was nothing hidden in the decorative jars, no safe behind the bland oil painting, nothing lurking in the recesses of the leather couch, no hollow places under the carpet. But a section of the picture-sandstone wall beside Prott's desk was thick with the oils and acids of his touch.

A laser beam had carefully sawn an irregular curve around the radiating iron crystals that formed one of the "pictures" in the stone. The resulting thin plate of rock covered a shallow cavity in the wall's cladding. Sparta had to play with the oddly shaped plate a moment before she was able to dislodge it: the trick was to press a lower corner and let the featherweight slab fall into her hand.

Inside the cavity were two objects, a microchip recording and a gun.

The gun was .22 caliber, a long-barreled target pistol uncleaned since its last use. It smelled of stale propellant and uranium oxide.

Sparta bent close to it, peered at it microscopically, sniffed it. Prott had handled it, but not recently. Less recent were other chemical signatures, two of them pronounced. One she did not know. The other she could not believe, did not want to believe. . . .

She bent to the chip. Prott's signature was as fresh here as his fingerprints on the door lock. He had recorded the chip shortly before he was killed.

She placed it in Prott's desktop terminal. She let her PIN spines emerge and inserted them into the ports, and then she went into trance and absorbed the contents of Prott's last chip.

15

Here begins the recording, synthesized in the voice of Wolfgang Prott:

If you are what I think you are, Inspector, you will have found these: the gun that murdered Morland and Chin, and an eyewitness account of the scene a few seconds after they were murdered.

I hope you don't find these things. You'll have no cause to look for them unless I haven't given them to you in person. In which case I'm probably dead. That is not a remote possibility, so I'm taking the precaution of recording this.

We have the same enemy, you and I. I speak of the *prophetae* of the Free Spirit. They did those things to you I don't fully understand, those things that make you so "lucky" and will have allowed you to find my hiding hole and this document. Because of those same people—through no direct means, but by necessity—I have become what I have become. No, I won't apologize for my sickly personality; after all, I've worked decades to perfect it.

Oh yes, I really am the odious hotelier I seem to be; the resume of my undistinguished career is quite accurate, as far as it goes. But after hours I pursue a . . . let's call it a hobby. I don't mean only the pursuit of women, although I try hard to give that impression. And apparently I succeed.

My primary . . . interest . . . has been to interdict the illegal trade in fossils and artifacts on Mars. This hotel I manage was a nexus for smuggling when I arrived here a year ago. No longer.

Smuggling still occurs on Mars, of course. How could it not? Otherwise-respectable people, museum directors and the like, will use the most extraordinary egocentric and ethnocentric excuses to justify their theft of cultural objects—usually claiming that they can better protect them or better appreciate them or show them off to better advantage than their rightful owners. But these sanctimonious deals are no longer made on the premises of the Mars Interplanetary Hotel. A smuggler on Mars needs to be much cleverer today than before I arrived.

Because of my interest in these matters, I had been following Dewdney Morland's career for some years before I arrived here—for some years before he showed any interest in Mars, in fact.

Morland had legitimate-seeming credentials, and his vita, quite unremarkable, looked no odder than that of many academics. He studied topics that seemed, to uninitiates, obscure and unrelated, but there was a plausible and respectable theme to his researches, being the relationship of artifacts to the tools used to shape them. It was only shortly before he came to Mars that he became interested in Culture X, however.

There are . . . were . . . only a dozen or so people throughout the solar system who claimed expertise in Culture X. It may have been Morland's misfortune to boast that he had joined them, for he and all but one of the others, Professor Forster, are dead now. And Morland was no expert.

The thing about Morland, not apparent to many people, was that valuable objects tended to disappear from the places where he did his research. He did his research on Cro-Magnon calendar bones at the Musée de l'Homme in Paris. A week after he'd wrapped up his work, a collection of valuable 20th-century ethnographic films was discovered missing. Fortunately no information was lost, for the films had long ago been transferred to more permanent media, but the acetate originals would have been extremely valuable to specialist collectors. No one suspected Morland at the time, and indeed no connection has ever been proved.

A year later, Morland was working on Anasazi artifacts at the University of Arizona. This time an extraordinary assemblage of pottery disappeared from the vaults. Here priceless information *was* lost with them, but although there was a thorough investigation, again nothing could be proved. Two years later, about the time Morland was visiting New Beirut, the Lebanese lost several unique items of Hellenistic gold jewelry from the Museum of Surviving Antiquities. In this instance the objects' aesthetic value exceeded their scholarly value, but the loss was nevertheless significant, and a blow to that struggling institution.

You will have no difficulty understanding that once objects of this kind are taken there is little likelihood they will ever be seen again. For a thief to dispose of a previously unknown artifact is relatively easy, but to try to fence one—sell one, I mean—which has already been catalogued, if it is well known, invites instant arrest.

Consequently, thefts of famous objects are almost always commissioned; the stolen goods go straight into the vaults of the wealthy but discreet pirates who finance the jobs, there to be gloated over in private.

In the case of Dewdney Morland we had a scholar of middle rank and modest income, with access to first-rate museums. Even on the face of it he was not, shall we say, unapproachable.

Strict liability laws forbid the spreading of unprovable allegations, but word manages to get to those who need to know. Museum people talk to each other, and some of them talk to me. The news that Morland had obtained permission to investigate the Martian plaque made my flesh creep. He'd never been stupid enough to steal the things he was ostensibly studying, but perhaps his successes had emboldened him.

The Martian plaque was not housed in a museum with other valuables; if it were to be stolen, it would have to be through a direct assault. I had nothing to go on but my suspicions, and I could not even share these with the local authorities without giving myself away. Nevertheless, I passed hints to Darius Chin—anonymously—and he followed up on them on his own.

Morland stayed here at the hotel. There was a regrettable mix-up while his luggage was being fetched from the shuttleport—a mix-up that allowed me to ascertain that he was carrying nothing suspicious and that his instruments were exactly what they seemed—interferometers and the like. But to make up to Morland for the hotel's error, I saw to it that he got a better room than he had paid for, plus very close personal attention.

He was not a pleasant man. He was rude to me, rude to the staff, loud and contentious with everyone. I find it difficult to understand how he could have done any work at all at night, for he spent most of his afternoons drinking. Indeed, on the night he was murdered he accosted Dr. Sayeed in the lobby and became so abusive that other guests complained, and the clerk threatened to remove him.

Putting up with him was doubly frustrating, for it appeared that if Morland was not innocent, he was maddeningly clever. The illegal devices I had left in his room and sometimes managed to get onto his person reported his whereabouts and his conversations faithfully. There was nothing suspicious in any of his actions.

I reluctantly determined to befriend the man. He had let drop that he was an excellent shot, that he considered himself something of a marksman. He bragged about it. I take it he was a hunter of deer and other controlled species on Earth.

Now, shooting has long been a pursuit of mine, a sort of hobby. Of course there is nothing to hunt on Mars, but target shooting is a popular sport here, and I offered to escort Morland to the hotel's range and teach him to use a pistol. He condescended to accept.

I took a mean pleasure in the fact that he was predictably inept at first; he wasn't used to a pistol and he wasn't used to the gravity of Mars. His first few dozen rounds came nowhere near the target. Shortly, however, I was struck by his rapid progress. Even during our first session, he showed noticeable improvement.

And from the start he was obsessed with beating me at my own game. When he asked if he could borrow one of my pistols—as you see, they are rather nicer pieces than those kept at the range for the use of guests—I didn't know how to refuse. He intended to spend the daylight hours at practice, he said, hours when I was working and he could not.

After a couple of days we met again, and Morland gave me quite a demonstration, cutting out the bull's-eyes with astonishing precision. To observe his skill was a useful reminder for me; we habitually assume that people who look athletic are skillful athletes in all ways and that people who don't look athletic have no physical skill whatever. But nothing prevents a fat, short-breathed, pasty-faced fellow with high blood pressure from having the gift of deadly aim.

He wasn't quite good enough to beat my score

that day, but he came close. We agreed to a rematch and wagered a bottle of Dom Pérignon on the outcome. He must have been confident; for him the champagne was a costly prize, whereas I could appropriate a bottle from dining room stores.

That night he and Darius Chin were murdered.

I was there, Inspector.

Alas, not soon enough to prevent the deaths of those two men—but I arrived soon enough to recover the murder weapon, the one you have in your hand now. Yes, it is my gun, the gun I loaned to Morland.

It happened this way: late that night I had intended to stop at the Phoenix Lounge to have a word with the bartender when I saw what I thought was a ghost, a man I had thought long dead. But this man is hard to mistake. He is a small man, fastidious in his manners, always expensively dressed, with curly bright orange hair that he keeps trimmed close to his skull.

He is one of the few *prophetae* I can recognize on sight, and the deadliest of their assassins.

I had just come in from inspecting the hotel's heat exchangers and was still in my pressure suit. The orange man was leaving the Phoenix Lounge. He put on his pressure suit in the cloak room and mingled with the group of guests who were going out on the town. I followed.

He didn't stay with the others. I am not without skill in stalking, and I know the pressure tubes of Labyrinth City well. It was quickly apparent that he was making his way by a roundabout route to the Town Hall.

I paused to let him get a few steps ahead. As you know, the only approach to the hall through the tubes is from the Council of Worlds executive building—that stretch is exposed and fairly well lit. After a minute or so I moved as close as I dared.

The pressure lock to the hall was still open; it's

a busy lock during office hours and it operates on a slow cycle. I saw no movement inside the building, so I went toward it.

At that moment the alarm sounded.

I almost turned and ran rather than be caught there, but I feared disaster. I ran to the end of the short corridor, into the central dome. You have a good idea of what I found, I think: those horrible bright spotlights on Morland, where he lay in his blood. And the bare cushion where the Martian plaque had rested only moments before.

Then more alarms went off, and I felt pressure loss—someone had opened an outside lock. I sealed up and ran through the dome, down the apse. . . .

I almost slipped in Dare Chin's blood. A glance told me he was beyond help. Ahead of me the door of the outer lock was closing. I ran toward it.

I stumbled again. My own gun was lying on the floor inside the door.

If I were to have any hope of catching the killer, I could not hesitate another second. But if I failed to catch him . . . leaving my own gun at the scene of the double murder . . .

I bent to pick up the pistol. Meanwhile the pressure door sealed. I punched the keys and waited the necessary seconds until it recycled and opened.

I fled into the night. Now *I* was the fugitive.

Had the orange man seen me following him? I didn't know then, and I don't know now. Did the orange man know who I was? I didn't know then, but now I fear the answer is yes. Did the orange man know I had recovered the weapon that incriminated me? I didn't know—I didn't even know if he knew the gun was mine.

But it was the orange man I feared then, and him I fear now.

I cautiously made my way back to the hotel. I put the pistol where you found it, took off my pressure suit, and later had what I hoped seemed like a relaxed nightcap in the lounge. It was a terrible alibi, no alibi at all. I could easily have been placed at the scene of the crime. But paradoxically I was not worried about that, for I had had time to consider that the taking of the Martian plaque was much too important to be left to the local patrollers or even the local Space Board detachment. Someone would be sent from Earth Central.

It was that person I wanted to see, and anything that pointed the finger at me—the lack of an alibi, for example—would get me to that person sooner.

Two weeks passed, filled with the bumbling inquiries of the locals. They searched this office, but never suspected this hiding place you have found so easily. I did my best to appear guilty.

If you had arrested me the day you arrived, I could have told you all this before. I wouldn't be taking the precaution of making this recording.

Now the precaution is necessary. You have been gone for days. If I don't speak to you within the next few hours, I fear it will be too late. I saw the orange man again today, caught a fleeting glimpse of him in a crowd of tourists at the shuttleport terminal.

One last thing. We have a acquaintance in common, you and I. You know him as your commander, your superior in the Board of Space Control. He is more than that, but I will leave the rest for him to tell, if he chooses. If necessary, I would like to be remembered to him.

Here ends the recording. . . .

16

Sparta pocketed the chip when it popped from the computer. She looked at Prott's target pistol, still in its hiding hole. Prott's apt description had confirmed the evidence of her senses, the evidence she had not wanted to accept. *The orange man.* The fussy, dapper, deadly little orange man.

And now she could sort out that faint and menacing presence, separate it even from the overwhelming odor of blood in the air. It was *his* smell, and to Sparta it was primal—as indelible and menacing as the smell of a dire wolf to a caveman.

Years ago, Sparta, disabled because her working memory had deliberately been destroyed, had been a patient in a sanatorium in Colorado. The orange man had come there to kill her. A doctor had died trying to save her. Three years before that, she had seen the orange man with her father and mother in Manhattan—the last time she could remember having seen either of her parents alive. But her subconscious told her there was more that it had to give up in memory, if only she could free it.

The orange man. From Prott's chip she knew what must have happened the night Morland and Chin were killed. Proving it would be more difficult.

She keyed the phonelink on the desk. "Get me Lieutenant Polanyi. At home, if necessary. Inspector Troy calling, on urgent official business."

She walked a sleepy Polanyi and two of the local patrollers around Prott's office, rehearsing the evidence with them. They bent and peered at the unfortunate hotel manager's body; thereafter, while one of them photogrammed the dead man from every possible angle, the others stepped carefully around him.

She showed them the secret compartment with the pistol in it—it took only seconds on the computer terminal to establish that the gun was in fact registered to Prott—but she made no mention of the chip she'd found with it. She had an odd distaste for outright lies; without saying so, she let the lieutenant believe that Prott had conveyed his suspicions to her before their dinner appointment.

"You believed his story?" Polanyi didn't bother to hide his skepticism. "Did anyone else see this so-called orange man?"

"I don't know yet, Lieutenant," Sparta said coolly. "I haven't questioned the bartender in the Phoenix Lounge or any of the other potential witnesses. I should think you and your colleagues are competent to handle that."

"If somebody else did the shooting, how did he happen to be in possession of the murder weapon?"

"That would have come out if he'd kept our dinner appointment, I'm sure. Meanwhile it's clear that Prott didn't shoot *himself*. Not with this gun or any other."

The chubby lieutenant conceded the point sourly—by saying nothing.

"The shuttleport, Lieutenant?" Sparta suggested quietly. "The truck terminals? Wouldn't it be good to search for a man of that description before he gets away?''

''We aren't stupid, Inspector. Every route out of Labyrinth City has been under constant surveillance since the night of the murders. We've been particularly vigilant about traffic off the planet. If this so-called orange guy murdered Prott, I guarantee you he's not getting off Mars.''

Which would have to satisfy her for the time being. There were moments when all one could do was wait; wait and answer bureaucracy's questions.

The bureaucracy had lots of questions. Hours passed before she stumbled exhausted to her bed in the hotel.

Morning.

Still half asleep, she groped for the burbling commlick. ''Ellen Troy here. Who's calling?''

''It's Blake, Ellen.''

''Blake? Is this a secure line?''

''I'm not scrambling, but it doesn't matter. My cover's blown so high it must be orbiting the planet.''

Her voice softened to a whisper. ''It's good to hear you.''

''Mutual.''

Blake was standing in a big steel shed, looking out a thick glass window at a raw dirt runway recently bulldozed from the sand and sprayed with polymer hardener. Out on the pad, ground crew in pressure suits were fueling a silver spaceplane, the *Kestrel*. Its swing-wings were extended and drooping; vapor billowed from the big hoses that pumped liquid hydrogen and oxygen into its booster tanks.

''When did you get in?'' Sparta's voice came over the field commlink's tinny speaker.

''We pulled in about three hours ago in the pitch

dark. It's light now. I'm out at the landing strip trying to cadge a lift out of here. They've got Khalid in the clinic for observation, but he's in pretty good shape. You?"

"I got back here yesterday. If I'd known it was all right to get in touch with you . . ."

"No problem. We heard on the link that you were all right. That was some flying."

"I was lucky. How did they find out about you?"

"Lydia Zeromski sort of talked me into confessing." He turned away from the window and the man who glanced at him curiously from behind the counter of the operations shed. "Apparently I wasn't the first Mycroft—somebody in the local Space Board used this I.D. before, to play dirty tricks on the PWG."

"That's a violation of Space Board policy."

He smiled. "In that case I want to watch you skin somebody's butt for it. Right now, just get me out of here."

"Don't you like the accommodations?" He could hear the answering smile in her voice.

"Far be it from me to complain." He looked around at the steel walls painted hospital green and white, at the torn charts and clipboards of yellow fax sheets hanging from nails. "The camp is a bit low on Taittinger at the moment, otherwise it's a charming spa, rather like the Gulag Archipelago. Lacking only the scenic Siberian snow."

"So what's keeping you?"

"I'm sure the roughnecks around here would be delighted to see the last of me, no problem there. And Lydia's my buddy now—she decided not to leave my bones to the wind—she'll give me a ride back when she leaves in a couple of days. But there's nothing out of here until then."

"What about the MTP? Aren't they going to pick up Khalid?"

"Khalid says he wants to stick around a while—

he was headed this way anyway. They're sending a marsplane for him next week. Marsplanes, after your experience . . . anyway, I was hoping to hitch a ride on Noble's executive spaceplane.''

''You know Noble. Can you reach him?''

''Unfortunately my old friend's been out of touch the last few months. I told the guys here at the field the whole truth, that I'm assisting the very important investigations of the very important Inspector Ellen Troy of the Board of Space Control, which even without Jack Noble to vouch for me makes me very important myself, and that I require immediate transportation to Labyrinth City.''

''What did they tell you?''

Blake looked at the two hairy characters behind the counter; the female was less friendly looking than the male. ''They were, shall we say, amused. Something about the cost of liquid hydrogen. Maybe if you backed me up . . .''

''I'll do that. Right now I need to talk to you about something else. I'm switching to command channel.''

''I'll hold my ears.''

The commlink squeaked and phased back in.

''Do you read me, Blake?''

''This must be going through three different satellites. . . .''

''Do you read me?''

''You're phasing, but I can read you—''

''All right—''

''What have you got?''

''—I can't prove it yet,'' she said, ''but as far I'm concerned the murders of Morland and Chin are solved. Khalid and Lydia Zeromski had nothing to do with it.''

''Shrewd, Ellen. That much I had figured out for myself.''

She ignored his sarcasm. ''Dewdney Morland was planning to steal the Martian plaque, with an accomplice. Morland was supposed to be the victim of an anonymous attacker—he was expecting to get drugged, probably. But instead his accomplice killed him." Sparta briefly recited the contents of Prott's chip, his identification and pursuit of the orange man. "Prott didn't mention hearing any shots at all, just the alarm sounding. That's when he ran into the hall and found Morland's body, then Chin's."

"You think Chin was dead before Prott heard the alarm?" Blake glanced at the desk, keeping his voice low.

"Yes, Chin must have gotten suspicious and arrived on the scene before the rendezvous."

"You think *Morland* shot Chin?" Blake whispered.

"Yes. He was a brand-new sharpshooter. And when the orange man arrived, he had an extra murder on his hands and an unwanted murder weapon to dispose of. Morland must have told him the gun was Prott's. . . ."

"Did the guy know that Prott was tailing him?"

"I don't know, and it doesn't matter. He must have told Morland to sit down in front of the plaque's display case, as if he were still studying it—he probably said he was going to knock him unconscious with Prott's gun. But when Morland bent over the plaque, he killed him."

"He grabbed the plaque—"

"Which set off the alarm—"

"And left Prott's gun by the lock as evidence. Does he know that Prott picked it up a few seconds later?"

"I don't think so," said Sparta. "I think he waited around for a couple of days, hoping Prott would be charged with the murders. When he realized that that part of the scheme had failed—that the local patrollers hadn't found a murder weapon—it was too late: you and I were already on our way to Mars.''

"*You* were on your way to Mars. Nobody knew about me,'' Blake said. "And if you're right, this guy knows who Inspector Ellen Troy really is.''

"He's been hiding on Mars ever since.''

"Waiting for a chance to kill you. *He* put that pulse bomb in Khalid's plane.''

"I'm sure of it. When that failed to kill me, he decided to kill Prott before Prott could say anything to me about him. That time he succeeded.''

"Not completely. You know who he is now.''

"But not where he is.''

"You'd better watch your step until I get back there.''

He heard her smile. "You mean I need all the help I can get?''

"I meant . . .''

"I know, Blake.''

"One unanswered question—''

"What did he do with the plaque?''

"Right,'' said Blake. "What do you think?''

"It's probably still on Mars.'' Her voice betrayed her doubt. "They claim the off-planet security's been tight.''

"At least it's a good bet it's on Mars. The guy's still here over two weeks later; he'd have been long gone if he weren't still waiting for a chance to get the plaque off the . . .'' Blake's voice faltered.

"What is it?'' she demanded.

"Just that . . . I was just remembering a conversation I overheard in a bar out at the shuttleport,'' he whispered. "Some women were talking about the black market, stuff stolen from the storage depots. . . .''

"What about it?''

"Somebody stole a bunch of sounding rockets, penetrators. They couldn't figure out what anyone would want with penetrators.''

"Solid-fuel rockets?"

"I don't know the specs, but if the rockets were big enough—"

"The escape velocity of Mars is only—"

"—maybe one of them could have launched that plaque into orbit."

"Prott saw the orange man at the spaceport yesterday," she said. "Get back here as soon as you can. I'll commandeer Noble's executive plane."

"You make me feel so important."

Sparta laughed. "I've got to keep you out of trouble. I don't want you going anywhere without me again."

In her hotel room, Sparta broke the commlink and keyed the camp's airstrip dispatcher on an open channel. With her other hand she was dragging her clothes from the closet and throwing them on the bed.

"Is this the Noble Water Works camp one dispatcher? Inspector Ellen Troy, Board of Space Patrol. Official business . . ."

She made sure Blake would get his ride. She dressed quickly and then called Lieutenant Polanyi.

"Any progress?"

The Space Board lieutenant did not look happy to hear from her. "Affirmative. The bartender confirms that there was a man matching the description you gave us—red-haired, of small stature, expensively dressed—in the Phoenix Lounge on the night of the murders. But he wasn't registered at the hotel or anywhere else that we can determine. No one remembers seeing him before that, and no one's seen him since."

"What about security?"

"We and the local patrol have had people at the shuttleport and the truck terminals ever since the murders, Inspector, as I explained before. There's been a satellite alert on unscheduled traffic from the surface. Nothing's left the planet, and nothing's left Mars Station, since yesterday afternoon.'' Polanyi caught himself. ''One exception . . .''

''What exception?''

''Well, there's no possible connection, Inspector. The freighter *Doradus* launched yesterday morning, but they're still in Mars space.''

''Still in Mars space?'' The remark triggered a vague memory. ''What happened?''

''They had a premature main engine cutoff during launch. They indicate MECO was due to a computer glitch and they can probably handle it on board. The only thing they have to worry about is bumping Phobos.''

For an invisibly brief fraction of a second Sparta's face became a neutral mask. The thing that was tugging at her memory sprang into consciousness— a remark made by Captain Walsh on the Space Board cutter that had carried her and Blake to Mars Station: ''. . . *We could have dumped him on Phobos, picked him off on the next orbit. . . . I just thought of it this minute. Phobos looks pretty good on this approach. . . .*''

Polanyi was still talking. ''. . . but they can easily avoid Phobos with steering verniers, and if they can't fix their glitch right away, another half orbit will take them back to Mars Station. . . .''

But Sparta wasn't listening. She interrupted Polanyi's explanation. ''Lieutenant, I need a vessel that can get me into orbit. Right now.''

''What did you say?''

''A shuttle, a spaceplane, anything. Whatever's on the runway. You get it for me. Use authority of eminent domain. I want to strap into it as soon as I get to the spaceport.''

''Inspector, I . . .''

''No time for explanations. This is triple-A priority, Lieutenant Polanyi. A direct order to be confirmed by Earth Central. Do it first and get the confirmation later. Do it *now*."

She keyed off the link and grabbed her pressure suit.

She knew where the Martian plaque was, and she intended to get to it before *Doradus* did.

PART 5

HIDE
AND
SEEK

17

The surface of the moon Phobos is hereby declared restricted, by authority of the Board of Space Control. Unauthorized parties landing on Phobos are subject to arrest.

The announcement repeated itself automatically on the navigation advisory channel, a channel automatically monitored by every spacecraft in Mars space.

It alternated with a second message: *Mars Cricket to Mars Station unit, Board of Space Control: officer requires immediate assistance at Phobos Base. Code Yellow.*

The commander of the *Doradus* arrived on the bridge less than a minute after the first reception. He settled into the command couch behind the pilot and engineer, smoothing his thick gray hair along the sides of his patrician head. He had an air of distinction unusual for the captain of a space freighter, and his freshly scrubbed crew in their crisp white uniforms more nearly resembled the crew of a private yacht.

The commander listened to the transmission. ''You've jammed it, of course?''

''Yes, sir. We instituted electronic countermeasures after the first transmission. We believe we successfully intercepted at least the second part of the transmission, the request for assistance. We have sent an ECM missile to substitute for the originating vessel's transponder codes.''

''Won't they detect the missile?''

''We don't believe the originating vessel has the equipment to detect ECM.''

''Who is the originating vessel?''

''The *Mars Cricket* is a planetary shuttle, sir.''

''Any response from Mars Station?''

''No indication they received the message, sir.''

''The shuttle's trajectory?''

''It is now closing on Phobos. Computer tracks its trajectory back to Labyrinth City.''

''It came up from Mars.''

''Yes sir. Doppler indicates that on its present course it will rendezvous with Phobos in approximately thirty minutes.''

''Our estimated arrival time?''

''Sir, we have been following our original flight plan. Our unpowered elliptical orbit—''

''Yes, yes—''

''—puts our near approach to Phobos in just under two hours.''

''Abandon the plan. Proceed on a powered trajectory to Phobos rendezvous. If pressed by traffic control, reply that we thought we'd fixed our engine problems but were wrong. What's the best estimate?''

The pilot tapped briefly at the mounded keyboard of the navigational computer. The display was instantaneous. ''With continuous acceleration and deceleration, forty-nine minutes to orbit—matching and rendezvous, sir.''

''Execute the program.''

''Yes sir.'' The pilot hit the acceleration warning siren. Below the flight deck the other crewmembers scrambled for their couches.

''As soon as ignition sequence is completed, I want you to retract the camouflage cowling.''

''Yes, sir.''

''Fire control is to arm two torpedoes.''

* * *

Sparta was alone in the commandeered shuttle, calculating her own high-energy flight path directly from the instrument readings faster than the ship's computers could do it for her. Through the shuttle's narrow quartz windows she could already see the cratered black rock that was Phobos.

Equally demanding of her attention was the blip of *Doradus*, bright on her navigation flatscreen, although in line of sight from Sparta's point of view the freighter itself was still below the horizon of Mars. Mars Station had just sunk below the opposite horizon, but navigation satellites kept watch on Mars space and every object in it and automatically relayed positional data to all ships through Mars Station traffic control.

To accomplish this, traffic control needed cooperation in the form of transponder beams—or without such cooperation, traffic control needed a target big enough for radar to see. The *Mars Cricket* and the freighter *Doradus* were too big to escape detection even without transponders.

But Sparta knew that an object had landed on Phobos two weeks ago which had escaped detection. Penetrators weren't big enough to be seen on wide-field radar, and they announced themselves only if they were programmed to do so.

A penetrator—more formally, a solid-fuel penetrometer rocket—was meant to be fired from an orbiter or a marsplane *into* Mars, not out into space. Only a tiny portion of the dry planet had actually been visited by humans. In the huge remaining expanse the penetrometers served as remote sensing stations for regions not yet entered by explorers on the ground.

The armored, arrowhead-shaped payload sections of the rockets were built to withstand the shock of driving deep into solid rock without destroying the sturdy instruments contained within them. The tail sections, equipped with wide fins like an arrow's feathers, broke off when the heads slammed into the rock; the tail stayed on the surface, paying out a cable as the head dove into the ground and deploying a radio antenna to send telemetry to remote receivers. The transmitter conveyed seismic and geological data from the buried intruments.

Rip the scientific intruments out of a penetrator and you had a cavity big enough to contain the Martian plaque. Fire the penetrator straight up, and you had enough energy to reach the orbit of Phobos.

The friable carbonaceous stuff on that moon, struck head on, would have eagerly swallowed the rocket's head. Program the tail section to send a coded signal, and you could locate your buried treasure at leisure.

The Martian plaque had been sent off Mars the same night it was stolen. No radar, no navigational computer had even noticed its passing. The plaque had been waiting on Phobos for *Doradus* to pick it up ever since.

Doradus had waited until Mars Station and Phobos, in their close but not matching orbits around Mars, had traveled almost to opposite sides of the planet. When at last the two bodies had glided into the right relative positions, a convenient engine failure upon launch allowed *Doradus* to drift in leisurely and quite innocent fashion to a near rendezvous with the little moon.

No one would have noticed when a landing party left *Doradus* for a quick visit to the surface of Phobos. No one would have been suspicious when, soon after the party had returned to the ship, the freighter's engine-control problem had been corrected and she blasted for the asteroids.

Sparta reached to the command console of the *Mars Cricket* and hit switches. The shuttle's maneuvering system rockets ignited like mortars. Through the windows, the stars wheeled as the winged craft rotated on its yaw axis. Another burst of mortar fire and the stars stopped turning.

She punched the main engine triggers and shoved slowly on the throttles. In seconds Sparta's weight went from nothing to six times normal, crushing her into the acceleration couch. The *Mars Cricket* was standing on its tail, rapidly decelerating to match orbits with Phobos.

A few minutes now and she would be leaving the craft empty in space. She had received no acknowledgment of her call to Mars Station for assistance. She recalled Blake's complaint about his too-much-used cover and wondered whether he was really the victim of incompetence. Had he been betrayed? She knew from experience that the Free Spirit could penetrate any government agency they wished to.

She was not seriously concerned for her own safety, though; her loud and repeated public declaration, designating Phobos a restricted area and announcing a Space Board presence on the little moon, should deter *Doradus*. She had only to land on Phobos first and begin her search for the plaque.

She would have seized *Doradus* and placed its crew in detention if she'd had a scrap of evidence. But she had only informed intuition. The Space Board could place *Doradus* under permanent surveillance later.

The thing was to locate the plaque. Sparta had no doubt that if the crew of *Doradus* succeeded in getting to the plaque first, the precious object would be too well hidden by the time the freighter reached its Mainbelt destination for even the most thorough customs inspection to discover it.

Worse, if the crew of the *Doradus* were resigned to losing the plaque forever, once under acceleration they might simply eject it on a random trajectory that sooner or later would carry it into interstellar space.

The roar of the *Mars Cricket*'s main engines was suddenly silenced, leaving her ears ringing. Outside the quartz windows the surface of Phobos had blacked out every star, filling the field of view. She entered station-keeping instructions into the computer, unstrapped, and climbed down into the crew airlock.

Inside the cramped lock she sealed her helmet and pulled the hatch shut behind her, twisting its wheel to seal it. Warning lights shifted from green to yellow. She hit the buttons and pumps began to suck the air out of the lock.

Her suit was the high-pressure kind, with mechanical joints that didn't stiffen under atmospheric air pressure; it was made for emergency work in deep space when there was no time for the long prebreathing period needed to purge nitrogen from the bloodstream. Her compressed air tanks were full; her suit gauges showed she could survive on the surface of Phobos for six hours. Her backpack maneuvering unit was fully charged with gas.

On the wall of the lock there was a bag of fine mesh, containing emergency tools: recoilless wrenches, tape, adhesive patches, gel sealant, wires, connectors, a laser welder with a charged power pack. She unclipped the tool kit and waited for the pumps to stop.

The red warning sign came on: DANGER, VACUUM. She lifted the safety lock from the wheel of the outer hatch, twisted it, and pushed the thick round door outward. Half a kilometer below was a black sea of dust and craters. She got her boots on the lip of the hatch and pushed off gently. When she was well free of the *Mars Cricket* she used the suit's maneuvering jets to descend slowly toward Phobos.

She moved cautiously across the narrow strait of vacuum, listening over her short-range suitcomm as the *Mars Cricket* continued to broadcast her automated navigation warning and her call for help to all the vessels and satellites in near space. The shuttle was her commlink to Mars Station; as long as it was in her line of sight, it could relay her suit-comm channel to the satellites orbiting Mars.

Why hadn't Mars Station responded to her "officer needs assistance" message? She was beginning to wonder how much good the commlink through the shuttle would do her, if she needed it.

Sparta's boots touched down gently on the dusty surface of Phobos; she could feel the crunch of the meteorite-blasted dirt through her toes. Head up, she checked her position. The only light was the ocher radiance of Mars, looming above the nearby horizon, filling a third of the sky; the sun was below the horizon. But marslight was quite sufficient for her purposes, and she could see very well. She stood in the center of an irregular plain about two kilometers across, surrounded by groups of low hills over which she could leap rather easily if she wished. The hills were, in fact, crater rims. The highest of them, silhouetted against Mars, was the rim of Stickney, where the structures of Phobos Base stood more perfectly preserved than the graves of lost explorers in the Arctic ice.

She moved off toward the base and found her first step taking her high into vacuum. She remembered hearing a story long ago about a man who had accidentally jumped off Phobos. That wasn't really possible—though it would have been on Deimos—as the escape velocity here was still faster than a person in a spacesuit could run. But unless she was careful she might easily find herself at such a height that it would take hours to fall back to the surface unaided, a risk she could not afford to take. She had a limited amount of maneuvering gas, and she intended to conserve it. Until reinforcements arrived she had to consider the possibility that *Dor-*

adus had defied her warning. She had no intention of exposing herself in space.

With three long bounds Sparta quickly gained the heights of Stickney's rim. She stabilized herself on the edge of the deep crater and turned to look up at the *Mars Cricket* hanging upside down in space, its stubby white wings gleaming in marslight against the powdered-sugar stars.

As she looked, a streak of light bisected the black sky and touched the shuttle. Instantly a ball of radiance burst so brightly that Sparta barely had time to hurl herself backward over Stickney's rim. The autopolarizers in her faceplate saved her eyes, but debris from the blast riddled the landscape. Chunks of metal bounced off the rim where she had been standing; at well over escape velocity they rushed on into space.

At ground zero under the *Mars Cricket*, she would have been torn to pieces. This time her good luck was only that.

The crew of *Doradus* were too disciplined to cheer unless the commander indicated that cheering was in order; nevertheless, murmurs of enthusiasm were heard on the bridge.

When the fire control officer confirmed that the *Mars Cricket* had been destroyed, the commander maintained a demeanor of judicious calm. With luck, the meddlesome Space Board officer had still been aboard.

Unfortunately, he could not count on it.

Communications had no indication that Mars Station traffic control had detected the firing of the torpedo. The satellites surrounding Mars had not been designed for weapons detection or electronic warfare. But the commander could not count on that either.

Phony signals from an ECM drone were intended to persuade traffic control that the shuttle still existed; the decoy had followed the lethal torpedo toward the doomed shuttle and had begun broadcasting imitation *Mars Cricket* transponder code and a characteristic radar signature as it looped slowly away from Phobos. How long could it be before someone decided to question the odd trajectory of the commandeered shuttle? What had the Space Board officer who'd commandeered it already said to the people on the ground? These were exceedingly worrisome questions.

Behind his patrician mask, the commander of the *Doradus* was a frightened man.

From the moment he'd first heard the order restricting landing on Phobos, he'd had to resist a powerful temptation to obey it. The warning made no mention of the Martian plaque; why should he risk discovery of his ship? It would have been simple enough to stick to the cover story of engine failure, return to Mars Station for "repairs," and wait for another day to retrieve the plaque.

For *Doradus* was not what she seemed. She had the lines of a typical atomic freighter, with forward crew module and cargo holds separated from the aft fuel tanks and engines by a long central boom, but these clumsy lines disguised her true power. Her big fuel tanks were segmented, carrying fuel for two separate propulsion systems: her atomic engines were supplemented by a fusion torch comparable to those which powered the Space Board's sleek cutters. Hidden in her cargo holds there were not only ECM drones and EW decoys, but ultra-velocity torpedoes and slow SADs, search-and-destroy missiles.

It was not for this simple mission to Phobos that the clumsy-looking *Doradus* had been secretly armed with enough weapons and electronics to destroy a Space Board cutter or an entire space station, and the commander could plausibly argue to those who had equipped him and sent him here that the risk of jeopardizing that later, greater mission was too great.

But the commander knew what the navigation warning really meant. The Space Board investigator—her name was Troy, he'd been given a file on her—had certainly deduced the truth.

Far worse than to reveal the secrets of *Doradus*, far worse than to fall into the hands of the Space Board, would be to fall into the hands of his colleagues . . . if he failed to use every means at his disposal to recover the Martian plaque. No artifact in the solar system was more precious to the *prophetae* or more nearly an object of their worship.

Doradus would be an invincible devourer of armed cutters and space stations when the millenarian day arrived, but how well would the formidable ship do against one woman on a rock? Of all the machines of transport ever invented, a space freighter was surely the least maneuverable.

Doradus could descend right down to the crater rims, search the surface of Phobos with optical and infrared sensors and radar, and eradicate anything that moved. But this Troy person could make half a dozen circuits of the little world while the crew was persuading *Doradus* to make one.

A spaceship accelerates along its major axis, and any significant deviation from a straight course demands turning the ship, using the attitude-control jets or, in an emergency, the backup gyros, so that the main engines can blast in a different direction. A typical freighter like the one *Doradus* pretended to be has a mass of several thousand tonnes, which does not make for rapid footwork. Moreover, so far as maneuverability is concerned, it isn't the mass but the moment of inertia that matters most, and since a freighter is a long, thin object, shaped like a dumbbell, its moment of inertia is colossal.

In any event a freighter's main engine is far too powerful for fine maneuvers; for minor orbital translations—such as spiraling around an asteroid or small moon—the small rockets of the maneuvering system are used. But to translate *Doradus* through even a few degrees of arc on maneuvering rockets alone took several minutes.

In the ordinary way these disadvantages are not grave—certainly not for a freighter which expects to have cooperation from the object with which it seeks to rendezvous. Nor for a disguised warship which intends to sneak up on its foes or, failing that, to destroy them from thousands of kilometers away, as *Doradus* had just destroyed the *Mars Cricket*.

But for the target to move in circles of ten kilometers radius was definitely against the rules, and the commander of the *Doradus* felt aggrieved. Troy was down there, he felt it in his bones. And she was not playing fair.

Outside on the raw strip at the pipeline head, the *Kestrel* was ready for launch. In the morning light vaporous wisps of orange writhed over the surface of its booster tanks.

Inside the ops room of the makeshift landing strip, Blake shook hands with Khalid. "Soon as you get back we'll hold a reunion," Blake said, then lowered his voice. "I can't give you the details, but I can tell you this: Ellen has solved the case."

"Then you may not be long on Mars, my friend."

"I promise I won't let her leave before you get back, no matter *what* comes up."

Khalid smiled, and his liquid brown eyes closed in recollection of better times. "I trust your word." He glanced up through the window at an impatient ground crewman who was beckoning from beside the spaceplane's open lock. "Your hosts are eager to leave for Labyrinth City. Perhaps you should not give them an excuse to leave you behind."

Blake squeezed Khalid's hand for the last time and turned away. He sealed up his pressure suit as he stepped into the lock; in less than a minute he was striding across the blowing sand toward the waiting spaceplane.

The crewman gave him a boost into the lock and followed him inside, helping him into his seat in the plane's small cabin. Blake glanced forward to the flight deck, but its door was closed. The ground crewman saw to it that Blake was strapped securely into his acceleration couch and then quickly retreated, snugging the double hatches of the airlock behind him.

The pilot did not bother to use the comm system; the only launch announcement came from the computer's synthesized voice: ''Prepare for launch. The time is T minus thirty seconds.''

Half a minute later the booster rockets exploded and the spaceplane tore down the runway and lifted off abruptly.

The plane angled steeply back. Blake found himself peering straight up—the angle of attack was *too* steep, and the acceleration was crushing. Then, just as abruptly, the engines' thunder ceased. The plane leaped as the boosters fell away. A huge weight lifted from Blake's chest—

No longer crushed, he now felt disoriented by weightlessness. This was no low-level trajectory to Labyrinth City . . . Blake woke to the first hint that something was wrong.

Before he could free himself from his acceleration harness the door of the flight deck opened. Blake peered straight at the pilot he had not met before, and the first thing he noticed was the barrel of the .38 caliber Colt Aetheweight semiautomatic pistol that was aimed at his nose.

What he noticed next was the smiling face of the man holding it, a small fellow with curly orange hair who was wearing a roomy flying jacket that appeared to be tailored from camel's hair—worth more than a grade six plumber made in a year.

''Don't bother to get up, Mr. Redfield,'' said the orange man. ''There's really no place for you to go.'' The dapper little fellow allowed himself a broader grin. ''Not just yet, anyway.''

Blake almost lost his temper then, something that happened when he felt like an idiot. ''In here you wouldn't dare pull the . . .''

''Forgive me for disillusioning you,'' said the orange man, ''but there is no danger to the hull of this fragile craft. I assure you that if I am forced to shoot you, the bullet will stop in your heart.''

For a full minute Sparta lay facedown, eyeing the blinking readouts clustered beneath the chin of her helmet. Her suit was intact; she had suffered no damage in the explosion.

She fell into a split-second trance. Her soul's eye ran the partial differential equations she needed to estimate the arrival of *Doradus* in the near vicinity of Phobos: thirteen minutes.

She pushed up lightly and lifted herself out of the coal-black dust of Stickney. She peered over the crater's rim. Nothing moved on the black plain.

The suitcomm of her emergency spacesuit, though short ranged, was sensitive to an unusually wide band of the radio spectrum—but she could hear only one thing of interest on it—what sounded like the ghost of the *Mars Cricket*, still aloft and drifting slowly away from Phobos, its transponder signaling normally.

So *Doradus* had sent a decoy to take the shuttle's place. Even that signal faded rapidly. Her radio's range was indeed severely limited.

She would have given much for the microwave sensitivity that had been ripped from her when the pulse bomb exploded in Khalid's marsplane; she might then have been able to pick up a hint of the position of the *Doradus*, and had she chosen to beam signals of her own, she might have tried playing a few games with its electronic systems. She might even, with her own internal structures, have been able to detect the coded short-range transmission from the buried penetrator.

Those chances were history now. Isolated inside her suit from every other sensory medium, she was dependent upon her eyes. But they were very good eyes.

She had thirteen minutes in which to locate the penetrator and the plaque it contained before she had to cope with *Doradus* at close range.

While flying the *Mars Cricket* into orbit she had mentally run estimates of the penetrator's likely flight path. The thrust of the little solid-fuel rocket was more than sufficient for it to achieve the 2.1 kilometers per second orbital velocity of Phobos. The robber would have wanted to get the plaque off Mars as quickly as possible; that meant a high-energy parabolic orbit. Fired from somewhere near Labyrinth City as Phobos was high in the sky, the rocket's flight would have appeared almost vertical. The impact presumably would have been somewhere on the eastern half of the overtaking moon, its leading half.

Sparta was just inside the western rim of Stickney. A few long cautious bounds took her down into the crater's eight-kilometer–wide bowl and, some minutes later, up its far side. As she flew she moved toward the sub-Mars point of Phobos, the place on the tidally locked moon that always faced the planet. It marked the little moon's prime meridian; somewhere within the more than 500 hundred square kilometers of misshapen hemispheroid beyond it, the penetrator was surely buried.

Sparta paused beside the long-abandoned radio tower on Stickney's rim, a gleaming relic of the first human exploration of Mars. The little hut at its base had a bronze plaque beside the hatch: "Here men and women first erected a permanent structure on a body beyond the orbit of Earth." It was a qualified distinction—that bit about "beyond the orbit of Earth'' was meant to exclude the moon—but a worthy distinction nevertheless.

As Sparta gazed upon the pocked and grooved landscape commanded by the tower, she sensed something besides fear for her safety or anger at her attackers. She sensed exhilaration. When *Doradus* had failed in its sneak attack, the initiative had passed to her.

Already Mars was waning visibly as Phobos swept toward the night side of the planet. She could make out the lights of an isolated settlement far over her head, gleaming faintly in the twilight of the Martian outback. All else was stars and silence and a lumpy horizon, so near it seemed she could almost touch it.

Mars, overhead, was a very useful clock. When it was half full the sun would rise, and quite probably, if it had not risen already, the *Doradus* would rise with it. The ship already knew or would soon learn the location of the buried penetrator and would put down a party to retrieve it.

She tugged the net bag of tools behind her as she entered the danger zone. The landing of a search party would not be a problem; it would be an opportunity.

From his command couch the commander of the *Doradus* could see over the heads of the pilot and engineer to an unobstructed view of the high-resolution flatscreen that stretched across the width of the bridge, displaying a telescopic view of approaching Phobos. A slowly widening cloud of sparkling dust was suspended above the moon's limb—the remains of the *Mars Cricket*.

''Have we acquired a signal from the objective?''

''Not yet, sir. We are still overtaking. The objective is not yet within line of sight.''

The commander thrust his chin into his hand, brooding.

Somewhere down there—most likely in the eastern hemisphere—was a half-buried set of tiny rocket fins supporting a wire-thin radio aerial. *Doradus* had to stimulate the target to reveal itself by sending a coded transmission; they had to pinpoint its location optically; they had to land people to dig it up and get it back to the ship before Mars Station traffic control began questioning what was going on out here.

One more thing they had to do before they left— they had to find Troy and make sure she would not give away any secrets.

The surface area of Phobos was over a thousand square kilometers. If Troy had survived, she was somewhere down there waiting. It seemed prudent to assume she was armed.

Considering the weapons the *Doradus* carried, this last consideration might seem beside the point to some of his colleagues. The commander hoped he never had to explain to them why it was very far from being so. In the ordinary course of business, sidearms and other portable weapons are as much use in space combat as cutlasses and crossbows, perhaps even less so. A handgun is a dangerous thing aboard a spaceship or a space station—or an airplane, for that matter—for it is quite capable of punching a hole through the metal skin that keeps in pressurized air. For that reason, working handguns were universally barred in space.

As it happened, the commander of the *Doradus*— quite by chance and strictly against regulations— had a Luger pistol and a hundred rounds of ammunition stored in his cabin; the gun was an heirloom, inherited from an ancestor who had served under Viscount Montgomery of Alamein. As for the ammunition that went with it—well, guns and ammunition were a sort of hobby of the commander's. And in any event the finger of a spacesuit glove doesn't fit into the trigger guard of a Luger.

How would Troy be armed? Except on Earth, Board of Space Control personnel resorted to only three kinds of weapons, and then only in pressing need. In artificially pressurized environments, they used guns that fired rubber bullets; their punch was enough to knock people down but leave vital structures undamaged. But if sidearms were needed in vacuum—a rare occasion—laser rifles might be called into play; they were recoilless and if held on target long enough could cut a hole through sheet aluminum or even the layered fabric and metal of a spacesuit. But lasers exhausted their charges in seconds; they were also awkward and massive, and therefore generally useless.

For the worst work the Space Board issued shotguns. Shotguns had the distinct disadvantage of propelling the user backward when fired, but they could rip open a spacesuit, and at close range aim wasn't much of a problem.

The *Doradus* carried three shotguns modified for use in space.

"What is the status of the landing party?"

The voice came back from the crew deck. "Suited up and standing by, sir, at the main airlock." There were two men and two women in the party, old space hands and dedicated members of the Free Spirit.

"Break out the shotguns," the commander ordered. "The party is to go down armed."

"Yes sir."

"Sir," said the pilot, "we have acquired the objective's signal."

A squeak and chatter of telemetry issued from the speakers, earlier than expected.

"On the western hemisphere?"

"The near southwest quadrant, sir. Apparently the penetrator rocket somewhat overshot its target."

* * *

The terminator of Mars was now a perfectly straight line overhead, and at almost the same moment the sun came up—not so much like thunder as like a salvo of atomic bombs. The sun seemed smaller here than from Earth or Port Hesperus, but unfiltered by atmosphere it was blindingly bright.

The filter of Sparta's helmet visor had instantly adjusted to the glare. No sign of *Doradus* on the too-bright horizon . . . Sparta sought the shadow of a nearby crevice, one of the peculiar linear grooves that streak Phobos like furrows in a ploughed field.

Whatever had hit Phobos hard enough to make Stickney's big crater had almost squashed the moon, like hitting a watermelon with a mallet. The dust-filled grooves that radiated from Stickney, some of them up to a couple of hundred meters wide, were the scars of the encounter—splits in the moon's rind.

Up to her knees in the soft powder that filled the shallow trench, Sparta peered over the edge and scanned the horizon all around her. Her gaze lifted to sweep across the sky overhead. She was reluctant to move into full sunlight, for *Doradus* was no doubt equipped with powerful optics. With her own right eye Sparta could match them, if she knew where to look. But just now she could see nothing but stars.

She turned up her suitcomm to maximum volume but got nothing but static on the standard channels. She tuned it down again. Unless they were keeping radio silence, the landing party would have to communicate over standard suitcomm channels. To locate them she had to keep her suitcomm open and get within range.

Doradus must have rendezvoused with Phobos by now. The big ship was not afraid of her—she was hiding from it, it wasn't hiding from her, and its one overriding task was to recover the penetrator.

If she could not see it from her present position, it was more likely behind her than in front of her.

She could sit here, exposed in sunlight, or she could retreat with the terminator line that marked the creeping edge of dawn. On a planetoid where flying was easy, it was equally easy to keep up with the sun. Cautiously launching herself along an almost horizontal trajectory, she began to circumnavigate her world.

She skirted Stickney to the north this time. The narrowing crescent of Mars rose and, as she kept moving, began to sink again, until only one vast horn reared itself enigmatically against the stars. It irked her that she could see no sign of *Doradus*. The ship was painted the standard white, and anywhere above the horizon it would be a bright beacon.

She paused, instinctively sinking into the blacker shadow of a nearby hummock. Doubt assailed the dictates of logic: what if she'd moved in the wrong direction? What if *Doradus* was stalking *her*, circling the moon behind her?

Just then she glanced up, and her heart skipped a beat. Something quite large was eclipsing the stars almost vertically over her head, moving swiftly across them. How could she have blundered right under the belly of the monster?

In a fraction of a second she realized the black shadow slipping across the sky was not *Doradus* at all, but something almost as deadly—something far smaller and far closer than that first startled glance had suggested. If she had correctly identified its silhouette, the thing floating above her was a search-and-destroy missile.

Sparta froze in place. With the suit's chin switch she instantly shut off all her life-support systems. The suitcomm shut down with them. If she did not move, if the SAD got past her before she was forced to gulp air, the infrared radiation from her space-suit's life-support systems might escape its notice.

She was good at holding still and holding her breath.

If *Doradus* was using the kind of SADs used by the Board of Space Control—supposedly highly classified arms, unavailable for purchase on the open market—they had certain limitations. Unlike torpedoes, SADs did not home on a specific target. They were designed to move slowly, to lie in wait, to detect programmed activities: the firing of a steering motor, the swivel of an antenna, the escape of organic vapor—the signs of life in space. Their primary sensory organ was a video eye. Only when that eye could plainly identify a prepro-grammed target, or detect movement, or deduce an anomalous contrast ratio within the field of view, would it focus its other sensors. SADs were not at their best when searching for a woman hiding in a dark jungle of rocks—a woman who could see them first.

With a brief glow of its steering jets, the SAD moved on. Sparta switched on her suit pumps and allowed herself to breathe again.

The incident confirmed her suspicion that the *Doradus* was interested in more than simply recov-ering the plaque; it also needed to eliminate her as a witness. There are more men on the chessboard now, Sparta thought, and the game is a little dead-lier. But the initiative is still mine.

The SAD kept going until its silhouette vanished in the night sky to the southeast; since the missile was traveling an almost straight course in the low gravitational field, it would soon be leaving Phobos behind, unless. . . . Sparta waited for what she knew would happen next. In a few moments she saw it, the brief stab of steering jets: the projectile was swinging slowly back on its course.

At almost the same moment she saw another

faint flare far away in the southwest corner of the sky. She wondered just how many of the infernal machines were in action.

She considered what she knew of *Doradus*—there were not so many freighters in space that an officer in her job could not remember the basic facts about them all, even without an enhanced memory. *Doradus* had been built ten years ago at the New Clyde Shipyards, one of the oldest and most respected of the private shipyards orbiting Earth. It was an average-sized vessel for a freighter, unusual at the time only in that it had a somewhat higher ratio of fuel-to-payload mass than was customary. The crew complement was ten, also unusually large—the minimum and customary crew being three—but because *Doradus* was intended specifically to serve the burgeoning settlements of the Mainbelt, it was not illogical that it should sacrifice a bit of carrying capacity for speed, or that it should have a crew large enough to be self-sufficient where docking and cargo-handling facilities were primitive.

The ship's history since then had been uneventful, although Sparta recalled that its maiden voyage had kept it away from Earth for three full years. Sparta wondered just where it had gone during that cruise and how it had spent its time. She had no doubt that some considerable period had been spent secretly converting *Doradus* into a pirate ship.

Even with an extra-large crew it seemed unlikely that *Doradus* had more than one fire-control officer, whose computer would have difficulty simultaneously keeping track of more than half a dozen SADs in a small area—for the greatest challenge of working with SADs was to prevent them from blowing one another up.

Sparta herself could keep track of that many SADs if she could find them. With a bit of luck, that would be no problem—and at the same time, she would find *Doradus.* Somewhere not far away the *Doradus* was pumping out radio power, at frequencies from a kilohertz on up. She switched on her suit's broadband comm unit again and began cautiously to explore the spectrum.

She quickly found what she was looking for—the raucous whine of a pulse transmitter not far away. She was picking up a subharmonic, but that was good enough: the *Doradus* had betrayed itself. As long as the ship kept a data channel open to its missiles, Sparta would know exactly where it was.

She moved cautiously toward the south, *listening* to the transmitter whine with superhuman sensitivity, analyzing what she heard at lightning speed. With an oscillation imperceptible to ordinary ears the signal alternately faded and increased sharply; the pulsed signal was interfering with itself as Sparta moved with respect to the ship, and the width of the diffraction zones gave her the relative velocity. From the increasing signal strength she knew she was getting closer to *Doradus.* She should see it—

—there. The *Doradus* was hanging just above the southern horizon, perhaps five kilometers above the surface, rimlit in marslight.

Sparta guessed that *Doradus* had made contact with the penetrator rocket and was station-keeping above it, at a sufficient distance that its optical and other sensors could sweep most of the southern hemisphere of Phobos. The scheme gave her an advantage—any landing party would have a long way to go to get to the surface.

Sparta had another advantage, due not to the tactics of *Doradus* but to plain honest luck. It was "winter" on the southern hemisphere of Phobos; Sparta no longer had to worry about the rapidly revolving sun, which had sunk below the northern horizon. It would be dark in this neighborhood for a long time.

Sparta settled down comfortably where she could just see the freighter above the horizon. When the landing party left the ship, the patrolling SADs—most of them, anyway—would have to be inactivated. Then she could move in.

She didn't have long to wait.

The sound of the missile-control transmitter suddenly died. A moment later a bright circle opened in the ochre-shadowed sphere of *Doradus*'s crew module.

With her macrozoom eye zeroed in on the airlock, Sparta could see as clearly as if she were floating only a dozen meters away. The round hatch swung fully open and four space-suited figures emerged, one coming quickly after the other. Sparta noted with interest that their spacesuits were black—and that they were carrying weapons. These people took their piracy seriously.

Gas jets puffed, and the four began their descent.

Taking advantage of every crater and hillock, Sparta moved forward, skimming Phobos like a low-flying grasshopper. She tuned her suitcomm back to standard communication channels and was rewarded with a terse vocal hiss: *Right ten degrees.*

A woman's voice. The suited figures above her, black cutouts against the stars, spiraled down like slow-motion skydivers.

When they hit the dusty surface Sparta was already in position, belly down behind a massive block of rock which glistened like coal. She was not a hundred meters from the landing site. She watched as three of the party fanned out, taking up positions in a rough circle around the fourth, who disappeared over the lip of one of the moon's big radiating grooves.

Another burst on the commlink, a man's voice: *We have located the objective.*

Almost five minutes passed without further communication. The three crewmembers standing guard bounced nervously, rising a meter or two above the black dirt with each step. Below the edge of the groove, out of sight, the fourth was presumably digging.

The next move was up to Sparta. The timing was tricky.

She had the laser welder from the tool kit out and ready, cradled in her arms. The welder was not an ideal rifle. While it had a power-pack as massive as any rifle's, it had no provision for aim at a distance; Sparta's right eye was her telescopic sight. And though a laser beam spreads very little in the vacuum of space, the welder's optics were designed for optimum focus a few centimeters in front of its barrel.

The power reserves wouldn't allow keeping a beam on three distant spacesuits, one after the other, long enough to burn a significant hole in each, but Sparta had no desire to kill anyone in the landing party. She only needed to disable them.

The objective is in my possession. Returning to the ship.

Before the man who had been busy excavating the buried head of the penetrator could reappear above the rim of the trench, Sparta shot the nearest guard. She heard the woman's scream over the suitcomm channel.

Sparta's laser had illuminated the woman for the briefest fraction of a second, not her torso but through the glass of her visor; before the visor glass could react to the light, the brightness of a dozen suns had exploded inside the unfortunate woman's eyes.

The others on guard instinctively tried to wheel; it was a mistake which sent both of them spinning out of control. Sparta got one of them before she had completed even a single rotation; she heard the woman's scream over the suitcomm.

The second guard, a man, compounded his mistake by firing his shotgun. Paradoxically, the ill-considered act almost saved him, for he was propelled starward by the gun's recoil. Sparta held her aim for an agonizing two seconds as he tumbled away, before his visor came around to face her; evidently he had not yet figured out his companions' mistake, for he had failed to darken the glass manually.

He too wailed when the light burst in his head.

Landing party, come in. . . .

We are under attack. Send in SADs.

Sparta smiled grimly. She could take out the eyes of a SAD as efficiently as she'd blinded the guards. There were an estimated half a dozen SADs out there on the perimeter. She checked her power pack. Well, as long as she didn't miss even once . . .

The man who now clutched the Martian plaque rocketed straight up out of the rill where he'd been hiding. Whether by luck or good sense, his back was to Sparta; he could not be blinded. Nevertheless Sparta aimed the laser welder and fired a sustained burst.

Five seconds passed. Her target rose farther and farther above the surface. Ten . . . her laser power ran out, and at the same moment the gas reservoir in the man's maneuvering pack overheated and exploded.

The force of the explosion sent him hurtling back toward Phobos. Sparta had already tossed the useless bulky laser behind her and launched herself on an intercepting trajectory.

They closed on each other with slow precision. The man was alive, and would stay alive if *Doradus* rescued him while there was still air in his suit. Sparta was satisfied that she had not murdered a man; she was otherwise uninterested in his fate.

She was interested only in the precious object he gripped in his right glove.

He saw her coming, but he could do nothing except writhe helplessly, out of control.

SADs target on me! Danger of capture!

At the last second he threw the gleaming mirror as hard as he could, away from him. In his panic he threw it almost at her, down toward the surface of the moon. Sparta clutched at the plaque and missed. She swung her booted feet around and kicked the man's helmet, launching herself off him in the direction of the speeding plaque, nimbly evading the clutch of his gloves. She boosted herself at maximum power with her gas jets.

The seconds passed with interminable slowness. Sparta overtook the plaque shortly after it struck the surface, throwing up a cloud of coal-black dust that hung suspended in vacuum. She launched herself from the surface with one arm, like a diver moving along the bottom of the sea, and snatched the tumbling mirror before it bounced farther. With a burst of her jets she drove herself on toward the nearest crater.

The helplessly struggling crewman hit dirt a few seconds later and rebounded into space. If *Doradus* had any interest in rescuing the landing party, that interest was subordinate to the desire to destroy Sparta—and apparently the plaque with her, if necessary. Sparta had distanced herself from the crewman by almost a hundred meters when the first SAD came in. The missile found him, not her, and exploded in fury.

By then she was in a foxhole-sized crater. Shrapnel peppered the landscape around her. She heard long screams on her suitcomm radio as the other exposed members of the landing party were hit by the fragments of the warhead, their suits torn open, their life's blood and breath spilling into space.

Sparta felt the old anger rise, the rage she felt

against the people who had tried to kill her, the people who had murdered her parents. She would have let those crew people live. Not even their blindness would have been permanent. Their own commander had slaughtered them.

With effort she suppressed her adrenalin surge. She switched her suitcomm channel back to the SAD command frequency. It was child's play to evade the missiles; she had only to stay silent and still when they were within range, move cautiously when they were distant. How long could *Doradus* afford to cause havoc in near-Mars space? Sooner or later, Mars Station would be alerted.

Meanwhile, let *Doradus* think it had killed her, too. Let anyone aboard dare come to confirm it.

Before she left the scene of the carnage she added a shotgun to her kit.

19

Blake sat under the eye of the orange man's pistol for half an hour. Toward the end of the flight there was a brief moment of vertigo while the space-plane spun on its axis. Shortly afterward the sensation of weight was restored as the *Kestrel* began to decelerate.

The natty little red-haired man was undisturbed by any of this. He perched comfortably on the edge of the flight-deck door when the plane stood on its tail, trusting the plane's computers to handle the details, never wavering in his aim. He'd answered none of Blake's questions, had made no move to come closer to Blake or to turn away, had hardly registered more than a slight smile when Blake complained that his bladder was full and he desperately needed to make a trip to the head. He had given Blake not the slightest chance to escape the pistol's bleak stare.

Then a signal chimed in the cabin of the small spaceplane.

"Time to put on your spacesuit," the orange man said cheerily. "You'll find it in the locker beside the airlock."

"Why should I put on a spacesuit?" Blake snapped.

"Because I'll shoot you if you don't."

Blake believed him. Still he tried. "Why do you *want* me in a spacesuit?"

"You'll learn that soon enough, if you choose to get into it by yourself. Although I admit that you would be *almost* as useful to me dead—should you require me to kill you now and stuff you into the thing myself."

Blake expelled his breath. "Why save you the trouble, if you're going to kill me anyway?"

"My dear Mr. Redfield! Your death is by no means inevitable—else I would not have bored myself to tedium, sitting here watching you all this time!" The man's grin was almost charming. "Have I motivated you sufficiently?"

Blake said nothing, but cautiously unloosed his harness. While the orange man watched from his overhead perch, Blake climbed down to the suit locker, opened it, and began struggling into the soft fabric suit that hung there.

"Do I have time for the prebreathe?" Blake asked. The suit was equipped for oxygen only, not built for the full air pressure which had been standard on Mars. Unless Blake purged his bloodstream of dissolved nitrogen—a process that required hours—the gas would bubble out of his blood under the suit's low oxygen pressure, giving him a painful case of the bends.

"You're being silly again, but it doesn't matter," the orange man remarked. "You won't have time to get the bends. A few minutes after you're through the lock we'll both know whether you are going to live or die."

"That's a comforting thought," Blake muttered.

"I regret to confess that your comfort, while it concerns me in the abstract, as a consideration pales by comparison to the larger aims to which it must be sacrificed."

Without a weapon of his own Blake couldn't think of a worthy reply to that baroque expression of sentiment, so he climbed into the spacesuit. Shortly after he was done, a second chime sounded.

"Hang on," the orange man said. "We're about to go weightless again."

The rumble of the *Kestrel*'s engines cut out a few seconds later. Blake and his captor were both adrift again. As before, the gun hardly wavered.

"Seal your helmet," said the orange man. "Now into the airlock. Right now—and close the hatch behind you."

Blake complied. If he'd had any thought of jamming the hatches, the orange man was too quick for him, flying down the short aisle and slamming the door behind him.

Before Blake could even grab the safety rail, the outer hatch, triggered from inside, slammed open. The air in the lock rushed out and he was propelled spinning into space, gasping for air. He stared desperately around him, trying to orient himself.

He saw the enormous crescent of Mars, filling much of the sky. He saw a huge black rock, crumpled and striated and cratered, which he knew must be Phobos. Behind him he saw the slim dart of the Noble Water Works executive spaceplane he had just exited so precipitously, its silvery skin reflecting the bright yellow sun and the red planet Mars.

And he saw a long white ship, a freighter, some five kilometers distant but moving slowly in his direction under maneuvering rockets.

He wished *he* had maneuvering rockets. Without them, he was probably going to die, and soon: the pressure gauge of his suit was already on emergency reserve. He calculated that he had at most five minutes to live under the partial pressure of oxygen remaining in his depleted tanks.

The outer hatch of the *Kestrel* closed firmly behind him.

* * *

Sparta had made her way cautiously northward, keeping a close eye on the heavens and a sensitive ear to the data channels that *Doradus* used to keep track of its hunting SADs. Once she noted a flare of light on the western horizon, its spectrum that of an exploding SAD, and she guessed that the exasperated fire-control officer had seen a humanlike shadow—or, more likely, that an overruled computer had allowed two SADs to home on each other's exhaust.

Only once did she see a missile drifting inquisitively overhead. Keeping perfectly still, with her spacesuit's systems in stasis, she was confident that she was undetectable. And once only, *Doradus* itself hove into view. Sparta froze between two rocks until it had sunk beneath the horizon again; its radio signals broke up and grew faint. Sparta thought the commander must be getting desperate, to be searching the landscape of the dark moon so randomly. But the position of the ship was no longer her primary concern—

—for she had reached her goal. On the sunlit rim of Stickney stood the bright aluminum domes of Phobos Base, untouched in half a century. Untouched and uncorroded.

Sparta needed to send a message farther than the comm unit in her space suit could transmit. What she needed was an amplifier and a big antenna.

On the radio mast of Phobos base a working dish was still mounted, aimed at a place in the sky where Earth had been half a century ago. Sparta pulled herself effortlessly up the tall mast and twisted the dish into a new alignment, pointing it in the general direction of the nearest of the synchronous communications satellites orbiting Mars. Anything approximating line of sight would do. The old dish's beam wasn't that tight.

She bounded down to the hut at the base of the

mast. She pushed open the unsealed hatch and entered the empty, airless building.

She closed the hatch behind her and turned on her helmet lamp. She saw the interior exactly as the Soviet and American explorers had left it—or at least as the monument's administrators wanted visitors to believe they had left it.

The garbage had been cleared away. A couple of stained coffee bulbs were prudently wired to the table. Checkpads were fastened to a desktop by eternally effective Velcro tabs, their ballpoint-ink entries still legible. A big plastic-covered map of Mars was bolted to the wall.

But here was the prize: a radio in pristine condition, mounted above the bench. A check of its power meter indicated that, after half a century, hordes of electrons still swarmed through its superconducting capacitors. Sparta had been prepared to sacrifice suit power if she had to, but it seemed that wouldn't be necessary.

The tool kit from the *Mars Cricket* yielded up what she needed to improvise connectors so she could plug her suitcomm into the antique amplifier. She hesitated a moment before sending her message. Once she started broadcasting, she would be as visible to *Doradus* as *Doradus* had been visible to her—more so, for her message would be picked up by communication satellites and rebroadcast, and to hear her *Doradus* wouldn't even have to be in line of sight.

Still, the cumbersome freighter would take its time crawling around the moon toward her. Even its SADs would take precious seconds to arrive on target. Sparta could call for help and still make her escape.

''Mars Station Board of Space Control, this is a Code Red emergency. Officer in trouble at Phobos Base. Requiring immediate assistance. Repeat, officer in trouble at Phobos Base. Require any available units to render immediate assistance. Mars Station Board of Space Control, this is a Code Red . . .''

She was startled by the voice that crackled in her ears: *Inspector Troy, this is Lieutenant Fisher, Mars Station Board of Space Control. We are here to render assistance. Give us your position, please.*

Her earlier message had been received after all. ''About time,'' she said. ''Where are you?''

Station-keeping, approximately above the sub-Mars point.

''Do you see *Doradus*?''

As we came in, Doradus *was proceeding under full power to high-orbit injection. They do not respond to queries.*

''Order *Doradus* impounded, triple-A priority.''

Wilco, Inspector.

''I'll meet you at Phobos Base. I want you to come alone.''

Say again.

''I want one officer on the surface, Lieutenant. One only.''

We'll do what you say, Inspector. . . .

She keyed off abruptly and left the radio hut, slamming the hatch behind her. She skimmed like a gliding bird down the smooth black inner walls of Stickney, alighting on the rim of a smaller, younger crater deep inside. She hooked herself into the makeshift foxhole with gloved hands, turned, and fixed her macrozoom eye on the shining structure she had just vacated.

Perhaps *Doradus* really was fleeing, maintaining communications silence. She could not see it from her position. Perhaps the Board of Space Control really was coming to the rescue, in the person of this Lieutenant Fisher. But Sparta knew the roster of the Mars Station unit. Yes, there was a Fisher based at Mars Station, but she was a clerk.

She waited to see whether a man or a missile would keep the rendezvous at Phobos Base.

Blake had been spinning helplessly for four minutes when the *Kestrel*'s hatch opened and a space-suited figure emerged. The orange man was wearing a high-pressure suit with a full maneuvering unit. He was carrying something Blake didn't recognize, but it looked like a gun. He aimed himself toward the limb of Phobos and jetted away. The hatch closed automatically behind him.

Blake's oxygen gauge glowed red for "empty."

The sun was behind the spacesuited figure as it swept over the edge of Stickney under full maneuvering jets and homed on the radio shed at Phobos Base. Sparta watched as "Fisher" landed expertly outside the shed, opened its hatch, and disappeared inside. A few seconds later the hatch opened and he reemerged.

He was half a kilometer away, but to her eye he might be standing half a meter away. She could not see his face through his reflective visor, but she knew he was no member of the Space Board. He was holding a laser rifle.

Troy—or should I call you Linda?—I'm sure you can see me. And I know you have the plaque. If you give it to me now, I may still have time to save Blake Redfield's life.

His voice in her helmet made her scalp crawl, but she said nothing. Let the orange man come to her.

How long can you wait, Linda? My oxygen tanks are full. You've been up here for hours. I'll find you eventually—when you're dead—so why not give up now and save Blake? The poor fellow is adrift in space without a maneuvering unit, without a friend in sight, with no pressure in his tanks.

Let him come to her . . .

Oh, I understand—you think perhaps this is just a clever fiction. But remember? You yourself demanded that the Noble Water Works put its executive spaceplane at the dis-

posal of Mr. Redfield. You should have inquired who the pilot was—not that the name would have meant anything to you—and of course, I was happy to oblige you. You can see the Kestrel *just about now, I think, if you are more or less where I suspect you are. It should be rising in the east.*

The bright dart of a spaceplane had indeed crept into view above the eastern crater rim. When Sparta looked closer, she could see a tiny white dot hovering beside it, almost lost in the starry background.

Blake and I came to understand each other rather well during our flight. I assure you that he is pining for my return.

"Here I am," said Sparta. She straightened slowly, keeping her boots in touch with the ground. Her lower body was protected by the rim of the small crate. Let the orange man come to her . . .

Ah . . . show me the plaque, dear.

"As soon as you have it, you'll kill me."

I'm afraid you're right. I deeply regret I haven't managed to do the job properly before now.

"Why should I believe that you'll save Blake?"

Because I don't kill for amusement, Linda. I will save him if I can. I cannot guarantee that it isn't already too late.

Very slowly she reached into her thigh pocket and pulled out the plaque. Its unmarred surface glittered in the bright sun, a shining star against the coal-black slopes of Stickney.

Thank you, dear. He raised his rifle quickly, smoothly, and took aim. His gloved finger squeezed the trigger as—

—a lance of light speared him.

With deadly precision Sparta had directed the plaque's reflection straight into his eyes. She saw him flinch and spin away. While the filtered sun was not bright enough to blind him through his visor—not for more than a moment or two—his vision must be full of dancing corruscations.

She hated what she did next, for Sparta would risk her own life rather than kill another person— but she had no right to sacrifice Blake to her desperate ideals. She raised the shotgun at her side and sited it with inhuman accuracy at the confused man above her. The explosion drove her back against the crater wall. The shot pattern sped toward its target with no drag and insignificant deflection.

But he'd been quick. As he'd jerked himself away from the painful brightness of the mirror he'd dived for the ground. Sparta's blast tore a ragged hole through the venerable aluminum of the Phobos Base radio hut behind where his helmet had been. By the time she'd recovered her balance and jacked a second shell into the gun, he was out of sight.

His suitcomm still reached her. *A brave try, Linda. Between the two of us we would have an interesting contest. But we are not the only two people involved.*

Black spots were dancing in front of Blake's eyes. The aching pressure to open his mouth and gasp for air was becoming unbearable. He knew that if he did so, there would be no air to breathe. He also knew—although it took extreme effort to persuade himself of this truth—that the blood's dissolved oxygen lasts many minutes beyond the brain's conviction that one is suffocating.

The modern spacesuit is the product of over a century of development, and one of the earliest improvements was the perfection of the interchangeable life-support unit. Unlike the spacesuits of the 1980s and '90s, the tanks on pressure suits and deep-space suits could readily be traded in vacuum.

Blake's tank was empty, so he'd taken it off.

He held his breath while he spun slowly in space. He let himself spin once, then again, counting as precisely as he could: "One, one thousand, two, one thousand, three, one thousand . . ." If anoxia overcame him the counting would amount to nothing, but at the moment he still trusted his reason. He was feeling anything but euphoric.

When his back was to the spaceplane, he hurled the pack away from him as hard as he could. It massed a fraction of what he and the rest of the suit massed together, and it tumbled away fast. He moved backward more slowly—but just as inevitably.

He grinned. Good ol' Isaac Newton.

By the time he reached the *Kestrel* he was turned half toward it. There were no handholds on the streamlined surface of the spaceplane, but he caught the leading edge of its swing wing and held on for his life. The recessed handle of the airlock was just beyond his grasp, but by now this was all starting to seem like fun. Blake giggled. He wished he didn't feel so damn good. That meant he was going to die real soon. What a gas . . . !

He let go and floated toward the handle. He got hold of it. Now what?

Oh, yeah. *Twist* it, you nut.

He twisted it. The hatch sprang open in his face so hard he broke into more paroxysms of giggles. Somehow a strap on his sleeve got caught in the handle. It saved his life; the opening hatch would have pushed him off to Phobos.

He climbed into the airlock and slapped drunkenly at the buttons on the wall. The hatch closed behind him. Air spewed into the airlock.

None of it reached him inside his suit. The world had narrowed to a tiny point of light before he remembered to unlatch his helmet.

Calling the pilot of the Kestrel. *This is Blake Redfield calling the pilot of the Noble spaceplane. This is going out over all channels, Red. I'm talking to you, but every ship in Mars space is hearing what I'm telling you. Everybody in that freighter is hearing what I'm telling you. Everybody in Mars Station Traffic Control is hearing what I'm telling you. I'm sitting in the lefthand seat of your plane, Red, and you'd better hope somebody comes to take you off that rock, because I'm not letting you back inside.*

Sparta recognized his voice before the first sentence had left his mouth. "Blake, hear me. Blake, this is Ellen. Hear me."

Ellen!

"Take immediate evasive action. You are a target. Take immediate evasive action. Do you read me? Do you understand? You must take . . ."

She saw the rockets of the spaceplane burst into blue flame. He'd understood enough to act on her warning. She waited in agony as the *Kestrel* wheeled in the sky . . . waiting for the incoming torpedo from *Doradus*.

Within the last few seconds *Doradus* itself had risen in the east, within easy range of the *Kestrel*.

A burst of scrambled communication came over her commlink. And at that moment she saw the orange man rise from his hiding place and begin to *run*—run along the north rim of Stickney in astonishing strides, one, two, three—a hundred meters, two hundred at a leap—then stretch like a longjumper and soar right off the surface of the moon. The gas jets of his maneuvering unit puffed and augmented his takeoff. His white-suited figure dwindled in the direction of *Doradus*.

She held him in her sights. The shotgun blast, unhindered by atmosphere, undeflected by strong gravity, would have intercepted him at any point on his trajectory. The pattern would have spread and spread; perhaps only one massive pellet would have impacted his helmet. That would have been enough.

She lowered the gun.

Almost before the *Doradus*'s airlock hatch had

closed behind him, there was a sudden blast of steering jets and the pirate ship's main drive burst forth in the fury and splendor of fusion exhaust. In seconds *Doradus* was shrinking sunward, free of Phobos at last. Sparta wondered if the ship's commander were thankful to leave, even in defeat, this miserable lump of rock that had so annoyingly balked him of what should have been easy prey.

Meanwhile the *Kestrel* was spinning like a top.

"Blake, try to get control of that thing and park it long enough for me to come up and get aboard."

I'm trying, Ellen, I'm trying.

A female voice broke into the suitcomm channel. *Inspector Troy. Inspector Troy. This is Inspector Sharansky, Board of Space Control. We are responding to your request for assistance. Please advise. Inspector Troy . . .*

"This is Troy."

Troy? Is you?

"Is me. Sharansky, I've got one thing to say to you."

Go ahead, please.

"Great timing."

20

The channels in the metal were different from each other but all the same height and width and depth. They ran in straight lines. There were three dozen different kinds of them, but they repeated themselves in various sequences until the total number of them, etched in the metal, was a thousand and more. . . .

Sparta caught herself drifting and made an effort to concentrate. Less than a meter in front her, overhead spotlights focused their beams on the shining Martian plaque, which rested on a velvet cushion under a dome of laser-cut Xanthian crystal, glittering as if it had never been disturbed, never even been touched.

Sparta and Lieutenant Polanyi stood alone in the empty room. The members of the official delegation which had restored the relic to its shrine, local dignitaries all—the mayor had gotten a fast liner back from his leadership conference in order to preside—had finally drunk the last bottle of champagne and made their separate ways home.

"As soon as we get out of here we can set the alarms."

She nodded. "Sorry for the delay, Lieutenant. In all the excitement I never stopped to look at the thing. An odd relic."

"That's true enough. Can't scratch it, but some-

257

thing busted it once. Must have been quite a crunch.''

Sparta glanced at the young Space Board officer. ''What do you know of its lore?''

''The 'lore' is mostly made up by the tour operators, I think.'' He was as bored as he sounded; he recited the facts as if reading from a file. ''No one ever found out where it came from—somewhere near the north pole; that's all anyone knows. The man who found it hid it, told no one the circumstances of its discovery—it was found in his effects after his death. There were rumors of a hoard of alien objects, but in ten years nothing else has ever come to light. The brochures call the thing the 'Soul of Mars.' Poetic name for a broken plate.''

She contemplated the etched surface of the plaque. ''Do you really think it came from Mars?'' she asked. ''Do you think it was made on Mars?''

''I'm no expert in these matters, Inspector.'' Polanyi didn't bother to hide his impatience.

''I don't think it's from here,'' she said.

''Oh? What makes you think not?''

''Just a feeling I get,'' she said. ''Well, thanks for indulging me. Let's set the alarms so you can go home.''

A scream of self-destructing synthekords on the sound system maintained the requisite noise level in the Park-Your-Pain, even as the hoarse yells of conversation fell silent around the four newcomers, who opened their faceplates and pushed into the crowd.

''Don't worry. With me, you are safe.'' Yevgeny Rostov threw a massive paw around Sparta's shoulders and crushed her to his side. Behind him, Blake and Lydia Zeromski pressed close together in his wake.

Yevgeny glared at the other patrons as he moved toward the bar. ''Not all cops are tools of capitalist-imperialists," he shouted. "This is brave woman. She brought back Martian plaque. All are comrades here."

The people in the bar peered curiously at Sparta for long seconds; Blake too got his share of odd glances, but he was used to the place by now. Everybody gradually lost interest and resumed yelling at each other over the music.

"So, Mike, you are not fink after all? Another cop!" The four new friends reached the sanctuary of the stainless steel bar. "I buy you beer anyway." Yevgeny released his hold on Sparta and walloped Blake on the shoulder hard enough to send him staggering.

The bartender didn't bother to ask what anybody wanted; he poured Yevgeny's regular for them all. Four foaming mugs of black, bitter bock appeared on the bartop.

"Lydia, we toast to getting these people off our planet as soon as possible."

Sparta raised her mug gingerly. Blake was more enthusiastic. "Thanks, comrade," he shouted. "To the next shuttle out of here."

Four mugs collided with enough force to slop foam.

"But do me a favor, Yevgeny," Blake yelled. "Don't think of me as a cop. This is just a hobby."

Sparta laughed. "You said it. Amateur night on Mars."

"You blow up truck yards for a *hobby?*" Lydia shouted, loud enough to be heard above the rocket-scream of the synthekords.

Blake's eyes widened with innocence. *Blow up what?* he mouthed, voiceless.

"I forgot," Lydia yelled at him, eyeing Sparta. "We shouldn't talk about it where somebody might be listening."

"I'll second that!" Blake shouted back. "To local

776 of the Pipeline Workers Guild, long may it live and prosper!''

He was greeted with cheers from everyone within a meter's distance—a half a dozen or so, the only ones who could hear him.

His companions grinned and shook their heads. Sparta sniffed the black beer and declined to drink. Blake stuck his face into the foam far enough to get a mustache, but he only pretended to sip. Meanwhile Yevgeny was pouring the contents of his mug down his open throat; he slammed the empty mug on the steel bartop and raised four fingers imperiously.

''No you don't,'' Blake shouted. ''Not for me.''

''What's for you? When it's your turn again, I let you know.''

''Yevgeny, one question before we get out of here—''

''What's that, my feeble friend?''

''After all your years on Mars, why do you still have that awful accent? I mean, does that help your credibility with the comrades or something?''

Yevgeny reared back, affronted—

—and when he leaned down to push his face up to Blake's there was fire in his eyes and his bushy brows were poised to fly right off his forehead. ''Why, whatever could have motivated you to cast aspersions upon my perspicacity, Mr. Redfield?'' His voice was pitched to carry no farther than Blake's ears. ''Did you suppose that I was some sneaking impersonator like yourself?''

''You old fox''—Blake broke up laughing—''You did it.''

''Did . . . *it?*'' The eyebrows climbed higher.

''Told the truth. And you *still* never used an article.''

''Article?'' Yevgeny straightened up and roared. ''What is such thing as *article?*''

* * *

Sparta and Blake hunched against the wind, pushing their way along the shuttleport's sandy streets.

"Your place or mine?" he asked. "Or am I presuming?"

"How about your cubicle at the hive? A luxury hotel gets so boring."

"Knowing you, you might mean that."

"Don't worry," she said, "I won't . . ." At that moment she gasped and stumbled against him, clutching herself with both arms as if she'd been struck under the heart.

Blake grabbed her. "Ellen! What's wrong? Ellen!" She went limp in his arms and collapsed; he lowered her slowly to the sand. She stared at him through her glass faceplate, but her open mouth made no sound.

She could be the greatest of us
She resists our authority

The lights over the operating table were arranged in a circle, like the rolling pictureless videoplates at the Park-Your-Pain, like the spotlights that ringed the Martian plaque.

The rank smell of onions threatened to suffocate her. Her mind's eye involuntarily displayed complex sulfer compounds as the circle of lights above her began to swirl in a golden spiral.

Blake was with her. She'd been conscious enough to insist on it before she would let them operate. They put him at her left shoulder, where he could hold her hand in both of his.

William, she's a child

As the darkness closed in she clutched Blake's hand harder, clinging to it to keep from falling.

To resist us is to resist the Knowledge

She was sliding under. She was falling up into the spiral.

She lost her grip on Blake's hand. Around her shapes swarmed in the maelstrom.

The shapes were signs. The signs were the signs of the plaque. The signs had meaning.

The meaning sprang at her. She tried to call out, to shout a warning.

But when the blackness closed over her, only one image remained, an image of swirling clouds, red and yellow and white, boiling in an immense whirlpool, big enough to swallow a planet. She left herself then, and fell endlessly into them. . . .

The medicos didn't let Blake see what was going on; they protected his assumed squeamishness with a curtain of fabric that screened Sparta's body from the neck down.

The cut was bloodless and swift; the microtome scalpel paralyzed the edges of the wound as it sliced through skin and muscle and membrane. Sparta lay open from breastbone to navel.

"What the *hell* is this stuff?" the young surgeon muttered angrily, his voice muffled inside his clear-film sterile suit. He caught his assistant's nervous glance toward Blake. He growled and said, "Biopsy. I want to know what it is before we close."

At his terse orders they pulled her open and held her open with clamps; he went in with scalpel and scissors and tongs. He removed as much of the slippery, silvery tissue as he could reach, working with quick precision around the blood vessels and packed organs.

Sheets of the stuff lay on the tray like a beached jellyfish, trembling and iridescent.

By the time the surgeon had cleaned the last accessible speck of it from beneath the muscular canopy of Sparta's diaphragm, the technician had returned with a laser-spectrometer analysis and a computer-generated graph: the substance was a long-chain conducting polymer of a kind neither

the technician nor the surgeon had ever encountered before.

"All right, we'd better close. For now. I want
this woman under intensive surveillance until we
hear what the research committee makes of this."

The healing instruments passed over the wound,
reknitting the severed blood vessels and nerves, re-
sealing the skin, salving the flesh with growth fac-
tors that would erase all signs of the scar within a
few weeks.

With Blake walking beside the gurney, still holding Sparta's unfeeling hand, they wheeled her out
of the operating theater. The surgeon and his assis-
tants tidied up and left soon after.

A man stood in the darkness of the gallery above
the theater, peering down through its glass roof.
Blue eyes glittered in his sun-blackened face, and
his iron-gray hair was cut to within a few millimeters of his scalp. He wore the dress-blue uniform
of a full commander of the Board of Space Patrol;
there were not many ribbons over his breast
pocket, but those he wore testified to supreme
courage and deadly skill.

The commander turned to an officer who stood
farther back in the shadows. "Get hold of that
readout, then wipe the machine's memory. This
information is not to go to any hospital committee." His voice was gravel, the texture of waves
beating on a rocky beach.

"What of those who operated on her, sir?"

"Explain it to them, Sharansky."

"You know what surgeons are like, sir. Especially young ones."

Yes, he knew. Surgeons like that bright young
guy had saved his life more than once. All they
wanted in return was worship. "Try explaining
first. If they don't see the point . . ." He fell silent.

Sharansky let the silence stretch for several seconds before she said, "Understood, sir."

"Good for you. If you have to go that far, watch the dosage," he growled. "We don't want them to forget how to do what they're good at."

"Yes sir. And Inspector Troy, sir?"

"We'll get her out of here tonight."

"Mr. Redfield, sir?"

The commander sighed. "Sharansky, if I didn't like your cousin Proboda so much, I'd bust you for that stupid stunt. Vik may be a dumb hero, but you're just plain dumb."

"Sir! Is stupid right word? Maybe miscalculation . . ."

"Bull. You didn't like the guy and you don't like the unions. You had three I.D.'s in your pocket and you gave him the one you knew would get him in trouble."

She drew herself up stiffly. "I thought to create diversion, sir. Away from Inspector Troy's investigation."

"The next lie will be your last in this service, Sharansky."

She didn't answer for a long time. Then she said, "Understood, sir."

"Good." For a moment he favored her with a freezing stare. "Humans are funny, Sharansky, they need funny things," he said, and then abruptly turned away. "She's definitely a human being, despite what they tried to do to her. And whatever you or I think of this guy Redfield, right now she needs him."

EPILOGUE

Thus the Martian plaque was returned to Mars. Two years later . . .

On a country estate southwest of London an elegant middle-aged man in a shooting outfit stalks the autumn woods. Beside him, not far away, is his host, an older gentleman, Lord Kingman. Slender shotguns rest easily in the two men's arms; their bag is a small but varied one—three grouse, four rabbits, and a couple of pigeons—and contrary to the dark forecasts of their colleagues, both their dogs are still alive, questing eagerly ahead through the aromatic underbrush.

Nothing about the younger man, whose closest associates call him Bill, betrays the complexity of his thoughts or the ambiguity of his feelings upon this occasion. For all the world he could be just another aristocratic English shooter out for a genteel bit of small-animal slaughtering.

As for Lord Kingman, with his leonine head of gray hair he is an even more imposing figure of mature manhood. Until the moment he sees the gray squirrel.

The squirrel sees the men at the same moment. Perhaps it knows it is marked for immediate execution as a result of the damage it has done to the trees on the estate; perhaps it has already lost close relatives to Kingman's gun. Whatever its reasons, it wastes no time in observation, but in three leaps reaches the base of the nearest tree and vanishes behind it in a flicker of gray.

The effect on Kingman is electrifying; his gun comes up as quickly as if the dogs had flushed a pheasant. He keeps his gun aimed at that part of the trunk where he expects the squirrel to reappear and begins ever so slowly to circle the tree, step by cautious step.

The dogs must be used to this sort of thing; they immediately go off and settle among the ferns, resting their chins on their paws, where they peer up at Kingman in resignation and wait for the drama to play itself out.

For his part, the best Bill can do is keep out of Kingman's line of fire, staying as quiet as possible while circling with him.

The squirrel's face appears for a moment round the edge of its shield a dozen feet from the ground and Kingman instantly lets off a blast, then pumps and ejects and aims again in a swift and practiced series of motions—he is an excellent shot—but he holds his fire, for his target has vanished. Sawdust drifts from the rip in the bark where the squirrel's head had been (rather more damage to the tree than the squirrel could have done, Bill thinks), but no small body tumbles to the ground.

Though they continue to circle, Kingman with his gun leveled hopefully, they never see the squirrel again.

Kingman is very thoughtful as they walk back across the lawn toward the magnificent old house. "That tree-rat!" he says with sudden vehemence (he has always called them tree-rats, he has earlier confided to Bill, on the grounds that people are too sentimental to condone the shooting of dear little squirrels). "Reminded me of a very peculiar experience I had year before last."

Bill is pretty sure he knows what is coming, and he doesn't want to hear it. Kingman's circumstances are awkward, but there is nothing Bill can do for him—or so he would protest if asked—and he hopes Kingman won't put him in the position of refusing a host's request.

He is saved, temporarily at least, by the appearance of two other shooters, Jurgen and Holly, just coming around the far side of the house. The two of them were hunting the western half of the estate while Bill and Kingman took the east. From the looks of things the west will be devoid of bird life for years to come; Jurgen, shouting a hearty "Hola," brandishes what looks to be several generations of a once-populous grouse family, strung up in bunches by their feet.

Holly is trim and deadly looking in spotless doeskin jodhpurs and a white silk blouse. A silver-chased under-and-over rests in the crook of her arm, and two of Kingman's hounds stalk at her heels. Perhaps she has given her kills to Jurgen to carry for her, or perhaps she has simply let them lie where they fell, preferring not to soil her shooting outfit.

For Jurgen's shooting jacket is covered with blood and feathers; that and the fierce grin that stretches his ruddy cheeks make him look quite the fell huntsman—which he is, although his hunting is usually not done in the woods. He yells at Kingman in his too-jolly, German-accented notion of British upper-class speech: "Simply marvelous place you've got here, Lord Kingman. Very good of you to have us."

Kingman glances at his companion, pained. "Nothing, really," he mutters, by which Bill suspects he means that if it were up to him, he'd have nothing to do with bloody Jurgen and his ilk. But Kingman is no longer the ruler of his own fate. "Let's give these to the cook, shall we?"

"I'll be going on up then," Holly says. "Until this evening." She waves with two fingers and ascends the curving stone stairs to the wide back porch; Jurgen follows her, his gaze resting heavily on her swaying hips.

Kingman leaves the dogs with the kennel keeper and goes in through the kitchen entrance; he and Bill hand their victims to Mrs. McGrath, who receives them without too much enthusiasm—all that bird shot to be dug out—and then they part company.

Bill walks slowly up the broad staircase to his rooms. He checks his watch. The business meeting is set for six o'clock—an exploratory affair this first evening, with the hard choices deferred until tomorrow. Dinner is to be promptly at eight. Whatever his failings as a strategist, Bill reflects, Kingman knows how to do things in a civilized way.

Before anything else there is the ceremony, of course. There are few better places for it; the sanctuary at Kingman's, while small, is one of the oldest surviving in the Athanasian Society, the earlier ones on the Continent having been destroyed in the Terrors. The vaulted ceiling is patterned with the Starry Cross in gold leaf on blue—and a remarkably accurate rendition it is, given that Europeans were unfamiliar with the southern skies when this crypt was built.

Jurgen reads the dedication. A stranger would be surprised to see how the man's intelligence shines through his lumpishness when he is in the grip of the Knowledge. Finally they all speak the Words of Affirmation—"All Will Be Well"—and drink from the Chalice, in this case an iron vessel, a Hittite piece which is the crown of Kingman's collection.

They exchange their robes for regular clothing and

reassemble in the library, beneath oak shelves filled with a good many real printed books bound in tooled leather. Besides the four of them who fancy themselves shooters—Kingman and Bill attired rather tweedily, Jurgen in something that looks like an American cowboy outfit, and Holly again in white, this time a pristine cotton sari befitting a maharani—the other members of the executive committee present are Jack and Martita.

Jack, who has the look of an aging fighter, is as usual dressed like a Manhattan banker. Martita is as naturally pale as Holly is dark and like her seeks the maximum effect from contrast, on this occasion by wearing a rough-woven woolen outfit that sets off her fine gold hair.

Although Martita's costume is paramilitary, her combativeness is genuine. "We have come some way from the debacles of the last two years, but not far enough," she announces, as the butler is still bringing drinks. "Our program—largely *your* program, Bill, but correct me if I'm wrong"—she gives him an arch stare—"failed pathetically in execution, however sensible it may have seemed at the time."

"I hardly think it's necessary to rehearse old misfortunes. We are all thoroughly familiar with the relevant issues," Bill replies, too stiffly. Is anything less dignified than wounded dignity?

Martita will not be put off. "I think we could all benefit from a thorough review of our predicament . . ."

"For Knowledge's sake, why do you think we're all here?" Bill grumbles.

". . . in order to assess any new plan with essential objectivity," she finishes.

"Get it off your chest, darling," says Jurgen, peering openly at her splendid chest.

Martita ignores him. "We failed in our first attempt to create an intermediary . . ."

"Now that is *very* old history," Bill mutters.

". . . and the latest efforts are untested."

"They will be tested soon," Bill replies. "In plenty of time."

"We have failed to conceal the identity of the home star," she goes on, "and we have failed to maintain the confidentiality of the sacred texts."

"As to the identity of the home star, our fears were groundless, but no one can be blamed," Jack says with his customary directness. "No one knows exactly where it is and no one will, unless and until there's a signal."

"That is not her point," Holly puts in. Her self-satisfied serenity can set one's teeth on edge—and has occasionally, Bill muses, driven him to the edge of violence. Nevertheless she is a logical person. "The point is our failure, a costly failure that has drawn attention to what we had hoped to hide."

"I agree with Jack," Jurgen says. "The home star is doing well enough at hiding itself."

"And immediately afterward, the debacle of the texts . . ." Martita continues—but then allows her words to trail off. No one fills the silence.

An angel chooses that moment to pass. The angel of death, no doubt.

Some call them the Free Spirit. Some call them Athanasians. Their attempt to destroy all existing copies of what the public has come to know as the Culture X writings—and to eliminate anyone who might have been able to reconstruct them from memory—was a bold and necessary effort, nor was it a *complete* failure. In the attempt Bill and his companions learned much that was necessary and might not otherwise have come to light.

They learned from the texts themselves. Some of what they learned was in the Knowledge, but some was not. Some that was in the Knowledge had been misinterpreted.

Yet against these gains, Bill reflects, what they

lost by their ill-conceived venture was undeniably greater.

Kingman, who has contributed nothing to the conversation so far except to direct the butler with minute nods and tilts of his leonine head, abruptly speaks. "It was a peculiar experience, very peculiar indeed. That damned tree-rat this afternoon—remember, Bill?—brought it vividly to mind."

Jurgen sees it coming, as Bill had earlier, and tries to head Kingman off. "Lord Kingman, the particulars of your experience are quite illuminating, *ja*, but the agenda possibly precludes . . ."

"Of course, if you'd rather I didn't . . ." Kingman is clearly nettled.

"No, please," Bill says hastily, seeing an opportunity where before he had seen only an embarrassment. Let Kingman tell his tale once again. Let them all again contemplate his debacle. "Martita has already rewritten the agenda, I think. So at your suggestion, my dear"—Bill graces her with a smile as poisonous as he can make it—"let us all exert ourselves to learn from the past." He turns to Kingman. "So please do go on. Tell us, just what connection is there between a gray squirrel and the fate of the most sacred of the texts?"

Kingman is greatly mollified. He settles deep into his leather armchair and, after refreshing himself with a sip from his jigger of Scotch, begins thoughtfully to speak. "I'm not sure I have all the names, but the times and places are vivid enough in memory. The story begins on Mars Station. . . ."

The minutes pass swiftly, and now it is almost eight o'clock. The servants have appeared in the shadowed doorways, quietly but anxiously seeking to remind the assembled party that dinner is about to be served.

But Kingman has paced himself well, and he is just now finishing his recitation. ". . . and so we were forced to retreat. We had no choice. It was the best and only course remaining to us."

There is a protracted moment of silence before Bill speaks. "Quite an interesting story, Rupert," he says, "and I see now how it ties up with that squirrel. There you were, with all that firepower, with one of the most powerful ships in the solar system under your command, and one unarmed woman on the surface of a puny little rock . . ."

"Bill, really . . ."

Sometimes when the red anger takes Bill he can't stop, and I . . . he, I mean . . . adds unnecessary insult to deserved injury. "Would you have done as well in her place? Do you think you would have been able to evade . . . not only evade, but *drive off* . . . the best machinery and people the Free Spirit could muster? How would you have done if you were the squirrel and she were the hunter?"

Kingman's lordly features sag; he turns pale. "She is not human, Bill." He gets stiffly to his feet. "We have you to thank for that."

Which neatly puts me in my place. Or so I . . . Bill, that is . . . concedes.

Our host—I mean, Bill's host, Bill's and the others'—marches out of the room, doing an old man's best to keep his shoulders squared in proper regimental fashion.

The others in the library look at me with varying degrees of disapproval. Only Jurgen is vulgar enough to laugh.

The next morning reveals one of those crisp October days when, despite the lazy sun, the haze in the air renders the landscape in the flat perspectives of an Oriental ink painting. I am enjoying the view from the terrace when Kingman comes out of the house. He seems unhappy to see me.

"Rupert," I say, "I really didn't intend to . . ."

"If you'll excuse me," he says, cutting off my

apology. "I believe I'll have another go at that tree-rat. Maybe I'll get him this time."

I watch a long time as he strides across the dewy lawn and into the ruddy bracken. Finally he disappears into the autumn woods on the far side of the shallow valley.

A few minutes later, I hear the shot. Not the roar of Kingman's shotgun, but the sharp crack of a pistol.

I stand at the stone railing, watching the bright speck of a yellow leaf fluttering to the ground at the edge of the distant woods. The others come out of the house one by one.

"Poor Kingman," says Jurgen, suppressing a giggle.

"He would have done better to run. When he knew it was . . . *her*," says Martita.

"The file he had on her was not complete," I say. "But that was no excuse. If he'd acted more quickly, he could have defeated her."

"Meaning, I suppose, that we would not have lost the *Doradus*? That half of its crew would not now be dead and the other half fugitives?"

Damn Martita. I refuse to reply.

"It's clear enough that she remembers what she was taught," Jack observes. "The Knowledge has not been erased in her."

"No matter. We are impervious now," I say, as firmly as I can. "The New Man is indestructible."

Jurgen snorts at me; he sounds like some bulky ungulate. "You've said *that* before. And been as wrong as Kingman." When he is in a very good mood his giggle uncannily resembles the whinny of a jackass. "Really, Bill, if Kingman must die for such a trivial mistake, why should we let *you* live?"

"*Let* me live?" I turn away from the fields and the forest to face them. "I think you can answer that for yourselves."

Until now they hadn't known how I was planning to deal with Kingman, or who I'd chosen to do the work. But I've just seen the man coming out of the woods—which is why I choose this moment to turn toward them. Against the colorful autumn leaves the man's curly red hair, his camel's hair coat, his pigskin gloves, make an unmistakable orange splotch on the landscape.

I've turned because I want to see the looks on their faces. They cringe quite satisfactorily—all of them except Jack Noble, who is my man now, now that he's been forced to go underground like me. The orange man is my man too, and they all know it.

Holly is the first to recover her aplomb. "So, Bill, on to Jupiter." She has the audacity to smirk at me. "But how do we know Linda won't be there ahead of us, as she was on Phobos?"

I can think of several answers to that. The least obscene finds voice before the others.

"Actually, my dear, I'm depending on it."

HIDE AND SEEK
AN AFTERWORD BY
ARTHUR C. CLARKE

The wise science fiction writer prefers to operate in galaxies far, far away and long, long ago, where he is safe from nagging critics—like the small boy who once told Ray Bradbury he had a satellite moving in the wrong direction. ("So I hit him.")

However, by exquisitely bad timing, the setting of *this* novel occurs practically next door and tomorrow afternoon. Desperate attempts to persuade publisher Byron Preiss to stop the countdown for a year or so have been of no avail. By the time these words appear in print, Paul and I may have to eat some of them.

How could I have dreamed when I wrote "Hide and Seek" back in 1948 that forty-one years later a Russian robot would be hopping across the face of Phobos, just like the character in my story? (As in the case of every space mission forecast, this sentence must be qualified by the incantation, "If all goes well.") For early in 1989—probably about the time I'm proofreading this book, dammit—two space probes will have made a rendezvous with Phobos, and one of them will have dropped a small "rover" which will explore the little world by jumping across it in twenty-meter hops, making a whole series of scientific measurements at each landing. (I will be quite embarrassed if, in the course of its wanderings, it encounters a large black monolith.)

When Phobos was discovered in 1877, it not only made obsolete Tennyson's "The snowy poles of moonless Mars," but it presented astronomers with a phenomenon they had never encountered before. Most satellites orbit their primaries at substantial distances, in a fairly leisurely manner; our own Moon takes almost thirty times longer to go around the Earth than Earth takes to revolve on its own axis. But here was a world where the "month" was shorter than the "day"! Mars rotates in twenty-four and a half hours (to the great convenience of future colonists, who need make only minor adjustments to their watches and circadian rhythms), yet Phobos circles it in only seven and a half!

Today, we are accustomed to artificial satellites which perform such feats, thus rising in the west and setting in the east (see Bradbury, *supra*), but the behavior of Phobos was quite a surprise to late-19th-century astronomers. It was also a bonus to such writers as Edgar Rice Burroughs; who can forget the hurtling inner moon illuminating the ancient sea beds of Barsoom?

Alas, Phobos doesn't hurtle very fast, and you'd have to watch for some time to see that it's moving at all. And it's a miserable source of illumination; not only is its apparent size a fraction of our Moon's, but it is one of the darkest objects in the Solar System, reflecting about as much light as a lump of coal. Indeed, it may be largely made of carbon, and altogether bears a close resemblance to the nucleus of Halley's Comet, as revealed by a whole flotilla of space probes in 1987. It's not much use, therefore, during the cold Martian nights, to warn travelers of approaching thoats, seeking whom they might devour.*

Tiny though it is—a battered ellipsoid whose longest dimension is less than thirty kilometers—Phobos may be destined to play a major role in the future of space exploration. After the Moon, it may be the next celestial body to know human visitors, since it is an ideal base for the reconnaissance of Mars.

Perhaps the first writer to suggest this was Laurence Manning, an early member of the American Rocket Society. In "The Wreck of the Asteroid" (*Wonder Stories*, 1932) his explorers first landed on Phobos and had a lot of fun bouncing around in its approximately one-thousandth-of-an-Earth gravity. Until one of them overdid it, achieved escape velocity—and started to fall helpless toward the looming face of Mars . . .

It's a nice, dramatic situation, which the author milked for all it was worth. The crew had to make an emergency takeoff and race after their careless colleague, hoping to catch up with him before he made yet another crater on Mars.

I hate to spoil the fun, but that just couldn't happen. Small though it is (about 20 meters a second, compared with Earth's 11,200) not even an Olympic high-jumper could attain the escape velocity of Phobos—especially when encumbered with a spacesuit. And even if he did, he would be in no danger of falling onto Mars—*because he would still have the whole of Phobos's eight thousand meters per second orbital velocity*. His trifling muscular contribution would make virtually no difference to that, so he would continue to move in just the same orbit as Phobos, but displaced by a few kilometers. And

---

*The erudite Sprague de Camp once pointed out a very peculiar feature of Barsoomian ecology: the fauna apparently consisted almost entirely of carnivores. The poor beasts must have suffered from acute malnutrition.

after one revolution, he'd be back just where he started. . . .

If you want further details, I refer you to "Jupiter V" (in *Reach for Tomorrow*) which takes place on what was, in pre–Voyager days, the innermost satellite of Jupiter, now renamed Amalthea. To fall onto Jupiter would be a much more spectacular fate than falling onto Mars; but it's even more difficult to do. ("If all goes well," the much-delayed Galileo Mission will demonstrate this feat in 1995).

"Hide and Seek" is not the only story of mine to deal with Phobos; in *The Sands of Mars* (1954), I brutally turned it into a minisun (by carefully unspecified technology) in order to improve the climate of Mars. It now occurs to me that this was a trial run for blowing up Jupiter in *2010: Odyssey Two*.

Soon after the appearance of "Hide and Seek," another British science fiction writer asked me rather suspiciously: "Have you ever read C.S. Forester's short story 'Brown on Resolution'?"

"No," I answered, truthfully enough. "I'm afraid I've never even read the Hornblower books. What's it about?"

Well, it seems that Brown was a British seaman in the First World War, armed with only a rifle, who managed to keep at bay a German cruiser from his various hideouts on a small, rocky island. (A rather similar story, one war later, was made into an excellent movie starring Peter O'Toole. In *Murphy's War*, the hero was still coping, more or less single-handed, with Germans; but being Irish he would have been just as happy fighting the Brits.)

I'm sorry to say that I still haven't gotten around to Forester's story and missed the chance of discussing "Brown" with him when we once dined together in the magnificent Painted Hall of the Royal Navy College at Greenwich. Which was a pity, as it would have given me a chance of trotting out one of my favorite quotations: ''Talent borrows—but Genius steals.''

Decades before the Viking spacecraft gave us our first close-up views of Phobos, it was obvious that a hunk of rock only a few times larger than Manhattan could possess no trace of atmosphere, still less harbor any life. Yet unless my memory has betrayed me completely, I seem to recall that Burroughs once had Mars invaded by maurading Phobians. The economics—not to mention the ecology—of such a microcivilization boggles the imagination. Once again, I fear, ERB hadn't done his homework.* Nevertheless, Phobos once featured rather spectacularly on the SETI (Search for Extra-Terrestrial Intelligence) agenda. Back in the sixties, the Russian astrophysicist Iosef Shkovskii—best known to the general public for his collaboration with Carl Sagan on SETI's sacred book *Intelligence in the Universe* (1966)—made an extraordinary suggestion about the little world, based on the long-established observation that it is slowly falling toward Mars.

I have never decided how seriously Iosef took his theory; he had a considerable sense of humor—which he needed to survive as a Jewish scientist in Stalin's time (and a lot later)—but this is how his argument went:

The slow descent of Phobos is due to the same effect that finally brings down close artificial satellites of Earth—the braking effect of the atmosphere. A satellite made of dense material will survive a long time; one with low mass per volume will be brought down more quickly, as was demonstrated

---

*I am still prepared to repeat a statement that I made many years ago: ERB is a much underrated writer. To have created the best-known character in Western (and perhaps world) fiction is no small achievement. The Mars novels, however, should be read before the age of sixteen: I hope to revisit Barsoom in my rapidly approaching second childhood.

by the ECHO balloon, and later by SKYLAB, which was essentially an empty fuel tank.

Working backward from the drag figures, Iosef calculated that the density of Phobos must be *much less than that of water*. This could only mean that it was hollow. . . .

Well, it seemed unlikely that Nature could make a hollow world some tens of kilometers across. Phobos must be a space station, presumably constructed by the Martians. Which, added another scientist, is why they're no longer around. They went broke building it.

Alas, the Viking photos showed that Phobos is undoubtedly a natural object, but its surface does show some puzzling peculiarities. Much of it is covered with parallel grooves several hundred meters wide, so that it looks like a ploughed field on a gigantic scale.

I cannot help recalling that when the Italian astronomer Schiaparelli reported "grooves" on Mars in 1877, he chose the unfortunate word "channels" to describe them. What a lot of trouble the mistranslation caused—and how chagrined Percival Lowell would have been to learn that his beloved canals have now turned up not on Mars, but on tiny Phobos.

Arthur C. Clarke
Colombo, June 1988

P.S.: Alas, Phobos 1 has just been lost, halfway through its mission; it was sent an incorrect instruction which caused it to close down completely, beyond hope of revival. I feel very sorry for the programmer concerned, who has to face the wrath of colleagues who've lost years of their lives' work.

Incidentally, something similar happened with Mariner 1, the first of the series of U.S. probes which eventually explored Venus, Mercury, and

Mars. It was lost soon after takeoff because a single comma had been omitted from a line of programming.

I'm keeping my fingers crossed for Phobos 2. How glad I am that I only have to *write* about these machines, not make them actually work. . . .

Colombo,
10 October 1988

RETURN TO AMBER...

THE ONE *REAL* WORLD, OF WHICH ALL OTHERS, INCLUDING EARTH, ARE BUT SHADOWS

ROGER ZELAZNY

The New Amber Novel

SIGN OF CHAOS 89637-0/$3.50 US/$4.50 Can
Merlin embarks on another marathon adventure, leading him back to the court of Amber and a final confrontation at the Keep of the Four Worlds.

BLOOD OF AMBER 89636-2/$3.95 US/$4.95 Can
Pursued by fiendish enemies, Merlin, son of Corwin, battles through an intricate web of vengeance and murder.

TRUMPS OF DOOM 89635-4/$3.50 US/$3.95 Can
Death stalks the son of Amber's vanished hero on a Shadow world called Earth.

The Classic Amber Series

NINE PRINCES IN AMBER 01430-0/$3.50 US/$4.50 Can
THE GUNS OF AVALON 00083-0/$3.50 US/$4.50 Can
SIGN OF THE UNICORN 00031-9/$2.95 US/$3.75 Can
THE HAND OF OBERON 01664-8/$3.50 US/$4.50 Can
THE COURTS OF CHAOS 47175-2/$3.50 US/$4.25 Can